PORTLAND (
LEARNING R

D0210715

WITHDRAWN

SHIP FEVER

ALSO BY ANDREA BARRETT

The Forms of Water
The Middle Kingdom
Secret Harmonies
Lucid Stars

ANDREA BARRETT

Ship Fever

and

Other Stories

W. W. Norton & Company / New York / London

Copyright © 1996 by Andrea Barrett

All rights reserved
Printed in the United States of America
First Edition

The text of this book is composed in 10½/14 Stemple Garamond
with the display set in Nuptial Script
Composition by Crane Typesetting Service, Inc.
Manufacturing by Courier Westford
Book design by Jaye Zimet

Library of Congress Cataloging-in-Publication Data

Barrett, Andrea.
    Ship fever and other stories / Andrea Barrett.
        p.   cm.
    1. Scientists—Social life and customs—Fiction.   2. Historical
fiction, American.   I. Title.
    PS3552.A7327S55   1996
    813'.54—dc20   95-14562
ISBN 0-393-03853-X

W. W. Norton & Company, Inc., 500 Fifth Avenue, New York, N.Y. 10110
W. W. Norton & Company Ltd., 10 Coptic Street, London WC1A 1PU

1   2   3   4   5   6   7   8   9   0

For Wendy Weil

Portions of this book have appeared previously in the following maga-zines: "The English Pupil" in The Southern Review; "The Littoral Zone" and "Soroche" in Story; "The Marburg Sisters" in New England Review; "The Behavior of the Hawkweeds" in The Missouri Review. My thanks to those magazines and their editors. "Rare Bird" first appeared in The Writing Path: An Anthology of New Writing from Writers' Conferences and Festivals (University of Iowa Press); my thanks to them as well.

"The Behavior of the Hawkweeds" was selected for Best American Short Stories, 1995 (Jane Smiley, Guest Editor).

Grateful acknowledgment is also made to the National Endowment for the Arts, for its generous support, and to the MacDowell Colony, for its gift of time and space.

Finally, my thanks to Margot Livesey, Ellen Bryant Voigt, Sarah Stone, and Carol Houck Smith, for their insightful reading and thoughtful sugges-tions.

Contents

SHIP FEVER

The Behavior of the Hawkweeds

For thirty years, until he retired, my husband stood each fall in front of his sophomore genetics class and passed out copies of Gregor Mendel's famous paper on the hybridization of edible peas. This paper was a model of clarity, Richard told his students. It represented everything that science should be.

Richard paced in front of the chalkboard, speaking easily and without notes. Like the minor evolutionist Robert Chambers, he had been born hexadactylic; he was sensitive about his left hand, which was somewhat scarred from the childhood operation that had removed his extra finger. And so, although Richard gestured freely he used only his right hand and kept his left in his pocket. From the back of the room, where I sat when I came each fall to hear him lecture, I could watch the students listen to him.

After he passed out the paper, Richard told the students his first, conventional version of Gregor Mendel's life. Mendel, he said, grew up in a tiny village in the northwestern corner of Moravia, which was then a part of the Hapsburg Empire and later became part of Czechoslovakia. When he was twenty-one, poor and desperate for further education, he entered the Augustinian monastery in the capital city of Brünn, which is now called Brno. He studied science and later taught at a local high school. In 1856, at the age of thirty-four, he began his experi-

PORTLAND COMMUNITY COLLEGE
LEARNING RESOURCE CENTERS

ments in the hybridization of the edible pea. For his laboratory he used a little strip of garden adjoining the monastery wall.

Over the next eight years Mendel performed hundreds of experiments on thousands of plants, tracing the ways in which characteristics were passed through generations. Tall and short plants, with white or violet flowers; peas that were wrinkled or smooth; pods that were arched or constricted around the seeds. He kept meticulous records of his hybridizations in order to write the paper the students now held in their hands. On a clear, cold evening in 1865, he read the first part of this paper to his fellow members of the Brünn Society for the Study of Natural Science. About forty men were present, a few professional scientists and many serious amateurs. Mendel read to them for an hour, describing his experiments and demonstrating the invariable ratios with which traits appeared in his hybrids. A month later, at the Society's next meeting, he presented the theory he'd formulated to account for his results.

Right there, my husband said, right in that small, crowded room, the science of genetics was born. Mendel knew nothing of genes or chromosomes or DNA, but he'd discovered the principles that made the search for those things possible.

"Was there applause?" Richard always asked at this point. "Was there a great outcry of approval or even a mutter of disagreement?" A rhetorical question; the students knew better than to answer.

"There was not. The minutes of that meeting show that no questions were asked and no discussion took place. Not one person in that room understood the significance of what Mendel had presented. A year later, when the paper was published, no one noticed it."

The students looked down at their papers and Richard finished his story quickly, describing how Mendel went back to his monastery and busied himself with other things. For a while he continued to teach and to do other experiments; he raised grapes and fruit trees and all kinds of flowers, and he kept bees. Eventually he was elected abbot of his monastery, and from that time until his death he was occupied with his administrative duties. Only in 1900 was his lost paper rediscovered and his work appreciated by a new generation of scientists.

When Richard reached this point, he would look toward the back of the room and catch my eye and smile. He knew that I knew what was in store for the students at the end of the semester. After they'd read the paper and survived the labs where fruit flies bred in tubes and displayed the principles of Mendelian inheritance, Richard would tell them the other Mendel story. The one I told him, in which Mendel is led astray by a condescending fellow scientist and the behavior of the hawkweeds. The one in which science is not just unappreciated, but bent by loneliness and longing.

I had a reason for showing up in that classroom each fall, and it was not just that I was so dutiful, so wifely. Richard was not the one who introduced Mendel into my life.

When I was a girl, during the early years of the Depression, my grandfather, Anton Vaculik, worked at a nursery in Niskayuna, not far from where Richard and I still live in Schenectady. This was not the only job my grandfather had ever had, but it was the one he liked the best. He had left Moravia in 1891 and traveled to the city of Bremen with his pregnant wife. From there he'd taken a boat to New York and then another to Albany. He'd meant to journey on to one of the large Czech settlements in Minnesota or Wisconsin, but when my mother was born six weeks early he settled his family here instead. A few other Czech families lived in the area, and one of those settlers hired my grandfather to work in a small factory that made mother-of-pearl buttons for women's blouses.

Later, after he learned more English, he found the nursery

job that he liked so much. He worked there for thirty years; he was so skilled at propagating plants and grafting trees that his employers kept him on part-time long past the age when he should have retired. Everyone at the nursery called him Tony, which sounded appropriately American. I called him Tati, a corruption of *tatínek*, which is Czech for "dad" and was what my mother called him. I was named Antonia after him.

We were never hungry when I was young, we were better off than many, but our daily life was a web of small economies. My mother took in sewing, making over jackets and mending pants; when she ironed she saved the flat pieces for last, to be pressed while the iron was cooling and the electricity was off. My father's wages had been cut at the GE plant and my older brothers tried to help by scrounging for odd jobs. I was the only idle member of the family, and so on weekends and during the summer my mother sometimes let me go with Tati. I loved it when Tati put me to work.

At the nursery there were fields full of fruit trees, peach and apple and pear, and long, low, glass houses full of seedlings. I followed Tati around and helped him as he transplanted plants or worked with his sharp, curved knife and his grafting wax. I sat next to him on a tall, wooden stool, holding his forceps or the jar of methylated spirits as he emasculated flowers. While we worked he talked, which is how I learned about his early days in America.

The only time Tati frowned and went silent was when his new boss appeared. Sheldon Hardy, the old chief horticulturalist, had been our friend; he was Tati's age and had worked side by side with Tati for years, cutting scions and whip-grafting fruit trees. But in 1931, the year I was ten, Mr. Hardy had a heart attack and went to live with his daughter in Ithaca. Otto Leiniger descended on us shortly after that, spoiling part of our pleasure every day.

Leiniger must have been in his late fifties. He lost no time telling Tati that he had a master's degree from a university out west, and it was clear from his white lab coat and the books in his office that he thought of himself as a scholar. In his office he sat at a big oak desk, making out lists of tasks for Tati with a fancy pen left over from better days; once he had been the director of an arboretum. He tacked the lists to the propagating benches, where they curled like shavings of wood from the damp, and when we were deep in work he'd drift into the glass house and hover over us. He didn't complain about my presence, but he treated Tati like a common laborer. One day he caught me alone in a greenhouse filled with small begonias we'd grown from cuttings.

Tati had fitted a misting rose to a pot small enough for me to handle, and I was watering the tiny plants. It was very warm beneath the glass roof. I was wearing shorts and an old white shirt of Tati's, with nothing beneath it but my damp skin; I was only ten. There were benches against the two side walls and another, narrower, propagating bench running down the center of the house. On one side of this narrow bench I stood on an overturned crate to increase my reach, bending to mist the plants on the far side. When I looked up Leiniger was standing across from me. His face was round and heavy, with dark pouches beneath his eyes.

"You're a good little helper," he said. "You help your grand-papa out." Tati was in the greenhouse next door, examining a new crop of fuchias.

"I like it here," I told Leiniger. The plants beneath my hands were Rex begonias, grown not for their flowers but for their showy, ruffled leaves. I had helped Tati pin the mother leaves to the moist sand and then transplant the babies that rooted from the ribs.

Leiniger pointed at the row of begonias closest to him, farthest from me. "These seem a little dry," he said. "Over here."

I didn't want to walk around the bench and stand by his side. "You can reach," he said. "Just lean over a little farther."

I stood up on my toes and bent across the bench, stretching the watering pot to reach those farthest plants. Leiniger flushed. "That's right," he said thickly. "Lean towards me."

Tati's old white shirt gaped at the neck and fell away from my body when I bent over. I stretched out my arm and misted the begonias. When I straightened I saw that Leiniger's face was red and that he was pressed against the wooden bench.

"Here," he said, and he made a shaky gesture at another group of plants to the right of him. "These here, these are also very dry."

I was afraid of him, and yet I also wanted to do my job and feared that any sloppiness on my part might get Tati in trouble. I leaned over once again, the watering pot in my hand. This time Leiniger reached for my forearm with his thick fingers. "Not those," he said, steering my hand closer to the edge of the bench, which he was still pressed against. "These here, these are very dry."

Just as the pot brushed the front of his lab coat, Tati walked in. I can imagine, now, what that scene must have looked like to him. Me bent over that narrow bench, my toes barely touching the crate and the white shirt hanging down like a sheet to the young begonias below; Leiniger red-faced, sweating, grinding into the wooden bench. And his hand, that guilty hand, forcing me towards him. I dropped the pot when I heard Tati shout my name.

Who can say what Leiniger had in mind? To Tati it must have looked as though Leiniger was dragging me across the begonias to him. But Leiniger was just a lonely old man and it seems possible to me, now, that he wanted only the view down my shirt and that one small contact with the skin of my inner arm. Had Tati not entered the greenhouse just then, nothing more might have happened.

But Tati saw the worst in what was there. He saw that fat hand on my arm and those eyes fixed on my childish chest. He had a small pruning knife in his hand. When he called my name and I dropped the pot, Leiniger clamped down on my arm. As I was tearing myself away, Tati flew over and jabbed his knife into the back of Leiniger's hand.

"*Nêmecky!*" he shouted. "*Prase!*"

Leiniger screamed and stumbled backward. Behind him was the concrete block on which I stood to water the hanging plants, and that block caught Leiniger below the knees. He went down slowly, heavily, one hand clutching the wound on the other and a look of disbelief on his face. Tati was already reaching out to catch him when Leiniger cracked his head against a heating pipe.

But of course this is not what I told Richard. When we met, just after the war, I was working at the GE plant that had once employed my father and Richard was finishing his thesis. After my father died I had dropped out of junior college; Richard had interrupted his Ph.D. program to join the Navy, where he'd worked for three years doing research on tropical fungi. We both had a sense of urgency and a need to make up for lost time. During our brief courtship, I told Richard only the things that I thought would make him love me.

On our second date, over coffee and Italian pastries, I told Richard that my grandfather had taught me a little about plant breeding when I was young, and that I was fascinated by genetics. "Tati lived with us for a while, when I was a girl," I said. "He used to take me for walks through the empty fields of Niskayuna and tell me about Gregor Mendel. I still know a pistil from a stamen."

"Mendel's my hero," Richard said. "He's always been my ideal of what a scientist should be. It's not so often I meet a woman familiar with his work."

"I know a lot about him," I said. "What Tati told me— you'd be surprised." I didn't say that Tati and I had talked about

Mendel because we couldn't stand to talk about what we'd both lost.

Tati slept in my room during the months before the trial; he was released on bail on the condition that he leave his small house in Rensselaer and stay with us. I slept on the couch in the living room and Leiniger lay unconscious in the Schenectady hospital. We were quiet, Tati and I. No one seemed to want to talk to us. My brothers stayed away from the house as much as possible and my father worked long hours. My mother was around, but she was so upset by what had happened that she could hardly speak to either Tati or myself. The most she could manage to do was to take me aside, a few days after Tati's arrival, and say, "What happened to Leiniger wasn't your fault. It's an old-country thing, what's between those men."

She made me sit with her on the porch, where she was turning mushrooms she'd gathered in the woods and laid out to dry on screens. Red, yellow, violet, buff. Some pieces were drier than others. While she spoke she moved from screen to screen, turning the delicate fragments.

"What country?" I said. "What are you talking about?"

"Tati is Czech," my mother said. "Like me. Mr. Leiniger's family is German, from a part of Moravia where only Germans live. Tati and Mr. Leiniger don't like each other because of things that happened in the Czech lands a long time ago."

"Am I Czech, then?" I said. "This happened because I am Czech?"

"You're American," my mother said. "American first. But Tati hates Germans. He and Leiniger would have found some way to quarrel even if you hadn't been there." She told me a little about the history of Moravia, enough to help me understand how long the Czechs and Germans had been quarreling. And she told me how thrilled Tati had been during the First World War, when the Czech and Slovak immigrants in America had banded together to contribute funds to help in the formation of an independent Czechoslovak state. When she was a girl, she said, Tati and her mother had argued over the donations Tati made and the meetings he attended.

But none of this seemed important to me. In the greenhouse, a policeman had asked Tati what had happened, and Tati had said, "I stuck his hand with my knife. But the rest was an accident—he tripped over that block and fell."

"Why?" the policeman had said. "Why did you do that?"

"My granddaughter," Tati had said. "He was . . . feeling her."

The policeman had tipped my chin up with his hand and looked hard at me. "Is that right?" he'd asked. And I had nodded dumbly, feeling both very guilty and very important. Now my mother was telling me that I was of no consequence.

"Am *I* supposed to hate Germans?" I asked.

A few years later, when Tati was dead and I was in high school and Hitler had dismembered Czechoslovakia, my mother would become loudly anti-German. But now all she said was, "No. Mr. Leiniger shouldn't have bothered you, but he's only one man. It's not right to hate everyone with a German last name."

"Is that what Tati does?"

"Sometimes."

I told my mother what Tati had shouted at Leiniger, repeating the foreign sounds as best as I could. My mother blushed. "*Nêmecky* means 'German,' " she said reluctantly. "*Prase* means 'pig.' You must never tell anyone you heard your grandfather say such things."

I did not discuss this conversation with Tati. All during that fall, but especially after Leiniger died, I'd come home from school to find Tati waiting for me on the porch, his knobby walking stick in his hands and his cap on his head. He wanted to walk, he was desperate to walk. My mother wouldn't let him leave the house alone but she seldom found the time to go out with him; my brothers could not be bothered. And so Tati waited for me each afternoon like a restless dog.

While we walked in the fields and woods behind our house, we did not talk about what had happened in the greenhouse. Instead, Tati named the ferns and mosses and flowers we passed. He showed me the hawkweeds—Canada hawkweed, spotted hawkweed, poor-Robin's hawkweed. Orange hawkweed, also called devil's paintbrush, creeping into abandoned fields. The plants had long stems, rosettes of leaves at the base, small flowerheads that resembled dandelions. Once Tati opened my eyes to them I realized they were everywhere.

"*Hieracium*," Tati said. "That is their real name. It comes from the Greek word for hawk. The juice from the stem is supposed to make your vision very sharp." They were weeds, he said: extremely hardy. They grew wherever the soil was too poor to support other plants. They were related to asters and daisies and dahlias—all plants I'd seen growing at the nursery— but also to thistles and burdocks. I should remember them, he said. They were important. With his own eyes he had watched the hawkweeds ruin Gregor Mendel's life.

Even now this seems impossible: how could I have known someone of an age to have known Mendel? And yet it was true: Tati had grown up on the outskirts of Brno, the city where Mendel spent most of his life. In 1866, when they first met, there was cholera in Brno, and Prussian soldiers were passing through after the brief and nasty war. Tati was ten then, and those things didn't interest him. He had scaled the white walls of the Augustinian monastery of St. Thomas one afternoon, for a lark. As he'd straddled the wall he'd seen a plump, short-legged man with glasses looking up at him.

"He looked like my mother's uncle," Tati said. "A little bit."

Mendel had held out a hand and helped Tati jump down from the wall. Around him were fruit trees and wild vines; in the distance he saw a clocktower and a long, low building. Where Tati had landed, just where his feet touched ground, there were peas. Not the thousands of plants that would have been there at the height of Mendel's investigations, but still hundreds of plants clinging to sticks and stretched strings.

The place was magical, Tati said. Mendel showed him the tame fox he tied up during the day but allowed to run free at night, the hedgehogs and the hamsters and the mice he kept, the beehives and the cages full of birds. The two of them, the boy and the middle-aged man, made friends. Mendel taught Tati most of his horticultural secrets and later he was responsible for getting him a scholarship to the school where he taught. But Tati said that the first year of their friendship, before the hawkweed experiments, was the best. He and Mendel, side by side, had opened pea flowers and transferred pollen with a camel-hair brush.

On the last day of 1866, Mendel wrote his first letter to Carl Nägeli of Munich, a powerful and well-known botanist known to be interested in hybridization. He sent a copy of his pea paper along with the letter, hoping Nägeli might help it find the recognition it deserved. But he also, in his letter, mentioned that he had started a few experiments with hawkweeds, which he hoped would confirm his results with peas.

Nägeli was an expert on the hawkweeds, and Tati believed that Mendel had only mentioned them to pique Nägeli's interest in his work. Nägeli didn't reply for several months, and when he finally wrote back he said almost nothing about the peas. But he was working on the hawkweeds himself, and he proposed that Mendel turn his experimental skills to them. Mendel, desperate for recognition, ceased to write about his peas and concentrated on the hawkweeds instead.

"Oh, that Nägeli!" Tati said. "Month after month, year after year, I watched Mendel writing his long, patient letters and getting no answer or slow answers or answers off the point.

Whenever Nägeli wrote to Mendel, it was always about the hawkweeds. Later, when I learned why Mendel's experiments with them hadn't worked, I wanted to cry."

The experiments that had given such tidy results with peas gave nothing but chaos with hawkweeds, which were very difficult to hybridize. Experiment after experiment failed; years of work were wasted. The inexplicable behavior of the hawkweeds destroyed Mendel's belief that the laws of heredity he'd worked out with peas would be universally valid. By 1873, Mendel had given up completely. The hawkweeds, and Nägeli behind them, had convinced him that his work was useless.

It was bad luck, Tati said. Bad luck in choosing Nägeli to help him, and in letting Nägeli steer him toward the hawkweeds. Mendel's experimental technique was fine, and his laws of heredity were perfectly true. He could not have known—no one knew for years—that his hawkweeds didn't hybridize in rational ways because they frequently formed seeds without fertilization. "Parthenogenesis," Tati told me—a huge, knobby word that I could hardly get my mouth around. Still, it sounds to me like a disease. "The plants grown from seeds formed this way are exact copies of the mother plant, just like the begonias we make from leaf cuttings."

Mendel gave up on science and spent his last years, after he was elected abbot, struggling with the government over the taxes levied on his monastery. He quarreled with his fellow monks; he grew bitter and isolated. Some of the monks believed he had gone insane. In his quarters he smoked heavy cigars and gazed at the ceiling, which he'd had painted with scenes of saints and fruit trees, beehives and scientific equipment. When Tati came to visit him, his conversation wandered.

Mendel died in January 1884, on the night of Epiphany, confused about the value of his scientific work. That same year, long after their correspondence had ceased, Nägeli published an enormous book summarizing all his years of work. Although many of his opinions and observations seemed to echo Mendel's work with peas, Nägeli made no mention of Mendel or his paper.

That was the story I told Richard. Torn from its context, stripped of the reasons why it was told, it became a story about the beginnings of Richard's discipline. I knew that Richard would have paid money to hear it, but I gave it to him as a gift.

"And your grandfather saw all that?" he said. This was later on in our courtship; we were sitting on a riverbank, drinking Manhattans that Richard had mixed and enjoying the cold spiced beef and marinated vegetables and lemon tart I had brought in a basket. Richard liked my cooking quite a bit. He liked me too, but apparently not enough; I was longing for him to propose but he still hadn't said a word. "Your grandfather saw the letters," he said. "He watched Mendel assembling data for Nägeli. That's remarkable. That's extraordinary. I can't believe the things you know."

There was more, I hinted. What else did I have to offer him? Now it seems to me that I had almost everything: youth and health and an affectionate temperament; the desire to make a family. But then I was more impressed than I should have been by Richard's education.

"More?" he said.

"There are some papers," I said. "That Tati left behind."

Of course I was not allowed in the courtroom, I was much too young. After Leiniger died, the date of the trial was moved forward. I never saw Tati sitting next to the lawyer my father had hired for him; I never saw a judge or a jury and never learned whether my testimony might have helped Tati. I never even learned whether, in that long-ago time, the court would have accepted the testimony of a child, because Tati died on the evening before the first day of the trial.

He had a stroke, my mother said. In the night she heard a

loud, garbled cry and when she ran into the room that had once been mine she found Tati tipped over in bed, with his head hanging down and his face dark and swollen. Afterwards, after the funeral, when I came home from school I no longer went on walks through the woods and fields. I did my homework at the kitchen table and then I helped my mother around the house. On weekends I no longer went to the nursery.

Because there had been no trial, no one in town learned of my role in Leiniger's death. There had been a quarrel between two old men, people thought, and then an accident. No one blamed me or my family. I was able to go through school without people pointing or whispering. I put Tati out of my mind, and with him the nursery and Leiniger, Mendel and Nägeli, and the behavior of the hawkweeds. When the war came I refused to listen to my mother's rantings. After my father died she went to live with one of my married brothers, and I went off on my own. I loved working in the factory; I felt very independent.

Not until the war was over and I met Richard did I dredge up the hawkweed story. Richard's family had been in America for generations and seemed to have no history; that was one of the things that drew me to him. But after our picnic on the riverbank I knew for sure that part of what drew him to me was the way I was linked so closely to other times and places. I gave Richard the yellowed sheets of paper that Tati had left in an envelope for me.

This is a draft of one of Mendel's letters to Nägeli, Tati had written, on a note attached to the manuscript. *He showed it to me once, when he was feeling sad. Later he gave it to me. I want you to have it.*

Richard's voice trembled when he read that note out loud. He turned the pages of Mendel's letter slowly, here and there reading a line to me. The letter was an early one, or perhaps even the first. It was all about peas.

Richard said, "I can't believe I'm holding this in my hand."
"I could give it to you," I said. In my mind this seemed perfectly reasonable. Mendel had given the letter to Tati, the sole friend of his last days; then Tati had passed it to me, when he was no longer around to protect me himself. Now it seemed right that I should give it to the man I wanted to marry.

"To me?" Richard said. "You would give it to me?"

"Someone who appreciates it should have it."

Richard cherished Tati's letter like a jewel. We married, we moved to Schenectady, Richard got a good job at the college, and we had our two daughters. During each of my pregnancies Richard worried that our children might inherit his hexadactyly, but Annie and Joan were both born with regulation fingers and toes. I stayed home with them, first in the apartment on Union Street and then later, after Richard's promotion, in the handsome old house on campus that the college rented to us. Richard wrote papers and served on committees; I gave monthly dinners for the departmental faculty, weekly coffee hours for favored students, picnics for alumni on homecoming weekends. I managed that sort of thing rather well: it was a job, if an unpaid one, and it was expected of me.

Eventually our daughters grew up and moved away. And then, when I was nearly fifty, after Richard had been tenured and won his awards and grown almost unbearably self-satisfied, there came a time when the world went gray on me for the better part of a year.

I still can't explain what happened to me then. My doctor said it was hormones, the beginning of my change of life. My daughters, newly involved with the women's movement, said my years as a housewife had stifled me and that I needed a career of my own. Annie, our oldest, hemmed and hawed and finally asked me if her father and I were still sharing a bed; I said we were but didn't have the heart to tell her that all we did was share it. Richard said I needed more exercise and prescribed daily walks in the college gardens, which were full of exotic specimen trees from every corner of the earth.

He was self-absorbed, but not impossible; he hated to see me suffer. And I suppose he also wanted back the wife who for years had managed his household so well. But I could no longer manage anything. All I knew was that I felt old, and that everything had lost its savor. I lay in the windowseat in our bedroom with an afghan over my legs, watching the students mass and swirl and separate in the quad in front of the library.

This was 1970, when the students seemed to change overnight from pleasant boys into uncouth and hairy men. Every week brought a new protest. Chants and marches and demonstrations; bedsheets hanging like banners from the dormitory windows. The boys who used to come to our house for tea dressed in blue blazers and neatly pressed pants now wore vests with dangling fringes and jeans with holes in them. And when I went to Richard's genetics class that fall, to listen to his first Mendel lecture, I saw that the students gazed out the window while he spoke or tipped back in their chairs with their feet on the desks: openly bored, insubordinate. A girl encased in sheets of straight blond hair—there were girls in class, the college had started admitting them—interrupted Richard mid-sentence and said, "But what's the *relevance* of this? Science confined to the hands of the technocracy produces nothing but destruction."

Richard didn't answer her, but he hurried through the rest of his lecture and left the room without looking at me. That year, he didn't give his other Mendel lecture. The students had refused to do most of the labs; there was no reason, they said, why harmless fruit flies should be condemned to death just to prove a theory that everyone already acknowledged as true. Richard said they didn't deserve to hear about the hawkweeds. They were so dirty, so destructive, that he feared for the safety of Mendel's precious letter.

I was relieved, although I didn't say that; I had no urge to leave my perch on the windowseat and no desire to hear Richard repeat that story again. It seemed to me then that he told it badly. He muddled the dates, compressed the years, identified himself too closely with Mendel, and painted Nägeli as too black a villain. By then I knew that he liked to think of himself as another Mendel, unappreciated and misunderstood. To me he looked more like another Nägeli. I had seen him be less than generous to younger scientists struggling to establish themselves. I had watched him pick, as each year's favored student, not the brightest or most original but the most agreeable and flattering.

That year all the students seemed to mutate, and so there was no favorite student, no obsequious well-dressed boy to join us for Sunday dinner or cocktails after the Wednesday seminars. As I lay in my windowseat, idly addressing envelopes and stuffing them with reprints of Richard's papers, I hardly noticed that the house was emptier than usual. But at night, when I couldn't sleep, I rose from Richard's side and went down to the couch in the living room, where I lay midway between dream and panic. I heard Tati's voice then, telling me about Mendel. I heard Mendel, frantic over those hawkweeds, trying out draft after draft of his letters on the ears of an attentive little boy who sat in a garden next to a fox. *Highly esteemed sir, your honor, I beg you to allow me to submit for your kind consideration the results of these experiments.* How humble Mendel had been in his address, and yet how sure of his science. How kind he had been to Tati.

Some nights I grew very confused. Mendel and Nägeli, Mendel and Tati; Tati and Leiniger, Tati and me. Pairs of men who hated each other and pairs of friends passing papers. A boy I saw pruning shrubs in the college garden turned into a childish Tati, leaping over a white wall. During a nap I dreamed of Leiniger's wife. I had seen her only once; she had come to Tati's funeral. She stood in the back of the church in a brown dress flecked with small white leaves, and when my family left after the service she turned her face from us.

That June, after graduation, Sebastian Dunitz came to us from his lab in Frankfurt. He and Richard had been corresponding and they shared common research interests; Richard had arranged for Sebastian to visit the college for a year, working with Richard for the summer on a joint research project and then, during the fall and spring semesters, as a teaching assistant in the departmental laboratories. He stayed with us, in Annie's old bedroom, but he was little trouble. He did his own laundry and cooked his own meals except when we asked him to join us.

Richard took to Sebastian right away. He was young, bright, very well-educated; although speciation and evolutionary relationships interested him more than the classical Mendelian genetics Richard taught, his manner toward Richard was clearly deferential. Within a month of his arrival, Richard was telling me how, with a bit of luck, a permanent position might open up for his new protegé. Within a month of his arrival, I was up and about, dressed in bright colors, busy cleaning the house from basement to attic and working in the garden. It was nice to have some company around.

Richard invited Sebastian to a picnic dinner with us on the evening of the Fourth of July. This was something we'd done every year when the girls were growing up; we'd let the custom lapse but Richard thought Sebastian might enjoy it. I fried chicken in the morning, before the worst heat of the day; I dressed tomatoes with vinegar and olive oil and chopped fresh basil and I made potato salad and a chocolate cake. When dusk fell, Richard and I gathered a blanket and the picnic basket and our foreign guest and walked to the top of a rounded hill not far from the college grounds. In the distance, we could hear the band that preceded the fireworks.

"This is wonderful," Sebastian said. "Wonderful food, a wonderful night. You have both been very kind to me."

Richard had set a candle in a hurricane lamp in the center of our blanket, and in the dim light Sebastian's hair gleamed like a helmet. We all drank a lot of the sweet white wine that Sebastian had brought as his offering. Richard lay back on his elbows and cleared his throat, surprising me when he spoke.

"Did you know," he said to Sebastian, "that I have an actual draft of a letter that Gregor Mendel wrote to the botanist Nägeli? My dear Antonia gave it to me."

Sebastian looked from me to Richard and back. "Where did you get such a thing?" he asked. "How . . . ?"

Richard began to talk, but I couldn't bear to listen to him tell that story badly one more time. "My grandfather gave it to me," I said, interrupting Richard. "He knew Mendel when he was a little boy." And without giving Richard a chance to say another word, without even looking at the hurt and puzzlement I knew must be on his face, I told Sebastian all about the behavior of the hawkweeds. I told the story slowly, fully, without skipping any parts. In the gathering darkness I moved my hands and did my best to make Sebastian see the wall and the clocktower and the gardens and the hives, the spectacles on Mendel's face and Tati's bare feet. And when I was done, when my words hung in the air and Sebastian murmured appreciatively, I did something I'd never done before, because Richard had never thought to ask the question Sebastian asked.

"How did your grandfather come to tell you that?" he said. "It is perhaps an unusual story to tell a little girl."

"It gave us something to talk about," I said. "We spent a lot of time together, the fall that I was ten. He had killed a man—accidentally, but still the man was dead. He lived with us while we were waiting for the trial."

Overhead, the first fireworks opened into blossoms of red and gold and green. "Antonia," Richard said, but he caught himself. In front of Sebastian he would not admit that this was something his wife of twenty-five years had never told him before. In the light of the white cascading fountain above us I could see him staring at me, but all he said was, "An amazing story, isn't it? I used to tell it to my genetics students every year, but this fall everything was so deranged—I left it out, I knew they wouldn't appreciate it."

"Things are different," Sebastian said. "The world is changing." He did not ask me how it was that my grandfather had killed a man.

The pace and intensity of the fireworks increased, until all of them seemed to be exploding at once; then there was one final crash and then silence and darkness. I had been rude, I knew. I had deprived Richard of one of his great pleasures simply for the sake of hearing that story told well once.

We gathered up our blanket and basket and walked home quietly. The house was dark and empty. In the living room I turned on a single light and then went to the kitchen to make coffee; when I came in with the tray the men were talking quietly about their work. "I believe what we have here is a *Rassenkreis*," Sebastian said, and he turned to include me in the conversation. In his short time with us, he had always paid me the compliment of assuming I understood his and Richard's work. "A German word," he said. "It means 'race-circle'—it is what we call it when a species spread over a large area is broken into a chain of subspecies, each of which differs slightly from its neighbors. The neighboring subspecies can interbreed, but the subspecies at the two ends of the chain may be so different that they cannot. In the population that Richard and I are examining. . . ."

"I am very tired," Richard said abruptly. "If you'll excuse me, I think I'll go up to bed."

"No coffee?" I said.

He looked at a spot just beyond my shoulder, as he always did when he was upset. "No," he said. "Are you coming?"

"Soon," I said.

And then, in that dim room, Sebastian came and sat in the chair right next to mine. "Is Richard well?" he said. "Is something wrong?"

"He's fine. Only tired. He's been working hard."

"That was a lovely story you told. When I was a boy, at university, our teachers did not talk about Nägeli, except to dismiss him as a Lamarkian. They would skip from Mendel's paper on the peas to its rediscovery, later. Nägeli's student, Correns, and Hugo de Vries—do you know about the evening primroses and de Vries?"

I shook my head. We sat at the dark end of the living room, near the stairs and away from the windows. Still, occasionally, came the sound of a renegade firecracker.

"No? You will like this."

But before he could tell me his anecdote I leaned toward him and rested my hand on his forearm. His skin was as smooth as a flower. "Don't tell me any more science," I said. "Tell me about yourself."

There was a pause. Then Sebastian pulled his arm away abruptly and stood up. "Please," he said. "You're an attractive woman, still. And I am flattered. But it's quite impossible, anything between us." His accent, usually almost imperceptible, thickened with those words.

I was grateful for the darkness that hid my flush. "You misunderstood," I said. "I didn't mean . . ."

"Don't be embarrassed," he said. "I've seen the way you watch me when you think I am not looking. I appreciate it."

A word came back to me, a word I thought I'd forgotten. "*Prase*," I muttered.

"What?" he said. Then I heard a noise on the stairs behind me, and a hand fell on my shoulder. I reached up and felt the knob where Richard's extra finger had once been.

"Antonia," Richard said. His voice was very gentle. "It's

so late—won't you come up to bed?" He did not say a word to Sebastian; upstairs, in our quiet room, he neither accused me of anything nor pressed me to explain the mysterious comment I'd made about my grandfather. I don't know what he said later to Sebastian, or how he arranged things with the Dean. But two days later Sebastian moved into an empty dormitory room, and before the end of the summer he was gone.

Nêmecky, prase; secret words. I have forgotten almost all the rest of Tati's language, and both he and Leiniger have been dead for sixty years. Sebastian Dunitz is back in Frankfurt, where he has grown very famous. The students study molecules now, spinning models across their computer screens and splicing the genes of one creature into those of another. The science of genetics is utterly changed and Richard has been forgotten by everyone. Sometimes I wonder where we have misplaced our lives.

Of course Richard no longer teaches. The college retired him when he turned sixty-five, despite his protests. Now they trot him out for dedications and graduations and departmental celebrations, along with the other emeritus professors who haunt the library and the halls. Without his class, he has no audience for his treasured stories. Instead he corners people at the dim, sad ends of parties when he's had too much to drink. Young instructors, too worried about their jobs to risk being impolite, turn their ears to Richard like flowers. He keeps them in place with a knobby hand on a sleeve or knee as he talks.

When I finally told him what had happened to Tati, I didn't really tell him anything. Two old men had quarreled, I said. An immigrant and an immigrant's son, arguing over some plants. But Tati and Leiniger, Richard decided, were Mendel and Nägeli all over again; surely Tati identified with Mendel and cast Leiniger as another Nägeli? Although he still doesn't know of my role in the accident, somehow the equation he's made between these pairs of men allows him to tell his tale with more sympathy, more balance. As he talks he looks across the room and smiles at me. I nod and smile back at him, thinking of Annie, whose first son was born with six toes on each foot.

Sebastian sent me a letter the summer after he left us, in which he finished the story I'd interrupted on that Fourth of July. The young Dutch botanist Hugo de Vries, he wrote, spent his summers searching the countryside for new species. One day, near Hilversum, he came to an abandoned potato field glowing strangely in the sun. The great evening primrose had been cultivated in a small bed in a nearby park; the plants had run wild and escaped into the field, where they formed a jungle as high as a man. From 1886 through 1888, de Vries made thousands of hybridization experiments with them, tracing the persistence of mutations. During his search for a way to explain his results, he uncovered Mendel's paper and found that Mendel had anticipated all his theories. Peas and primroses, primroses and peas, passing their traits serenely through generations.

I still have this letter, as Richard still has Mendel's. I wonder, sometimes, what Tati would have thought of all this. Not the story about Hugo de Vries, which he probably knew, but the way it came to me in a blue airmail envelope, from a scientist who meant to be kind. I think of Tati when I imagine Sebastian composing his answer to me.

Because it was an answer, of sorts; in the months after he left I mailed him several letters. They were, on the surface, about Mendel and Tati, all I recalled of their friendship. But I'm sure Sebastian read them for what they were. In 1906, Sebastian wrote, after Mendel's work was finally recognized, a small museum was opened in the Augustinian monastery. Sebastian visited it, when he passed through Brno on a family holiday.

"I could find no trace of your Tati," he wrote. "But the wall is still here, and you can see where the garden was. It's a lovely place. Perhaps you should visit someday."

The English Pupil

Outside Uppsala, on a late December afternoon in 1777, a figure tucked in a small sleigh ordered his coachman to keep driving.

"Hammarby," he said. "Please."

The words were cracked, almost unintelligible. The coachman was afraid. At home he had a wife, two daughters, and a mother-in-law, all dependent on him; his employers had strictly forbidden him to take the sleigh beyond the city limits, and he feared for his job. But his master was dying and these afternoon drives were his only remaining pleasure. He was weak and depressed and it had been months since he'd voiced even such a modest wish.

How could the coachman say no? He grumbled a bit and then drove the few miles across the plain without further complaint.

It was very cold. The air was crisp and dry. The sun, already low in the sky, made the fields glitter. Beneath the sleigh the snow was so smooth that the runners seemed to float. Carl Linnaeus, wrapped in sheepskins, watched the landscape speeding by and thought of Lappland, which he'd explored when he was young. Aspens and alders and birches budding, geese with their tiny yellow goslings. Gadflies longing to lay their eggs chased frantic herds of reindeer. In Jokkmokk, near the Gulf of Bothnia, the local pastor had tried to convince him that the clouds sweeping over the mountains carried off trees and animals.

He had learned how to trap ptarmigan, how to shoot wolves with a bow, how to make thread with reindeer tendons, and how to cure chilblains with the fat that exuded from toasted reindeer cheese. At night, under the polar star, the sheer beauty of the natural world had knocked him to the ground. He had been twenty-five then, and wildly energetic. Now he was seventy.

His once-famous memory was nearly gone, eroded by a series of strokes—he forgot where he was and what he was doing; he forgot the names of plants and animals; he forgot faces, places, dates. Sometimes he forgot his own name. His mind, which had once seemed to hold the whole world, had been occupied by a great dark lake that spread farther every day and around which he tiptoed gingerly. When he reached for facts they darted like minnows across the water and could only be captured by cunning and indirection. Pehr Artedi, the friend of his youth, had brought order to the study of fishes, the minnows included. In Amsterdam Artedi had fallen into a canal after a night of beer and conversation and had been found the next morning, drowned.

The sleigh flew through the snowy landscape. His legs were paralyzed, along with one arm and his bladder and part of his face; he could not dress or wash or feed himself. At home, when he tried to rise from his armchair unaided, he fell and lay helpless on the floor until his wife, Sara Lisa, retrieved him. Sara Lisa was busy with other tasks and often he lay there for some time.

But Sara Lisa was back at their house in Uppsala, and he was beyond her reach. The horses pulling him might have been reindeer; the coachman a Lapp dressed in fur and skins. Hammarby, the estate he'd bought as a country retreat years ago, at the height of his fame, was waiting for him. The door leading into the kitchen was wide and the sleigh was small. Linnaeus gestured for the coachman to push the sleigh inside.

The coachman was called Pehr; a common name. There had

been Artedi, of course, and then after him all the students named Pehr: Pehr Lofling, Pehr Forskal, Pehr Osbeck, Pehr Kalm. Half of them were dead. This Pehr, the coachman Pehr, lifted Linnaeus out of the sleigh and carried him carefully into the house. The kitchen was clean and almost bare: a rough table, a few straight chairs.

Pehr set Linnaeus on the floor, propped against the wall, and then he went back outside and unhitched the horses and shoved the sleigh through the door and in front of the stone fireplace. He was very worried and feared he had made a mistake. His master's face was white and drawn and his hand, gesturing from the sleigh to the door again and again, had been curled like a claw.

"Fire?" Linnaeus said, or thought he said. At certain moments, when the lake receded a bit and left a wider path around the shore, he was aware that the words coming out of his mouth bore little resemblance to the words he meant. Often he could only produce a syllable at a time. But he said something and gestured toward the fireplace, and Pehr had a good deal of sense. Pehr lifted Linnaeus back into the sleigh, tucked the sheepskins around his legs and his torso, and then built a fire. Soon the flames began to warm the room. The sky darkened outside; the room was dark except for the glow from the logs. Pehr went out to tend to the horses and Linnaeus, staring into the flames, felt his beloved place around him.

He'd rebuilt this house and added several wings; on the hill he'd built a small museum for his herbarium and his insect collection and his rocks and zoological specimens. In his study and bedroom the walls were papered from ceiling to floor with botanical etchings and prints, and outside, among the elms and beyond the Siberian garden, the glass bells he'd hung sang in the wind. In his youth he had heard the cries of ptarmigan, which had sounded like a kind of laughter. The fire was warm on his

face and his hands, and when Pehr returned from the horses
Linnaeus gestured toward his tobacco and his pipe.

Pehr filled the pipe, lit it, and placed it in his master's mouth.
"We should go back," he said. "Your family will be worried."
Worried was a kind word, Pehr knew; his master's wife would
be raging, possibly blaming him. They were an hour late already
and the sun was gone.

Linnaeus puffed on his pipe and said nothing. He was very
pleased with himself. The fire was warm, his pipe drew well, no
one knew where he was but Pehr and Pehr had the rare gift of
silence. A dog lying near the hearth would have completed his
happiness. Across the dark lake in his mind he saw Pompey, the
best of all his dogs, barking at the water. Pompey had walked
with him each summer Sunday from here to the parish church
and sat in the pew beside him. They'd stayed for an hour, ample
time for a sermon; if the parson spoke longer they rose and left
anyway. Pompey, so smart and funny, had learned the pattern
if not the meaning. When Linnaeus was ill, Pompey left for
church at the appropriate time, hopped into the appropriate
bench, stayed for an hour and then scampered out. The neighbors
had learned to watch for his antics. Now he was dead.

"Sir?" the coachman said.

His name was Pehr, Linnaeus remembered. Like Osbeck
and Forskal, Lofling and Kalm. There had been others, too:
those he had taught at the university in Uppsala and those he
had taught privately here at Hammarby. Germans and Danes,
Russians and Swiss, Finns and a few Norwegians; a Frenchman,
who had not worked out, and an American, who had; one En-
glishman, still around. And then there were those he had hardly
known, who had come by the hundreds to the great botanic
excursions he'd organized around the city. Dressed in loose linen
suits, their arms full of nets and jars, they had trailed him in a
huge parade, gathering plants and insects and herding around

him at resting places to listen to him lecture on the treasures they'd found. They were young, and when he was young he had often kept them out for twelve or thirteen hours at a stretch. On their return to the Botanic Gardens they had sometimes been hailed by a kettledrum and French horns. Outside the garden the band had stopped and cheered: *Vivat scientia! Vivat Linnaeus!* Lately there were those who attacked his work.

The coachman was worried, Linnaeus could see. He crouched to the right of the sleigh, tapping a bit of kindling on the floor. "They will be looking for you," he said.

And of course it was true; his family was always looking for him. Always looking, wanting, needing, demanding. He had written and taught and lectured and tutored, traveled and scrabbled and scrambled; and always Sara Lisa said there was not enough money, they needed more, she was worried about Carl Junior and the girls. Carl Junior was lazy, he needed more schooling. The girls needed frocks, the girls needed shoes. The girls needed earrings to wear to a dance where they might meet appropriate husbands.

The three oldest looked and acted like their mother: large-boned, coarse-featured, practical. Sophia seemed to belong to another genus entirely. He thought of her fine straight nose, her beautiful eyes. When she was small he used to take her with him to his lectures, where she would stand between his knees and listen. Now she was engaged. On his tour of Lappland, with the whole world still waiting to be named, he'd believed that he and everyone he loved would live forever.

Now he had named almost everything and everyone knew his name. How clear and simple was the system of his nomenclature! Two names, like human names: a generic name common to all the species of one genus; a specific name distinguishing differences. He liked names that clearly described a feature of the genus: *Potamogeton*, by the river; *Drosera*, like a dew. Names that honored botanists also pleased him. In England the

King had built a huge garden called Kew, in which wooden labels named each plant according to his system. The King of France had done the same thing at the Trianon. In Spain and Russia and South America plants bore names that he'd devised, and on his coat he wore the ribbon that named him a Knight of the Polar Star. But his monkey Grinn, a present from the Queen, was dead; and also Sjup the raccoon and the parrot who had sat on his shoulder at meals and the weasel who wore a bell on his neck and hunted rats among the rocks.

There was a noise outside. Pehr leapt up and a woman and a man walked through the door. Pehr was all apologies, blushing, shuffling, nervous. The woman touched his arm and said, "It wasn't your fault." Then she said, "Papa?"

One of his daughters, Linnaeus thought. She was pretty, she was smiling; she was almost surely Sophia. The man by her side looked familiar, and from the way he held Sophia's elbow Linnaeus wondered if it might be her husband. Had she married? He remembered no wedding. Her fiancé? Her fiancé, then. Or not: the man bent low, bringing his face down to Linnaeus's like the moon falling from the sky.

"Sir?" he said. "Sir?"

One of those moments in which no words were possible was upon him. He gazed at the open, handsome face of the young man, aware that this was someone he knew. The man said, "It's Rotheram, sir."

Rotheram. Rotheram. The sound was like the wind moving over the Lappland hills. Rotheram, one of his pupils, not a fiancé at all. Human beings had two names, like plants, by which they might be recalled. Nature was a cryptogram and the scientific method a key; nature was a labyrinth and this method the thread of Ariadne. Or the world was an alphabet written in God's hand, which he, Carl Linnaeus, had been called to decipher. One of his pupils had come to see him, one of the pupils he'd sent to all the corners of the world and called, half-jokingly, his apostles.

This one straightened now, a few feet away, most considerately not blocking the fire. What was his name? He was young, vigorous, strongly built. Was he Lofling, then? Or Ternström, Hasselquist, Falck?

The woman frowned. "Papa," she said. "Can we just sit you up? We've been looking everywhere for you."

Sophia. The man bent over again, sliding his hands beneath Linnaeus's armpits and gently raising him to a sitting position. He was Hasselquist or Ternström, Lofling or Forskal or Falck. Or he was none of them, because all of them were dead.

Linnaeus's mind left his body, rose and traveled along the paths his apostles had taken. He was young again, as they had been: twenty-five, thirty, thirty-five, the years he had done his best work. He was Christopher Ternström, that married pastor who'd been such a passionate botanist. Sailing to the East Indies in search of a tea plant and some living goldfish to give to the Queen, mailing letters back to his teacher from Cádiz. On a group of islands off Cambodia he had succumbed to a tropical fever. His wife had berated Linnaeus for luring her husband to his death.

But he was not Linnaeus. He was Fredrik Hasselquist, modest and poor, who had landed in Smyrna and traveled through Palestine and Syria and Cyprus and Rhodes, gathering plants and animals and keeping a diary so precise that it had broken Linnaeus's heart to edit it. Twice he had performed this task, once for Hasselquist, once for Artedi. After the drowning, he had edited Artedi's book on the fish. Hasselquist died in a village outside Smyrna, when he was thirty.

Of course there were those who had made it back: Pehr Osbeck, who had returned from China with a huge collection of new plants and a china tea-set decorated with Linnaeus's own flower; Marten Kahler, who'd returned with nothing. Kahler's health had been broken by the shipwreck in the North Sea, by the fever that followed the attack in Marseilles, by his endless, grinding poverty. The chest containing his collections had been captured by pirates long before it reached Sweden. Then there was Rolander, Daniel Rolander—was that the man who was with him now?

But he had said Ro . . ., Ro . . . *Rotheram, that's who it was, the English pupil.* Nomenclature is a mnemonic art. In Surinam the heat had crumpled Rolander's body and melted his mind. All he brought home was a lone pot of Indian fig covered with cochineal insects, which Linnaeus's gardener had mistakenly washed away. Lost insects and a handful of gray seeds, which Rolander claimed to be pearls. When Linnaeus gently pointed out the error, Rolander had left in a huff for Denmark, where he was reportedly living on charity. The others were dead: Lofling, Forskal, and Falck.

Sophia said, "Papa, we looked all over—why didn't you come back?"

Pehr the coachman said, "I'm sorry, he begged me."

The pupil—*Lofling?*—said, "How long has he been weeping like this?"

But Pehr wasn't weeping, Pehr was fine. Someone, not Pehr or Sophia, was laughing. Linnaeus remembered how Lofling had taken dictation from him when his hands were crippled by gout. Lofling was twenty-one, he was only a boy; he had tutored Carl Junior, the lazy son. In Spain Lofling had made a name for himself and had sent letters and plants to Linnaeus; then he'd gone to South America with a Spanish expedition. Venezuela; another place Linnaeus had never been. But he had seen it, through Lofling's letters and specimens. Birds so brightly colored they seemed to be jeweled and rivers that pulsed, foamy and brown, through ferns the height of a man. The letter from Spain announcing Lofling's death from fever had come only months after little Johannes had died.

There he sat, in his sleigh in the kitchen, surrounded by the dead. "Are you laughing, Papa?" Sophia said. "Are you happy?"

His apostles had gone out into the world like his own organs: extra eyes and hands and feet, observing, gathering, naming. Someone was stroking his hands. Pehr Forskal, after visiting Marseilles and Malta and Constantinople, reached Alexandria one October and dressed as a peasant to conceal himself from marauding Bedouins. In Cairo he roamed the streets in his disguise and made a fine collection of new plants; then he traveled by Suez and Jedda to Arabia, where he was stricken by plague and died. Months later, a letter arrived containing a stalk and a flower from a tree that Linnaeus had always wanted to see: the evergreen from which the Balm of Gilead was obtained. The smell was spicy and sweet but Forskal, who had also tutored Carl Junior, was gone. And Falck, who had meant to accompany Forskal on his Arabian journey, was gone as well—he had gone to St. Petersburg instead, and then traveled through Turkestan and Mongolia. Lonely and lost and sad in Kazan, he had shot himself in the head.

Outside the weather had changed and now it was raining. The pupil: Falck or Forskal, Osbeck or Rolander—*Rotheram, who had fallen ill several years ago, whom Sophia had nursed, who came and went from his house like family*—said, "I hate to move you, sir; I know you're enjoying it here. But the rain is ruining the track. We'll have a hard time if we don't leave soon."

Rolander? There was a story about Rolander, which he had used as the basis for a lecture on medicine and, later, in a paper. Where had it come from? A letter, perhaps. Or maybe Rolander had related it himself, before his mind disintegrated completely. On the ship, on the way to Surinam, he had fallen ill with dysentery. Ever the scientist, trained by his teacher, he'd examined his feces and found thousands of mites in them. He held his magnifying glass to the wooden beaker he'd sipped from in the night, and found a dense white line of flour mites down near the base.

Kahler lashed himself to the mast of his boat, where he remained two days and two nights without food.

Hasselquist died in the village of Bagda.

Pehr Kalm crossed the Great Lakes and walked into Canada.

In Denmark, someone stole Rolander's gray seeds, almost as if they'd been truly pearls.

Generic names, he had taught these pupils, must be clear and stable and expressive. They should not be vague or confusing; neither should they be primitive, barbarous, lengthy, or difficult to pronounce. They should have significant metaphorical or historical associations with the character of the genus. Another botanist had named the thyme-leaved bell-flower after him: *Linnaea borealis*. One June, in Lappland, he had seen it flourishing. His apostles had died in this order: Ternström, Hasselquist, Lofling, Forskal, Falck, and then finally Kahler, at home. His second son, Johannes, had died at the age of two, between Hasselquist and Lofling; but that was also the year of Sophia's birth. Once, when Sophia had dropped a tray full of dishes, he had secretly bought a new set to replace them, to spare her from her mother's wrath.

His apostles had taken wing like swallows, but they had failed to return. Swallows wintered beneath the lakes, or so he had always believed. During the autumn, he had written, they gather in large groups in the weeds and then dive, resting beneath the ice until spring. An English friend—Collinson, Peter in his own tongue but truly Pehr, and also dead—had argued with him over this and begged him to hold some swallows under water to see if they could live there. Was it so strange to think they might sleep beneath the water above which they hovered in summer? Was it not stranger to think they flew for thousands of miles? He knew another naturalist who believed that swallows wintered on the moon. But always there had been people, like his wife, who criticized his every word.

He had fought off all of them. The Queen had ennobled him: he was Carl von Linné now. But the pupils he'd sent out as his eyes and ears were dead. During his years in Uppsala he had written and lectured about the mud iguana of Carolina and Siberian buckwheat and bearberries; about lemmings and ants and a phosphorescent Chinese grasshopper. Fossils, crystals, the causes of leprosy and intermittent fever—all these things he had known about because of his pupils' travels. Over his bedroom door he'd inscribed this motto: "Live blamelessly; God is present."

A group of men had appeared to the left of the fire. Lofling, Forskal, Falck he saw, and also Ternström and Hasselquist. And another, whom he'd forgotten about: Carl Thunberg, his fellow Smalander.

Thunberg was back, then? Thunberg, the last he had heard, was still alive. From Paris Thunberg had gone to Holland. From Holland he had gone to the Cape of Good Hope, and then to Java and finally to Japan. In Japan he had been confined to the tiny island of Deshima, isolated like all the foreigners. So desperate had he been to learn about the Japanese flora that he had picked daily through the fodder the servants brought to feed the swine and cattle. He had begged the Japanese servants to bring him samples from their gardens.

Of all his pupils, Thunberg had been the most faithful about sending letters and herbarium specimens home. He had been scrupulous about spreading his teacher's methods. "I have met some Japanese doctors," he'd written. "I have been teaching them botany and Linnaean taxonomy. They welcome your method and sing your praises." He had also, Linnaeus remembered, introduced into Japan the treatment of syphilis by quicksilver. He had left Japan with crates of specimens; he'd been headed for Ceylon. But here he was, sharp-featured and elegant, leaning on the mantelpiece and trading tales with his predecessors.

"The people are small and dark and suspicious of us," he was saying. "They find us coarse. But their gardens are magnificent, and they have ways of stunting trees that I have never seen before."

"In Palestine," Hasselquist replied, "the land is so dry that the smallest plants send roots down for many feet, searching for buried water."

"The tropics cannot be described," Lofling said. "The astonishing fertility, the way the vegetation is layered from the ground to the sky, the epiphytes clumped in the highest branches like lace . . ."

"Alexandria," Forskal said. "Everything there is so ancient, so layered with history."

"My health is broken," Falck said; and Kahler said, "I walked from Rome almost all the way to Sweden."

In Lappland, Linnaeus said silently, *a gray gnat with striated wings and black legs cruelly tormented me and my most miserable horse.* His apostles did not seem to hear him. *A very bright and calm day*, he said. *The great Myrgiolingen was flying in the marshes.*

"We'll go home now, Papa," the tall woman said. "We'll put you to bed. Won't you like that?"

Her face was as radiant as a star. What was her name? Beside her, his apostles held leaves and twigs and scraps of blossoms, all new and named by them with their teacher's advice. They were trading these among themselves. A leaf from a new succulent for a spray from a never-seen orchid. Two fronds of a miniature fern for a twig from a dwarf evergreen. They were so excited that their voices were rising; they might have been playing cards, laying down plants for bets instead of gold. But the woman and the other pupil didn't seem to notice them. The woman and the other pupil were wholly focused on helping Pehr the coachman push the sleigh back outside.

The woman opened the doors and held them. Pehr and the

pupil pushed and pulled. The crisp, winy air of the afternoon had turned dank and raw, and a light rain was turning the snow to slush. Linnaeus said nothing, but he turned and gazed over his shoulder. The group gathered by the fireplace stepped back, displeased, when Pehr returned and doused the fire. Thunberg looked at Linnaeus and raised an eyebrow. Linnaeus nodded.

In the hands of his lost ones were the plants he had named for them: *Artedia*, an umbelliferous plant, and *Osbeckia*, tall and handsome; *Loeflingia*, a small plant from Spain; *Thunbergia* with its black eye centered in yellow petals, and the tropical *Ternstroemia*. There were more, he couldn't remember them all. He'd named thousands of plants in his life.

Outside, the woman and the pupil separated. *Sophia? Sophia, my favorite.* Sophia bundled herself into the borrowed sleigh in which she'd arrived; the pupil wedged himself into Pehr's sleigh, next to Linnaeus. In the dark damp air they formed a line that could hardly be seen: Pehr's sleigh, and then Sophia's, and behind them, following the cunning signal Linnaeus had given, the last sleigh filled with his apostles. Pehr huddled into his coat and gave the signal to depart. It was late and he was weary. To their left, the rain and melting snow had turned the low field into a lake. Linnaeus looked up at his pupil—*Rotheram? Of course it was him: the English pupil, the last one, the one who would survive him*—and tried to say, "The death of many whom I have induced to travel has turned my hair gray, and what have I gained? A few dried plants, accompanied by great anxiety, unrest, and care."

Rotheram said, "Rest your head on my arm. We will be home before you know it."

The Littoral Zone

When they met, fifteen years ago, Jonathan had a job teaching botany at a small college near Albany, and Ruby was teaching invertebrate zoology at a college in the Berkshires. Both of them, along with an ornithologist, an ichthyologist, and an oceanographer, had agreed to spend three weeks of their summer break at a marine biology research station on an island off the New Hampshire coast. They had spouses, children, mortgages, bills; they went, they later told each other, because the pay was too good to refuse. Two-thirds of the way through the course, they agreed that the pay was not enough.

How they reached that first agreement is a story they've repeated to each other again and again and told, separately, to their closest friends. Ruby thinks they had this conversation on the second Friday of the course, after Frank Kenary's slide show on the abyssal fish and before Carol Dagliesh's lecture on the courting behavior of herring gulls. Jonathan maintains that they had it earlier—that Wednesday, maybe, when they were still recovering from Gunnar Erickson's trawling expedition. The days before they became so aware of each other have blurred in their minds, but they agree that their first real conversation took place on the afternoon devoted to the littoral zone.

The tide was all the way out. The students were clumped on the rocky, pitted apron between the water and the ledges, peering into the tidal pools and listing the species they found. Gunnar was in the equipment room, repairing one of the sampling claws. Frank was setting up dissections in the tiny lab; Carol had gone back to the mainland on the supply boat, hoping to replace the camera one of the students had dropped. And so the two of them, Jonathan and Ruby, were left alone for a little while.

They both remember the granite ledge where they sat, and the raucous quarrels of the nesting gulls. They agree that Ruby was scratching furiously at her calves and that Jonathan said, "Take it easy, okay? You'll draw blood."

Her calves were slim and tan, Jonathan remembers. Covered with blotches and scrapes.

I folded my fingers, Ruby remembers. Then I blushed. My throat felt sunburned.

Ruby said, "I know, it's so embarrassing. But all this salt on my poison ivy—God, what I wouldn't give for a bath! They never told me there wouldn't be any *water* here. . . ."

Jonathan gestured at the ocean surrounding them and then they started laughing. *Hysteria*, they have told each other since. They were so tired by then, twelve days into the course, and so dirty and overworked and strained by pretending to the students that these things didn't matter, that neither of them could understand that they were also lonely. Their shared laughter felt like pure relief.

"No water?" Jonathan said. "I haven't been dry since we got here. My clothes are damp, my sneakers are damp, my hair never dries. . . ."

His hair was beautiful, Ruby remembers. Thick, a little too long. Part blond and part brown.

"I know," she said. "But you know what I mean. I didn't realize they'd have to bring our drinking water over on a boat."

"Or that they'd expect us to wash in the ocean," Jonathan

said. Her forearms were dusted with salt, he remembers. The down along them sparkled in the sun.

"And those cots," Ruby said. "Does yours have a sag in it like a hammock?"

"Like a slingshot," Jonathan said.

For half an hour they sat on their ledge and compared their bubbling patches of poison ivy and the barnacle wounds that scored their hands and feet. Nothing healed out here, they told each other. Everything got infected. When one of the students called, "Look what I found!" Jonathan rose and held his hand out to Ruby. She took it easily and hauled herself up and they walked down to the water together. Jonathan's hand was thick and blunt-fingered, with nails bitten down so far that the skin around them was raw. Odd, Ruby remembers thinking. Those bitten stumps attached to such a good-looking man.

They have always agreed that the worst moment, for each of them, was when they stepped from the boat to the dock on the final day of the course and saw their families waiting in the parking lot. Jonathan's wife had their four-year-old daughter balanced on her shoulders. Their two older children were leaning perilously over the guardrails and shrieking at the sight of him. Jessie had turned nine in Jonathan's absence, and Jonathan can't think of her eager face without remembering the starfish he brought as his sole, guilty gift.

Ruby's husband had parked their car just a few yards from Jonathan's family. Her sons were wearing baseball caps, and what Ruby remembers is the way the yellow linings lit their faces. For a minute she saw the children squealing near her sons as faceless, inconsequential; Jonathan later told her that her children had been similarly blurred for him. Then Jonathan said, "That's my family, there," and Ruby said, "That's mine, right next to yours," and all the faces leapt into focus for both of them.

Nothing that was to come—not the days in court, nor the days they moved, nor the losses of jobs and homes—would ever seem so awful to them as that moment when they first saw their families standing there, unaware and hopeful. Deceitfully, treacherously, Ruby and Jonathan separated and walked to the people awaiting them. They didn't introduce each other to their spouses. They didn't look at each other—although, they later admitted, they cast covert looks at each other's families. They thought they were invisible, that no one could see what had happened between them. They thought their families would not remember how they had stepped off the boat and stood, for an instant, together.

On that boat, sitting dumb and miserable in the litter of nets and equipment, they had each pretended to be resigned to going home. Each foresaw (or so they later told each other) the hysterical phone calls and the frenzied, secret meetings. Neither foresaw how much the sight of each other's family would hurt. "Sweetie," Jonathan remembers Ruby's husband saying. "You've lost so much weight." Ruby remembers staring over her husband's shoulder and watching Jessie butt her head like a dog under Jonathan's hand.

For the first twelve days on the island, Jonathan and Ruby were so busy that they hardly noticed each other. For the next few days, after their conversation on the ledge, they sat near each other during faculty lectures and student presentations. These were held in the library, a ramshackle building separated from the bunkhouse and the dining hall by a stretch of wild roses and poison ivy.

Jonathan had talked about algae in there, holding up samples of *Fucus* and *Hildenbrandtia*. Ruby had talked about the littoral zone, that space between high and low watermarks where organisms struggled to adapt to the daily rhythm of immersion and exposure. They had drawn on the blackboard in colored chalk while the students, itchy and hot and tired, scratched their arms and legs and feigned attention.

Neither of them, they admitted much later, had focused fully on the other's lecture. "It was *before*," Ruby has said ruefully. "I didn't know that I was going to want to have listened." And Jonathan has laughed and confessed that he was studying the shells and skulls on the walls while Ruby was drawing on the board.

The library was exceedingly hot, they agreed, and the chairs remarkably uncomfortable; the only good spot was the sofa in front of the fireplace. That was the spot they commandeered on the evening after their first conversation, when dinner led to a walk and then the walk led them into the library a few minutes before the scheduled lecture.

Erika Moorhead, Ruby remembers. Talking about the tensile strength of byssus threads.

Walter Schank, Jonathan remembers. Something to do with hydrozoans.

They both remember feeling comfortable for the first time since their arrival. And for the next few days—three by Ruby's accounting; four by Jonathan's—one of them came early for every lecture and saved a seat on the sofa for the other.

They giggled at Frank Kenary's slides, which he'd arranged like a creepy fashion show: abyssal fish sporting varied blobs of luminescent flesh. When Gunnar talked for two hours about subduction zones and the calcium carbonate cycle, they amused themselves exchanging doodles. They can't remember, now, whether Gunnar's endless lecture came before Carol Dagliesh's filmstrip on the herring gulls, or which of the students tipped over the dissecting scope and sent the dish of copepods to their deaths. But both of them remember those days and nights as being almost purely happy. They swam in that odd, indefinite zone where they were more than friends, not yet lovers, still able to deny to themselves that they were headed where they were headed.

Ruby made the first phone call, a week after they left the island. At eleven o'clock on a Sunday night, she told her husband she'd left something in her office that she needed to prepare the next day's class. She drove to campus, unlocked her door, picked up the phone and called Jonathan at his house. One of his children—Jessie, she thinks—answered the phone. Ruby remembers how, even through the turmoil of her emotions, she'd been shocked at the idea of a child staying up so late.

There was a horrible moment while Jessie went to find her father; another when Jonathan, hearing Ruby's voice, said, "Wait, hang on, I'll just be a minute," and then negotiated Jessie into bed. Ruby waited, dreading his anger, knowing she'd been wrong to call him at home. But Jonathan, when he finally returned, said, "Ruby. You got my letter."

"What letter?" she asked. He wrote to tell me good-bye, she remembers thinking.

"My *letter*," he said. "I wrote you, I have to see you. I can't stand this."

Ruby released the breath she hadn't known she was holding.

"You didn't get it?" he said. "You just called?" It wasn't only me, he remembers thinking. She feels it too.

"I had to hear your voice," she said.

Ruby called, but Jonathan wrote. And so when Jonathan's youngest daughter, Cora, later fell in love and confided in Ruby, and then asked her, "Was it like this with you two? Who started it—you or Dad?" all Ruby could say was, "It happened to both of us."

. . .

Sometimes, when Ruby and Jonathan sit on the patio looking out at the hills above Palmyra, they will turn and see their children watching them through the kitchen window. Before the children went off to college, the house bulged with them on weekends and holidays and seemed empty in between; Jonathan's wife had custody of Jessie and Gordon and Cora, and Ruby's husband took her sons, Mickey and Ryan, when he remarried. Now that the children are old enough to come and go as they please, the house is silent almost all the time.

Jessie is twenty-four, and Gordon is twenty-two; Mickey is twenty-one, and Cora and Ryan are both nineteen. When they visit Jonathan and Ruby they spend an unhealthy amount of time talking about their past. In their conversations they seem to split their lives into three epochs: the years when what they think of as their real families were whole; the years right after Jonathan and Ruby met, when their parents were coming and going, fighting and making up, separating and divorcing; and the years since Jonathan and Ruby's marriage, when they were forced into a reconstituted family. Which epoch they decide to explore depends on who's visiting and who's getting along with whom.

"But we were happy," Mickey may say to Ruby, if he and Ryan are visiting and Jonathan's children are absent. "We were, we were fine."

"It wasn't like you and Mom ever fought," Cora may say to Jonathan, if Ruby's sons aren't around. "You could have worked it out if you'd tried."

When they are all together, they tend to avoid the first two epochs and to talk about their first strained weekends and holidays together. They've learned to tolerate each other, despite their forced introductions; Cora and Ryan, whose birthdays are less than three months apart, seem especially close. Ruby and Jonathan know that much of what draws their youngest children together is shared speculation about what happened on that island.

They look old to their children, they know. Both of them are nearing fifty. Jonathan has grown quite heavy and has lost much of his hair; Ruby's fine-boned figure has gone gaunt and stringy. They know their children can't imagine them young and strong and wrung by passion. The children can't think—can't stand to think—about what happened on the island, but they can't stop themselves from asking questions.

"Did you have other girlfriends?" Cora asks Jonathan. "Were you so unhappy with Mom?"

"Did you know him before?" Ryan asks Ruby. "Did you go there to be with him?"

"We met there," Jonathan and Ruby say. "We had never seen each other before. We fell in love." That is all they will say, they never give details, they say "yes" or "no" to the easy questions and evade the hard ones. They worry that even the little they offer may be too much.

Jonathan and Ruby tell each other the stories of their talk by the tidal pool, their walks and meals, the sagging sofa, the moment in the parking lot, and the evening Ruby made her call. They tell these to console themselves when their children chide them or when, alone in the house, they sit quietly near each other and struggle to conceal their disappointments.

Of course they have expected some of these. Mickey and Gordon have both had trouble in school, and Jessie has grown much too close to her mother; neither Jonathan nor Ruby has found jobs as good as the ones they lost, and their new home in Palmyra still doesn't feel quite like home. But all they have lost in order to be together would seem bearable had they continued to feel the way they felt on the island.

They're sensible people, and very well-mannered; they remind themselves that they were young then and are middle-aged now, and that their fierce attraction would naturally ebb with time. Neither likes to think about how much of the thrill of their early days together came from the obstacles they had to overcome. Some days, when Ruby pulls into the driveway still thinking about her last class and catches sight of Jonathan out in the garden, she can't believe the heavyset figure pruning shrubs so meticulously is the man for whom she fought such battles. Jonathan, who often wakes very early, sometimes stares at Ruby's sleeping face and thinks how much more gracefully his ex-wife is aging.

They never reproach each other. When the tension builds in the house and the silence becomes overwhelming, one or the other will say, "Do you remember . . .?" and then launch into one of the myths on which they have founded their lives. But there is one story they never tell each other, because they can't bear to talk about what they have lost. This is the one about the evening that has shaped their life together.

Jonathan's hand on Ruby's back, Ruby's hand on Jonathan's thigh, a shirt unbuttoned, a belt undone. They never mention this moment, or the moments that followed it, because that would mean discussing who seduced whom, and any resolution of that would mean assigning blame. Guilt they can handle; they've been living with guilt for fifteen years. But blame? It would be more than either of them could bear, to know the exact moment when one of them precipitated all that has happened to them. The most either of them has ever said is, "How could we have known?"

But the night in the library is what they both think about, when they lie silently next to each other and listen to the wind.

It must be summer for them to think about it; the children must be with their other parents and the rain must be falling on the cedar shingles overhead. A candle must be burning on the mantel above the bed and the maple branches outside their window must be tossing against each other. Then they think of the story they know so well and never say out loud.

There was a huge storm three nights before they left the island, the tail end of a hurricane passing farther out to sea. The cedar trees creaked and swayed in the wind beyond the library windows. The students had staggered off to bed, after the visitor from Woods Hole had finished his lecture on the explorations of the *Alvin* in the Cayman Trough, and Frank and Gunnar and Carol had shrouded themselves in their rain gear and left as well, sheltering the visitor between them. Ruby sat at one end of the long table, preparing bottles of fixative for their expedition the following morning, and Jonathan lay on the sofa writing notes. The boat was leaving just after dawn and they knew they ought to go to bed.

The wind picked up outside, sweeping the branches against the walls. The windows rattled. Jonathan shivered and said, "Do you suppose we could get a fire going in that old fireplace?"

"I bet we could," said Ruby, which gave both of them the pretext they needed to crouch side by side on the cracked tiles, brushing elbows as they opened the flue and crumpled paper and laid kindling in the form of a grid. The logs Jonathan found near the lobster traps were dry and the fire caught quickly.

Who found the green candle in the drawer below the microscope? Who lit the candle and turned off the lights? And who found the remains of the jug of wine that Frank had brought in honor of the visitor? They sat there side by side, poking at the burning logs and pretending they weren't doing what they were doing. The wind pushed through the window they'd opened a crack, and the tan window shade lifted and then fell back against the frame. The noise was soothing at first; later it seemed irritating.

Jonathan, whose fingernails were bitten to the quick, admired the long nail on Ruby's right little finger and then said, half-seriously, how much he'd love to bite a nail like that. When Ruby held her hand to his mouth he took the nail between his teeth and nibbled through the white tip, which days in the water had softened. Ruby slipped her other hand inside his shirt and ran it up his back. Jonathan ran his mouth up her arm and down her neck.

They started in front of the fire and worked their way across the floor, breaking a glass, knocking the table askew. Ruby rubbed her back raw against the rug and Jonathan scraped his knees, and twice they paused and laughed at their wild excesses. They moved across the floor from east to west and later from west to east, and between those two journeys, during the time when they heaped their clothes and the sofa cushions into a nest in front of the fire, they talked.

This was not the kind of conversation they'd had during walks and meals since that first time on the rocks: who they were, where they'd come from, how they'd made it here. This was the talk where they instinctively edited out the daily pleasures of their lives on the mainland and spliced together the hard times, the dark times, until they'd constructed versions of themselves that could make sense of what they'd just done.

For months after this, as they lay in stolen, secret rooms between houses and divorces and jobs and lives, Jonathan would tell Ruby that he swallowed her nail. The nail dissolved in his stomach, he'd say. It passed into his villi and out to his blood and then flowed to bone and muscle and nerve, where the molecules that had once been part of her became part of him. Ruby, who always seemed to know more acutely than Jonathan that they'd have to leave whatever room this was in an hour or a day, would argue with him.

"Nails are keratin," she'd tell him. "Like hooves and hair. Like wool. We can't digest wool."

"Moths can," Jonathan would tell her. "Moths eat sweaters."

"Moths have a special enzyme in their saliva," Ruby would say. This was true, she knew it for a fact. She'd been so taken by Jonathan's tale that she'd gone to the library to check out the details and discovered he was wrong.

But Jonathan didn't care what the biochemists said. He held her against his chest and said, "I have an enzyme for you."

That night, after the fire burned out, they slept for a couple of hours. Ruby woke first and watched Jonathan sleep for a while. He slept like a child, with his knees bent toward his chest and his hands clasped between his thighs. Ruby picked up the tipped-over chair and swept the fragments of broken glass onto a sheet of paper. Then she woke Jonathan and they tiptoed back to the rooms where they were supposed to be.

Rare Bird

Imagine an April evening in 1762. A handsome house set in the gently rolling Kent landscape a few miles outside the city of London; the sun just set over blue squill and beech trees newly leafed. Inside the house are a group of men and a single woman: Christopher Billopp, his sister Sarah Anne, and Christopher's guests from London. Educated and well-bred, they're used to a certain level of conversation. Just now they're discussing Linnaeus's contention that swallows retire under water for the winter—that old belief, stemming from Aristotle, which Linnaeus still upholds.

"He's hardly alone," Mr. Miller says. Behind him, a large mirror reflects a pair of portraits: Christopher and Sarah Anne, painted several years earlier as a gift for their father. "Even Klein, Linnaeus's rival, agrees. He wrote that a friend's mother saw fishermen bring out a bundle of swallows from a lake near Pilaw. When the swallows were placed near a fire, they revived and flew about."

Mr. Pennant nods. "Remember the reports of Dr. Colas? Fishermen he talked to in northern parts claimed that when they broke through the ice in winter they took up comatose swallows in their nets as well as fish. And surely you remember reading how Taletini of Cremona swore a Jesuit had told him that the swallows in Poland and Moravia hurled themselves into cisterns and wells come autumn."

Mr. Collinson laughs at this, although not unkindly, and he looks across the table at his old friend Mr. Ellis. "Hearsay, hearsay," he says. He has a spot on his waistcoat. Gravy, perhaps. Or cream. "Not one shred of direct evidence. Mothers, fishermen, itinerant Jesuits—this is folklore, my friends. Not science."

At the foot of the table, Sarah Anne nods but says nothing. Pennant, Ellis, Collinson, Miller: all distinguished. But old, so old. She worries that she and Christopher are growing prematurely old as well. Staid and dull and entirely too comfortable with these admirable men, whom they have known since they were children.

Their father, a brewer by trade but a naturalist by avocation, had educated Christopher and Sarah Anne together after their mother's death, as if they were brothers. The three of them rambled the grounds of Burdem Place, learning the names of the plants and birds. Collinson lived in Peckham then, just a few miles away, and he often rode over bearing rare plants and seeds sent by naturalist friends in other countries. Peter Kalm, Linnaeus's famous student, visited the Billopps; Linnaeus himself, before Sarah Anne was born, once stayed for several days.

All these things are part of Sarah Anne's and Christopher's common past. And even after Christopher's return from Cambridge and their father's death, for a while they continued to enjoy an easy exchange of books and conversation. But now all that has changed. Sarah Anne inherited her father's brains but Christopher inherited everything else, including his father's friends. Sarah Anne acts as hostess to these men, at Christopher's bidding. In part she's happy for their company, which represents her only intellectual companionship. In part she despises them for their lumbago and thinning hair, their greediness in the presence of good food, the stories they repeat about the scientific triumphs of their youth, and the fact that they refuse to take her seriously. Not one of them has done anything original in years.

There's another reason, as well, why she holds her tongue on this night. Lately, since Christopher has started courting Miss Juliet Colden, he's become critical of Sarah Anne's manners. She does not dress as elegantly as Juliet, or comport herself with such decorum. She's forward when she ought to be retiring, he has said, and disputatious when she should be agreeable. He's spoken to her several times already: "You should wear your learning modestly," he lectures.

She does wear it modestly, or so she believes. She's careful not to betray in public those subjects she knows more thoroughly than Christopher. Always she reminds herself that her learning is only book-learning; that it hasn't been tempered, as Christopher's has, by long discussions after dinner and passionate arguments in coffeehouses with wiser minds.

And so here she is: learned, but not really; and not pretty, and no longer young: last month she turned twenty-nine. Old, old, old. Like her company. She knows that Christopher has begun to worry that she'll be on his hands for life. And she thinks that perhaps he's mentioned this worry to his friends.

They're fond of him, and of Burdem Place. They appreciate the library, the herbarium, the rare trees and shrubs outside, the collections in the specimen cabinets. They appreciate Sarah Anne as well, she knows. Earlier, they complimented the food, her gown, the flowers on the table and her eyes in the candlelight. But what's the use of that sort of admiration? Collinson, who has known her the longest, was the only one to make a stab at treating her the way they all had when she was a girl: he led her into quoting Pliny and then complimented her on her learning. But she saw the way the other men shifted uneasily as she spoke.

Despite herself, she continues to listen to the men's conversation. Despite her restlessness, her longing to be outside in the cool damp air, or in some other place entirely, she listens because the subject they're discussing fascinates her.

"I had a letter last year from Solander," Ellis says. "Regarding the November meeting of the Royal Society. There, a Reverend Forster said he'd observed large flocks of swallows flying quite high in the autumn, then coming down to sit on reeds and willows before plunging into the water of one of his ponds."

"More hearsay," Collinson says.

But Pennant says it might be so; either that or they slept for the winter in their summer nesting holes. "Locke says that there are no chasms or gaps in the great chain of being," he reminds them. "Rather there is a continuous series in which each step differs very little from the next. There are fishes that have wings, and birds that inhabit the water, whose blood is as cold as that of fishes. Why should not the swallow be one of those animals so near of kin to both birds and fish that it occupies a place between both? As there are mermaids or seamen, perhaps."

No one objects to the introduction of aquatic anthropoids into the conversation. Reports of them surface every few years— Cingalese fishermen swear they've caught them in their nets, a ship's captain spots two off the coast of Massachusetts. In Paris, only four years ago, a living female of the species was exhibited.

Collinson says, "Our friend Mr. Achard writes me that he has seen them hibernating in the cliffs along the Rhine. But I have my doubts about the whole story."

"Yes?" Pennant says. "So what do you believe?"

"I think swallows migrate," Collinson says.

While the servants change plates, replace glasses, and open fresh bottles of wine, Collinson relates a story from Mr. Adanson's recent *History of Senegal*. Off the coast of that land in autumn, he says, Adanson reported seeing swallows settling on the decks and rigging of passing ships like bees. Others have reported spring and autumn sightings of swallows in Andalusia and over the Strait of Gibraltar. "Clearly," Collinson says, "they must be birds of passage."

Which is what Sarah Anne believes. She opens her mouth and proposes a simple experiment to the men. "The swallow must breathe during winter," she says, between the soup and the roasted veal. "Respiration and circulation must somehow continue, in some degree. And how is that possible if the birds are under water for so long? Could one not settle this by catching some swallows at the time of their autumn disappearance and confining them under water in a tub for a time? If they are taken out alive, then Linnaeus's theory is proved. But if not . . ."

"A reasonable test," Collinson says. "How would you catch the birds?"

"At night," she tells him impatiently. Oh, he is so old; he has dribbled more gravy on his waistcoat. How is that he can no longer imagine leaving his world of books and talk for the world outside? Anyone might gather a handful of birds. "With nets, while they roost in the reeds."

Collinson says, "If they survived, we might dissect one and look for whatever internal structure made possible their under-water sojourn."

He seems to be waiting for Sarah Anne's response, but Christopher is glaring at her. She knows what he's thinking: in his new, middle-aged stodginess, assumed unnecessarily early and worn like a borrowed coat, he judges her harshly. She's been forward in entering the conversation, unladylike in offering an opinion that contradicts some of her guests, indelicate in suggesting that she might pursue a flock of birds with a net.

What has gotten into him? That pulse she hears inside her ear, the steady swish and hum of her blood, is the sound of time passing. Each minute whirling past her before she can wring any life from it; hours shattered and lost while she defers to her brother's sense of propriety.

. . .

Upstairs, finally. Dismissed while the men, in the library below, drink Christopher's excellent wine and avail themselves of the chamberpot in the sideboard. Her brother's friends are grateful for her hospitality, appreciative of her well-run household; but most grateful and appreciative when she disappears.

Her room is dark, the night is cool, the breeze flows through her windows. She sits in her high-ceilinged room, at the fragile desk in the three-windowed bay facing west, over the garden. If it were not dark, she could see the acres leading down to the lake and the low stretch of rushes and willows along the banks.

Her desk is very small, meant to hold a few letters and a vase of flowers: useless for any real work. The books she's taken from the library spill from it to the floor. Gorgeous books, expensive books. Her brother's books. But her brother doesn't use them the way she does. She's been rooting around in them and composing a letter to Linnaeus, in Uppsala, about the evening's dinner conversation. Christopher need never know what she writes alone in this room.

Some years ago, after Peter Kalm's visit, Sarah Anne's father and Linnaeus corresponded for a while; after expressing admiration for the great doctor's achievements this visit is what she first mentions. Some flattery, some common ground. She discusses the weather, which has been unusual; she passes on the news of Collinson's latest botanical acquisitions. Only then does she introduce the subject of the swallows. She writes:

Toward the end of September, I have observed swallows gathering in the reeds along the Thames. And yet, although these reeds are cut down annually, no one has ever discovered swallows sleeping in their roots, nor has any fisherman ever found, in the winter months, swallows sleeping in the water. If all the great flocks seen in the

autumn dove beneath the water, how could they not be
seen? How could none be found in winter? But perhaps the
situation differs in Sweden.
　　You are so well-known and so revered. Could you not
offer the fishermen of your country a reward, if they were to
bring to you or your students any swallows they found
beneath the ice? Could you not ask them to watch the lakes
and streams in spring, and report to you any sightings of
swallows emerging from the water? In this fashion you
might elucidate the problem.

She pauses and stares at the candle, considering what she observed
last fall. After the first killing frosts, the swallows disappeared along
with the warblers and flycatchers and other insectivorous birds
deprived of food and shelter. Surely it makes sense that they should
have gone elsewhere, following their food supply?

She signs the letter "S.A. Billopp," meaning by this not to
deceive the famous scholar but simply to keep him from dismissing her offhand. Then she reads it over, seals it, and snuffs her
candle. It is not yet ten but soon the men, who've been drinking
for hours, will be expecting her to rejoin them for supper. She
will not go down, she will send a message that she is indisposed.

She rests her elbows on the windowsill and leans out into
the night, dreaming of Andalusia and Senegal and imagining that
twice a year she might travel like the swallows. Málaga, Tangier,
Marrakech, Dakar. Birds of passage fly from England to the
south of France and from there down the Iberian peninsula,
where the updrafts from the Rock of Gibraltar ease them over
the Strait to Morocco. Then they make the long flight down the
coast of Africa.

A bat flies by, on its way to the river. She has seen bats
drink on the wing, as swallows do, sipping from the water's
surface. Swallows eat in flight as well, snapping insects from the
air. Rain is sure to follow when they fly low; a belief that dates
from Virgil, but which she knows to be true. When the air is

damp and heavy the insects hover low, and she has seen how the swallows merely follow them.

In the dark she sheds her gown, her corset, her slippers and stockings and complicated underclothes, until she is finally naked. She lies on the floor beside her desk, below the open window. Into her notebook she has copied these lines, written by Olaus Magnus, archbishop of Uppsala, in 1555:

> *From the northern waters, swallows are often dragged up by fishermen in the form of clustered masses, mouth to mouth, wing to wing, and foot to foot, these having at the beginning of autumn collected amongst the reeds previous to submersion. When young and inexperienced fishermen find such clusters of swallows, they will, by thawing the birds at the fire, bring them indeed to the use of their wings, which will continue but a very short time, as it is a premature and forced revival; but the old, being wiser, throw them away.*

A lovely story, but surely wrong. The cool damp air washes over her like water. She folds her arms around her torso and imagines lying at the bottom of the lake, wings wrapped around her body like a kind of chrysalis. It is cold, it is dark, she is barely breathing. How would she breathe? Around her are thousands of bodies. The days lengthen, some signal arrives, she shoots with the rest of her flock to the surface, lifts her head and breathes. Her wings unfold and she soars through the air, miraculously dry and alive.

Is it possible?

Eight months later, Sarah Anne and Christopher stand on London Bridge with Miss Juliet Colden and her brother John, all of them wrapped in enormous cloaks and shivering despite these. They've come to gaze at the river, which in this January of remarkable cold is covered with great floes of ice. An odd way, Sarah Anne thinks, to mark the announcement of Christopher and Juliet's engagement. She wishes she liked Juliet better. Already they've been thrown a great deal into each other's company; soon they'll be sharing a house.

But not sharing, not really. After the wedding, Juliet will have the household keys; Juliet will be in charge of the servants. Juliet will order the meals, the flowers, the servants' livery, the evening entertainments. And Sarah Anne will be the extra woman.

The pieces of ice make a grinding noise as they crash against each other and the bridge. Although the tall brick houses that crowded the bridge in Sarah Anne's childhood were pulled down several years ago and no longer hang precariously over the water, the view remains the same: downriver the Tower and a forest of masts; upriver the Abbey and Somerset House. The floating ice greatly menaces the thousands of ships waiting to be unloaded in the Pool. It is of this that John and Christopher speak. Manly talk: will ships be lost, fortunes destroyed? Meanwhile Juliet chatters and Sarah Anne is silent, scanning the sky for birds.

Wrynecks, white-throats, nightingales, cuckoos, willow-wrens, goatsuckers—none of these are visible, they've disappeared for the winter. The swallows are gone as well. An acquaintance of Christopher's mentioned over a recent dinner that on a remarkably warm December day, he'd seen a small group of swallows huddled under the moldings of a window at Merton College. What were they doing there? She's seen them, as late as October, gathered in great crowds in the osier-beds along the river—very late for young birds attempting to fly past the equator. In early May she's seen them clustered on the largest willow at Burdem Place, which hangs over the lake. And in summer swallows swarm the banks of the Thames below this very bridge. It's clear that they're attached to water, but attachment doesn't necessarily imply habitation. Is it possible that they are still around, either below the water or buried somehow in the banks?

If she were alone, and not dressed in these burdensome clothes, and if there were some way she could slip down one of the sets of stairs to the river bank without arousing everyone's attention, she knows what she would do. She'd mark out a section of bank where the nesting holes are thickest and survey each hole, poking down the burrows until she found the old nests. In the burrows along the river bank at home she's seen these: a base of straw, then finer grass lined with a little down. Small white eggs in early summer. Now, were she able to look, she believes she'd find only twists of tired grass.

The wind blows her hood over her face. As soon as she gets home, she thinks, she'll write another letter to Linnaeus and propose that he investigate burrows in Sweden. Four times she's written him, this past summer and fall; not once has he answered.

Christopher and John's discussion has shifted to politics, and she would like to join them. But she must talk to Juliet, whose delicate nose has reddened. Juliet's hands are buried in a huge fur muff; her face is buried in her hood. Well-mannered, she refuses to complain of the cold.

"You'll be part of the wedding, of course," Juliet says, and then she describes the music she hopes to have played, the feast that will follow the ceremony. "A big table," she says. "On the lawn outside the library, when the roses are in bloom—what is that giant vine winding up the porch there?"

"Honeysuckle," Sarah Anne says gloomily. "The scent is lovely."

She can picture the wedding only too clearly. The other attendants will be Juliet's sisters, all three as dainty and pretty as Juliet. Their gowns will be pink or yellow or pink and yellow, with bows down the bodice and too many flounces. The couple will go to Venice and Paris and Rome and when they return they'll move into Sarah Anne's large sunny bedroom and she'll move to a smaller room in the north wing. The first time Juliet saw Sarah Anne's room, her eyes lit with greed and pleasure. A few days later Christopher said to Sarah Anne, "About your room. . . ." She offered it before he had to ask.

"Christopher and I thought you'd like the dressing table your mother used," Juliet says. "For that lovely bay in your new room."

But just then, just when Sarah Anne thinks she can't bear another minute, along comes another of her dead father's elderly friends, accompanied by a woman. Introductions are made all around. Mr. Hill, Mrs. Pearce. Sarah Anne has always enjoyed Mr. Hill, who is livelier than his contemporaries, but he is taken away. The group splits naturally into two as they begin their walk back to the Strand. Mr. Hill joins Christopher and John, and Mrs. Pearce joins Sarah Anne and Juliet. But Mrs. Pearce, instead of responding to Juliet's remarks about the weather, turns to Sarah Anne and says, "You were studying the riverbank so intently when Mr. Hill pointed you out to me. What were you looking for?"

Her face is lean and intelligent; her eyes are full of curiosity. "Birds," Sarah Anne says impulsively. "I was looking for swallows' nests. Some people contend that swallows spend the winter hibernating either under water or in their summer burrows."

She explains the signs that mislead observers, the mistaken stories that multiply. At Burdem Place, she says, she heard a friend of her brother's claim that, as a boy, he found two or three swallows in the rubble of a church-tower being torn down. The birds were torpid, appearing dead, but revived when placed near a fire. Unfortunately they were then accidentally roasted.

"Roasted?" Mrs. Pearce says with a smile.

"Crisp as chickens," Sarah Anne says. "So of course they were lost as evidence. But I suppose it's more likely that they overwinter in holes or burrows, than that they should hibernate under water."

"Some people read omens in the movements of swallows," Mrs. Pearce says. "Even Shakespeare—remember this? 'Swallows have built in Cleopatra's sails their nests. The augeries say they know not, they cannot tell, look grimly, and dare not speak their knowledge.' Poetic. But surely we're not meant to believe it literally."

Sarah Anne stares. There's nothing visibly outrageous about Mrs. Pearce. Her clothing is simple and unfashionable but modest; her hair is dressed rather low but not impossibly so. "I believe that one should experiment," Sarah Anne says. "That we should base our statements on evidence."

"I always prefer to test hypotheses for myself," Mrs. Pearce says quietly.

Juliet is pouting, but Sarah Anne ignores her. She quotes Montaigne and Mrs. Pearce responds with a passage from Fontenelle's *Entretiens sur la pluralité des mondes.* "Do you know Mrs. Behn's translation?" Sarah Anne asks. At that moment she believes in a plurality of worlds as she never has before.

"Of course," says Mrs. Pearce. "Lovely, but I prefer the original."

Sarah Anne mentions the shells that she and Christopher have inherited from Sir Hans Sloane's collection, and Mrs. Pearce talks about her collection of mosses and fungi. And when Sarah Anne returns to the swallows and says that Linnaeus's belief in their watery winters derives from Aristotle, Mrs. Pearce says, "When I was younger, I translated several books of the *Historia Animalium.*"

Sarah Anne nearly weeps with excitement and pleasure. How learned this woman is. "How were you educated?" she asks.

"My father," Mrs. Pearce says. "A most cultured and intelligent man, who believed girls should learn as well as their brothers. And you?"

"Partly my father, partly my brother, before. . . . Partly by stealth."

"Well, *stealth,*" Mrs. Pearce says with a little smile. "Of course."

In their excitement they've been walking so fast that they've left Juliet behind. They hear the men calling them and stop. Quickly, knowing she has little time, Sarah Anne asks the remaining important question. "And your husband?" she says. "He shares your interests?"

"He's dead," Mrs. Pearce says calmly. "I'm a widow."

She lives in London, Sarah Anne learns, alone but for three servants. Both her daughters are married and gone. "I would be so pleased if you would visit us," Sarah Anne says. "We have a place just a few miles from town, but far enough away to have all the pleasures of the country. In the gardens there are some interesting plants from North America, and we've quite a large library. . . . "

Mrs. Pearce lays her gloved hand on Sarah Anne's arm. "I'd be delighted," she says. "And you must visit me in town. It's so rare to find a friend."

The others join them, looking cold and displeased. "Miss Colden," Mrs. Pearce says.

"Mrs. Pearce. I do hope you two have had a nice talk."

"Lovely," Mrs. Pearce says.

She looks over Juliet's head at Sarah Anne. "I'll see you soon." Then she hooks her hand into Mr. Hill's arm and walks away.

"Odd woman," John says. "Bit of a bluestocking, isn't she?"

"She dresses terribly," Juliet says, with considerable satisfaction. From the sharp look she gives Sarah Anne, Sarah Anne knows she'll pay for that brief bit of reviving conversation. But her mind is humming with the pleasure of her new friend, with plans for all they might do together, with the letter she'll write to Linnaeus the very instant she reaches home. She imagines reading that letter out loud to Mrs. Pearce, showing Mrs. Pearce the response she will surely receive.

.   .   .

"We should write him about that old potion," Mrs. Pearce says; and Sarah Anne says, "What?"

"For melancholy. Don't you know it?"

"I don't think so."

"It's a potion made partly from the blood of swallows. Birds of summer, symbols of ease—the potion is supposed to ease sadness and give wings to the feet."

"More likely than what he's proposing," Sarah Anne says, and Mrs. Pearce agrees.

It's September now—not the September following their meeting but the one after that: 1764. The two women are in an unused stable at Burdem Place, patiently waiting, surrounded by their equipment. It is just barely dawn. Down in the reeds, where the birds are sleeping, they've sent Robert the gardener's boy with a net and instructions. What they're talking about while they wait is the letter Sarah Anne received last week from Carl Linnaeus, in which he graciously but firmly (and in Latin; but Sarah Anne can read it), dismissed her theories and stated his absolute conviction that swallows hibernate under the water. The letter upset Sarah Anne, but she would not have done anything more than fume had Mrs. Pearce not been visiting. It was Mrs. Pearce—Catherine—who'd said, "Well. We'll just have to do the experiments ourselves."

On the wooden floor they've set the bottom half of a cask, which Robert has filled with water. Below the water lies a few inches of river sand; on the surface a board floats an inch from the rim. A large piece of sturdy netting awaits the use to which they'll put it. Inside the stable it's still quite dark; through the open door the trees are barely visible through the mist. Above them the house sleeps. Just after four o'clock, Sarah Anne rose in her new room and tapped once on the door of the room down the hall, where Catherine stays when she visits. Catherine opened the door instantly, already dressed.

Recently it has been easier for them to talk about the swallows than about the other goings-on at Burdem Place. Juliet's pregnancy has made her ill-humoured, and Christopher has changed as well. Sarah Anne knows she should have expected this, but still it has come as a shock. These days the guests tend to be Juliet's frivolous friends and not the older naturalists. Young, not old; some of them younger than Sarah Anne herself. For weeks at a time they stroll the grounds in fancy clothes and play games while Sarah Anne hovers off to the side, miserable in their company.

Who is she, then? She doesn't want to act, as Christopher does, the part of her parents' generation; but now she's found that she doesn't like her own peers either. She fits nowhere. Nowhere, except with Catherine. She and Catherine, tucked into a wing away from the fashionable guests, have formed their own society of two. But she suspects that, after the birth of Juliet's child, even this will be taken from her.

Christopher hopes for many children, an army of children. This child, and the ones that follow, will need a nurse and a governess, Juliet says. And a nursery, and a schoolroom. Sarah Anne has seen Christopher prowling the halls near her bedroom, assessing the space and almost visibly planning renovations. He's welcomed Catherine's frequent long visits—but only, Sarah Anne knows, because they keep her occupied and him from feeling guilty about her increasing isolation. The minute he feels pinched for space, he'll suggest to Sarah Anne that Catherine curtail her visits. And then it's possible he'll ask Sarah Anne to be his children's governess.

But Sarah Anne and Catherine don't talk about this. Instead they look once more at Linnaeus's letter, which arrived addressed to "Mr. S.A. Billopp" but which, fortunately, Christopher didn't see. They arrange their instruments on the bench beside them and shiver with cold and excitement. They wait. Where is Robert?

It was Catherine who first approached this weedy twelve-year-old, after Sarah Anne told her she'd once overheard him talking about netting birds for food in Ireland. Catherine told him that they required two or three swallows and would pay him handsomely for them; Robert seemed to believe they had plans to eat them. Still, at 4:30 he met them here, silent and secret. Now he reappears in the doorway, barefoot and wet to the waist. His net is draped over one shoulder and in his hands he holds a sack, which pulses and moves of its own accord.

"Robert!" Catherine says. "You had good luck?"

Robert nods. Both his hands are tightly wrapped around the sack's neck, and when Catherine reaches out for it he says, "You hold this tight, now. They'll be wanting to fly."

"You did a good job," Catherine says. "Let me get your money. Sarah Anne, why don't you take the sack?"

Sarah Anne slips both her hands below Robert's hands and twists the folds of cloth together. "I have it," she says. Robert releases the sack. Immediately she's aware that the sack is alive. Something inside is moving, leaping, dancing. Struggling. The feeling is terrifying.

"Thank you, Robert," Catherine says. Gently she guides him out the door. "You've been very helpful. If you remember to keep our secret, we'll ask you for help again."

By the time she turns back to Sarah Anne and takes the sack from her, Sarah Anne is almost hysterical.

"Nothing can satisfy but what confounds," Catherine says. "Nothing but what astonishes is true." Once more Sarah Anne is reminded of her friend's remarkable memory. When Catherine is excited, bits of all she has ever read fly off her like water from a churning lump of butter.

"All right now," Catherine says. "Hold the netting in both hands and pull it over the tub—that's good. Now fasten down the sides, all except for this little section here. I'm going to hold the mouth of the sack to the open part of the netting, and when

I say the word I'll open the sack and you drop the last lip of the netting into place. Are you ready?"

"Ready," Sarah Anne says. Her heart beats as if she has a bird inside her chest.

"*Now,*" Catherine says.

Everything happens so fast—a flurry of hands and cloth and netting and wings, loops of string and snagged skirts. Two swallows get away, passing so close to Sarah Anne's face that she feels the tips of their feathers and screams. But a minute later she sees that they've been at least partly successful. In the tub, huddled on the board and pushing frantically at the netting, are two birds. Steely blue, buff-bellied, gasping.

"They're so unhappy," Sarah Anne says.

"We must leave them," Catherine says. "If the famous Doctor Linnaeus is right, in our absence they'll let themselves down into the water and sleep, either on the surface of the river sand or perhaps just slightly beneath it."

"And if he's wrong?"

"Then we'll tell him so."

The day passes with excruciating slowness, chopped into bits by Juliet's rigid timetable: family breakfast, dinner, tea, and supper, long and complicated meals. After breakfast Juliet requires the company of Sarah Anne and Catherine in her dressing room, although Sarah Anne knows that Juliet is fond of neither of them. After tea, Christopher expects the women to join him in the library, where they talk and read the newspapers. Sarah Anne and Catherine have not a minute to themselves, and by supper they're wild-eyed with exhaustion and anticipation.

The next morning, when they slip out again before breakfast, the board over the tub is bare. Sarah Anne unfastens the netting, removes the dripping board, and peers down into the water. The swallows lie on the sand. But not wrapped serene in a cocoon of wings; rather twisted and sprawled. She knows before she reaches for them that they're dead. Catherine knows too; she stands ready with a penknife. They've agreed that, should the swallows die, they'll dissect one and examine its structures of circulation and respiration. They'll look for any organ that might make hibernation under water possible; any organ that might prove them wrong.

They work quickly. There isn't much blood. Catherine, peering into the open chest cavity, says, "It is very difficult to work without proper tools. Still. There is nothing out of the ordinary here. And there is no doubt that Linnaeus is wrong."

A four-chambered heart inside its pericardium; small, rosy, lobeless lungs. From the lungs, the mysterious air sacs extend into the abdomen, up into the neck, into the bones. There is no sign of a gill-like organ that might allow the bird to breathe under water. Sarah Anne is quite faint, and yet also fiercely thrilled. They've done an experiment; they've disproved an hypothesis. She says, "We will write to Linnaeus today."

"I think not," Catherine says. "I think it's time we made other plans."

What plans were those? Of course Christopher noticed that Mrs. Pearce returned to London in early October; he noticed, too, when Sarah Anne left Burdem Place a few weeks later for what she described as an 'extended visit' with her friend. All through November Christopher didn't hear from his sister, but he had worries of his own and thought nothing of her absence. In December, when he was in London on business, he stopped by Mrs. Pearce's house to find that her servants had been dismissed and her house was empty. Only then did he realize that his sister and her friend were simply gone.

Everyone had theories about their disappearance: Collinson,

Ellis, all the men. Foul play was suspected by some, although there was no evidence. But this is what Christopher thought, during the bleak nights of 1765 while Juliet was writhing with childbed fever, and during the even bleaker nights after her death, while his tiny son was wasting away. He imagined Sarah Anne and Mrs. Pearce—and who was Mrs. Pearce anyway? Where had she come from? Who were her people?—up before dawn in that London house, moving swiftly through the shadows as they gather bonnets, bags, gloves. Only one bag apiece, as they mean to travel light: and then they glide down the early morning streets toward the Thames. Toward the Tower wharf, perhaps; but it could be any wharf, any set of stairs, the river hums with activity. Ships are packed along the waterfront, their sails furled and their banners drooping; here a wherry, there a cutter, darts between them and the stairs. Some of the ships are headed for India and some for Madagascar. Some are going to the West Indies and others to Africa. Still others are headed for ports in the North American provinces: Quebec or Boston, New York or Baltimore.

Christopher believes his sister and her companion have boarded one of the ships headed for America. Once he overheard the two of them waxing rhapsodic over Mark Catesby's *Natural History*, talking in hushed tones about this land where squirrels flew and frogs whistled and birds the size of fingernails swarmed through forests so thick the sunlight failed to reach the ground. Catesby, Sarah Anne said, believed birds migrated sensibly: they flew to places where there was food.

Pacing his lonely house, miserable and broken, Christopher imagines the ship slowly moving down the Thames toward Dover and the Channel. There's a headwind and the tides are against them; the journey to Dover takes three days. But then the wind shifts and luck arrives. They fly past Portsmouth and Plymouth and Land's End, into the open ocean. The canvas billows out from the spars; the women lean against the railings, laughing.

That was the vision he had in mind when, a few years later, he sold both Burdem Place and the brewery and sailed for Delaware.

He never found Sarah Anne. But the crossing and the new world improved his spirits; he married a sturdy young Quaker woman and started a second family. Among the things he brought to his new life were two portraits—small, sepia-toned ovals, obviously copies of larger paintings—which surfaced much later near Baltimore. And if the faded notes found tucked in the back of Christopher's portrait are true, he made some modest contributions to the natural history of the mid-Atlantic states.

Sarah Anne's portrait bears only the date of her birth. Her letters were discovered in the mid-1850s, in the attic of a distant relation of the husband of Linnaeus's youngest daughter, Sophia. The British historian who found them was editing a collection of Linnaeus's correspondence, and from the handwriting and a few other hints, he deduced that "S.A. Billopp" was a woman, creating a minor furor among his colleagues. Later he was able to confirm his theory when he found Sarah Anne's journal at the Linnaean Society, jumbled among the collections left behind at Burdem Place. The last entry in Sarah Anne's journal was this, most likely copied there soon after she and Mrs. Pearce made their experiments with the swallows:

Collinson loaned me one of his books— An Essay towards the probable Solution of this Question, Whence come the Stork, etc; or Where those birds do probably make their Recess, etc. *(London, 1703)—with this passage marked for my amusement:*

"*Our migratory birds retire to the moon. They are about two months in retiring thither, and after they are arrived above the lower regions of the air into the thin aether, they will have no occasion for food, as it will not be apt to prey upon the spirits as our lower air. Even on our*

earth, bears will live upon their fat all the winter; and hence
these birds, being very succulent and sanguine, may have
their provisions laid up in their bodies for the voyage; or
perhaps they are thrown into a state of somnolency by the
motion arising from the mutual attraction of the earth and
moon."

He meant to be kind, I know he did. I cannot bear this
situation any longer. Catherine and I are meeting in town to
discuss the experiment she's proposed.

Soroche

Selling the house was remarkably easy. Zaga didn't tell her step-children what she was doing, and she didn't consult Joel's lawyer or his accountant. A few months after Joel's funeral, she sold the house for much less than her real-estate agent advised. Once she had a closing date she sold most of the furniture as well. She'd chosen every piece of it herself, except for the family heirlooms; she'd decorated each of the rooms and designed the kitchen in which she'd cooked the meals that had stunned Joel's friends but never truly made them like her. Joel had built the house for her, and she knew he'd assumed she would stay there. But in his absence the silent rooms seemed intolerable.

At night her dreams wound through blizzards and mountains she couldn't recognize. During the day she cleared out the house alone. Her stepchildren were nearby—Alicia lived in Meadow-brook and Rob in downtown Philadelphia—but they had hardly spoken to her since their father's death and she knew they wouldn't have offered to help even if they'd known about the sale. Vans came for the large pieces and men from the art museum crated the paintings Joel had bequeathed to them; room by room Zaga cleaned and wrapped and boxed. On the Wednesday evening before her forty-fourth birthday, she tackled Joel's walk-in closet. In the back, behind the overcoats, she found a carton of souvenirs from their trip to Chile in 1971.

A vicuna shawl, soft and light, bought in Santiago; two knitted ski caps Rob and Alicia had worn; a brochure showing the yellow hotel dwarfed by the mountains behind it. There were snapshots, which she vaguely remembered taking, of Joel and the children posed on the ski slopes in gaily colored outfits. And there was one picture of herself, which she'd never seen before, looking very young and miserable in the hotel lounge.

"For your baby," Dr. Sepulveda had said, on the snowy day when he'd captured her. A lifetime ago, and yet she remembered this perfectly clearly. "Someday you can show this to your child and tell him—or her, maybe you will have a little daughter?—how he was with you even here."

The envelope folded around the picture was addressed to Zaga in a spiky, European hand that could only have been Dr. Sepulveda's. She had never seen it; Joel must have intercepted it and then hidden the photo to spare her. If a letter had come with the photo it was lost.

On her first day in the Andes, the liquid and brilliant sky had made Zaga wildly euphoric. The peaks surrounding the Hotel Portillo were clean and white. The frozen lake gleamed like an eye below her room, and the top of Mt. Aconcagua rose in the distance like a moon. The slopes were dotted with skiers dressed in pink and green and blue, and although she couldn't ski and was afraid of heights and had never been athletic, the thin air made her feel at first that she could do anything.

The headache, the stiff neck, the burning cheeks and icy fingers came on the second day. When she tried to rise from her bed she threw up, and by mid-morning, when the children came in, she was as sick as she'd ever been.

They stood in the doorway, Rob and Alicia: Joel's children, not hers, red-cheeked and insubordinate and already dressed in their ski clothes. Joel had told them that they were not to go out alone until he'd had time to show them around. He was forty-two and panted each time he moved quickly. His children breathed easily and looked at Zaga with interest but no sympathy.

"Zaga's sick," Joel said, and Alicia said, "No kidding," and moved closer to the bed. Although she was only fourteen, she was three inches taller than Zaga and weighed thirty pounds more. There were long streaks bleached into her hair, from the hours she'd spent beside the pool, and her figure was so flamboyant that she made Zaga feel like a twig.

"You can't come skiing?" Rob asked Joel. He was twelve, Alicia's height already, and so strong that Joel had given up wrestling with him.

"Your stepmother's sick," Joel repeated. "No one's going anywhere until we get her fixed up."

Rob and Alicia exchanged a look. "We'll just go downstairs then," Alicia said. "Have some breakfast. Okay?"

Zaga leaned over and threw up again, diverting Joel's attention. The children moved out of the doorway but not, Zaga learned later, out of earshot. And so when Joel, holding Zaga's head over the wastebasket, said "Do you think it's morning sickness?" Alicia apparently heard every syllable.

All day Zaga lay in bed, dizzy and nauseated and only vaguely aware of Joel's comings and goings and of the scene Rob and Alicia made when Joel found them. They'd stormed off to the slopes without Joel and returned unrepentant, hours later. In the lounge, where Joel finally caught up with them, they had said the idea of a baby disgusted them.

"It's *so* gross," Alicia had said. Rob, ever practical, had apparently said only, "Where's it going to sleep?"

Joel imitated Alicia's disgusted squeal and Rob's nervous rumble as he described the scene to Zaga. "They'll come around," he said. "It's natural for them to feel this way—now they have proof that we sleep together."

Zaga had trouble smiling back at him, and by the time the hotel doctor arrived she was very weak.

"Dr. Sepulveda," he said. His face was lean and tanned and his hair fell back in a smooth black wave. He leaned over and rested his hand on her forehead. "You are feeling poorly?"

His short white jacket buttoned to one side and was starched and crisp. "Can you tell me your symptoms?" Lightly accented English, perfectly correct. Because Zaga couldn't speak, Joel told the doctor about the dizziness, the vomiting, the headache that spiked down the back of Zaga's neck and pierced her eyes.

"Yes?" Dr. Sepulveda said. He took her pulse and her temperature, looked in her throat and listened to her chest. Joel told him that Zaga was three months pregnant, and Dr. Sepulveda nodded and ran his fingers gently over her belly.

"You have *soroche*," he told her. Then he looked up at Joel and repeated the word. "*Soroche*. Altitude sickness. That's all."

"That's it?" Joel said. "No virus? There's nothing wrong with the baby?"

"The baby has nothing to do with this. She has all the classic symptoms."

He gave her two injections and then he left. An hour later she stopped throwing up; he returned the next morning and gave her two more shots and by nightfall she was almost well. The next day she dressed herself, after Joel and Alicia and Rob had gone out for the day. Then she began waiting for her time in Portillo to end.

Zaga knew she hadn't gotten what the house was worth, but at the closing, even the amount left after the broker's commission still took her breath away. She moved into a furnished apartment while she decided what to do. For nineteen years Joel had fussed about his health, but he'd never really been sick and she'd made no plans for a life without him.

He meant to retire young, he'd told her, during a quiet moment stolen from his sixtieth birthday party. They could travel again. Not the sort of family vacations they'd had for years, to Florida, Mexico, Maine—but a real trip, just the two of them. He didn't say, "We could go back to Portillo," but she knew it was on his mind. She'd thought about that: Portillo again, the way it was meant to be. Six days later a weak spot on the wall of his aorta had opened like a window.

Afterwards, when she'd woken each morning and found the undisturbed blankets beside her, his absence had seemed impossible. At dusk she'd strained her ears for the sound of his car pulling into the crescent driveway, and sometimes she'd called out his name in the empty rooms. But her first move eased her grief unexpectedly, and her second relieved her even more. Downtown, near the art museum, she found a lovely old building that had just been converted to condominiums. She bought a two-bedroom apartment on the fourth floor, overlooking the Schuylkill River: high ceilings, beautiful moldings, smooth oak floors. It cost so much less than the Merion house that she felt virtuous and thrifty.

Morning coffee in the sunny kitchen; a quiet browse through the papers and then a shower and some shopping or a walk. No meals to make, no garden to weed or guest room to rearrange. No guests. For nineteen years she had entertained Joel's friends and business associates; she had been famous for her parties and Joel had been proud of her success. Their closest moments had been spent on the sofa, going over menus and guest lists or rehashing the high points of a party just past, and she had never told him she knew that his friends still compared her unfavorably with his first wife.

Now she spent days alone in her new place and felt no desire to call anyone. She walked to Rittenhouse Square. She haunted the antique shops on Spruce and Lombard and then spent hours moving knicknacks here and pillows there. Silence, idleness, solitude. Where was Joel in all of this? Sometimes she walked the few blocks to the art museum and gazed at the statues or strolled through the hall in which the collection of Joel's grandfather's paintings hung.

Joel had taken her here on their fourth or fifth date, but he hadn't said a word about his family. He had let her admire the paintings and read the polished plaque in the front of the room. "Any relation?" she remembered asking, when she saw the identical last names—thinking of course not, or at most someone distant; laughing, joking. "My grandfather," he said, and only then had she realized how surely she was in over her head. She thought how her grandmothers might have done laundry for his family, and she dreaded what Joel might think of her father, who shed his clothes after work in the basement and then showered in a grimy stall, washing off layers of dust and mortar before entering the scrubbed and parsimonious upper floors.

But Joel had already told her he loved her by then. She was gentle, he said. And so flexible—she was as happy lying around in his old pajamas, eating muffins and reading the papers, as she was when he took her out to fancy nightclubs. She sang while she cooked. The rich, complicated meals she fixed, based on her grandmothers' recipes, made his eyes moist with pleasure.

In a bar off Rittenhouse Square, he courted her with recollections of his first visit to Portillo. He told her how, during the summer after he finished college, he'd found a spot on a freighter headed for Chile. He'd made his way to Santiago; then up the Andes and to the hotel, where he'd joined some old acquaintances. Just a handful of skiers, he said, back in those good old days. She could recall doing a quick calculation in her head as he spoke, and realizing that she'd been five at the time.

Endless white snowfields, he'd said, his hands moving in the smoky air. Daring stunts; condors soaring over the rocks. And although he was middle-aged and filled with the hectic despair of the newly divorced, his stories made him seem young. He *was* young, he said. He had married right after his trip to Portillo and had two children quickly. His wife had dumped him so she could discover herself.

"She wants to paint," he'd said bitterly, over a meal that Zaga made him: roast veal with fennel and garlic? Pork braised with prunes? "Watercolors," he'd said. "So she's got the house in Meadowbrook, which I'm still paying the mortgage on, and the kids are with her, and I'm stuck here."

'Here' was an airy two-bedroom apartment with an enormous kitchen, nicer than anything Zaga could afford. She was nothing like his first wife, Joel said, and she took this as a compliment. She was drawn by his stability, his solidity, the radiant success with which he managed his outward life. She was touched by his inability to cook or clean and by his obvious need for her. He reached across his sofa after their first visit with her family, and he lifted a strand of her hair and said, "Did you get this from some beautiful Lithuanian grandmother?"

She took this to mean that he accepted her background, and her. He bought her new clothes and then, in the galleries where he purchased paintings, introduced her as if he were proud. Two years later, when the huge house in Merion was almost done, she was thrilled when he proposed a delayed honeymoon in Portillo. Joel had been shaped by the Andes, she thought; perhaps the mountain air could transform her into someone from his world.

Then Rob and Alicia, unexpectedly abandoned by Joel's ex-wife, sailed into their lives like a three-masted ship from a foreign country. Their arrival changed the focus of the trip but made it seem even more important. By the time Zaga discovered she was pregnant, the plans were too far along to change without disappointing everyone.

Those early days came back to her one afternoon, over a lunch of salmon and asparagus salad in the museum café. She realized that she had not seen any of Joel's paintings anywhere.

She went back to the hall where his grandfather's collection hung, thinking Joel's bequests might have been mingled in. Then she walked more carefully from room to to room. Nothing. The next day she called the museum and made an appointment to meet the woman in charge of new acquisitions. The woman had an office so softly blue and gray that Zaga felt as if she'd been set inside a cloud.

There were some small financial difficulties, the woman murmured. She crossed her long, narrow legs and regarded her excellent shoes. Of course the museum was enormously grateful for the bequest. But so few people, outside the art world, understood the expenses involved with such a gift: cataloging, cleaning, reframing, lighting—her voice drifted off and so did her gaze, leaving Zaga to fill the empty space.

"You have an endowment, surely?" Zaga said. Joel had taught her a good deal and his friends had taught her more.

"Of course," the woman said. Her voice hovered between the purr she would have used with Joel and the bite she would have used on Zaga, had Zaga not been married to Joel. "But these are difficult times, and our budget is constantly being trimmed. . . ."

"Would a donation be useful?" Zaga asked. She felt a thrill as she said that. Joel had always made the big donations; of course he had, the money was his. But now Joel was gone and the money was hers.

When the woman smiled her teeth were perfectly white and straight. "Coffee?" she said. Zaga nodded and the woman summoned her assistant.

Three days before they were due to leave the Andes, a blizzard cut them off from the outside world. No traffic arrived or departed and there was nothing to do but wait. Joel and the children still skied, masked in goggles and wrapped in extra clothes, delighted at their extended vacation. Zaga sat, more and more frantic, at a table by the window in the lounge of the Hotel Portillo. Dr. Sepulveda, also trapped by the blizzard and unable to return to his home in Santiago, sometimes joined her. The first time he appeared at her table, he talked about the weather for a while and then fell silent and studied her face.

"You must be Slavic," he said. "With those cheekbones and that name." He lit a cigarette and turned from her face to the mountain. "Let me guess," he said. "Slovenian royalty. Ukrainian landowners. White Russian aristocrats fleeing the Bolsheviks."

"Lithuanian potato-and-cabbage peasants," she admitted. Was he teasing her? She had seen faces like his in the paintings of Spanish nobility that hung in the museum at home. "My parents were born in Philadelphia, but only just. I have a brother who's a bricklayer, like my father; another who's a cop. The big success is Timothy—he's an optometrist. My sister works part-time in a bakery, and I was working as a secretary in an art gallery when I met Joel."

"Really," the doctor said. "Among the modern languages, Lithuanian is the one most closely related to Sanskrit."

"I'll have to take your word for that," she said. "I hardly remember any of it."

"But your grandparents . . . ?"

"They never learned English well."

Outside, beyond the windows, the snow fell and fell and fell. The afternoon had only just started and there were hours to kill before Joel and the children returned from the slopes. There was nothing to do but talk, and so when Dr. Sepulveda said, "And what about your husband?" she answered him more fully than she might otherwise have done.

"Joel's grandfather was a chemist," she said. "He synthesized a drug used to treat ulcers, and then he started a pharmaceutical company to manufacture it. The family still owns most of the stock." When she mentioned the name of the company Dr. Sepulveda raised an eyebrow in recognition.

"Your husband runs it?"

"One of his cousins. But Joel's on the board of directors, of course, and he works there—all the cousins do. Joel's the vice-president for community relations."

"What does that mean?"

"He's the do-gooder," Zaga said. She would have given anything for a bottle of wine, green and slim on the table between them, but her doctor at home had forbidden alcohol. "He oversees all the nonbusiness stuff," she said. "The sports programs they sponsor, and the scholarships and grants and the corporate art program. Joel buys contemporary art for the offices, and he collects some privately."

"Very enlightened," the doctor murmured. "He must have a discriminating eye."

"And you?" Zaga said. "Are you married?"

He ordered more coffee for himself and, without consulting her, removed her cup and replaced it with a glass of fresh juice. "You shouldn't be having so much caffeine," he said. "Not in your condition." Then he turned to the window, where the bright figures of the skiers flashed against the snow. "Charles Darwin came by here," he said—the first time he mentioned that name, the first hint she had of the stories that were to come. "A century and a half ago, when these mountains were wilderness. He walked through the pass in the Cordillera near here, past Aconcagua and into Mendoza. Did you know that? If it wasn't snowing so hard, you could see the tip of Aconcagua from your chair."

Aconcagua; that chain of gentle, open-mouthed vowels could not be more different than what she remembered of her grandparents' speech. She rolled the word around in her mouth, and only when Dr. Sepulveda said, "Zaga?" did she hear the link to her own name.

. . .

The woman at the museum was very persuasive and Zaga, after an argument with her broker and a long phone call from her lawyer, wrote a substantial check. It was thrilling, inking that row of figures onto the smooth green paper. And she felt sure that Joel would have been pleased—he would have left the museum the funds to maintain the paintings had he not been overscrupulous about providing for her. But she had everything she needed. When her sister Marianna came to see the condominium, Zaga blithely told her about her gift.

"*How* much money?" Marianna said. "You gave that much to *strangers*?"

Zaga explained the situation: how there was money left from the sale of the house, how the museum needed it. "I'm fine," she told her sister. "Joel left me in good shape."

But Marianna wasn't worried about Zaga's financial stability. "You might have thought of *us*," she said, aggrieved and pink-faced, and then all the resentment she'd felt since Zaga's marriage came pouring out. Zaga, she said, had not been sufficiently generous.

"Look at your clothes," she said. Zaga could not see much difference between her blouse and jacket and Marianna's pretty sweater. "Look at your cars."

"I only kept one," Zaga protested. "Remember when I gave Dad the Oldsmobile?"

"Oh, please," Marianna said. "Big deal." And when Zaga reminded her that she and Joel had paid the hospital bills for her father's final illness, and also the live-in housekeeper who had made possible her mother's last days at home, Marianna only made a face. "What did that cost you?" she said. "What did you have to give up? Nothing."

"I had to ask Joel every time—you think that was easy?"

Marianna flicked her hand in front of her face, as if she were waving away a gnat. "Joel was a weenie," she said impatiently. "If you'll pardon me for saying so. We all knew he'd do whatever you asked. But things are different now. My kids are headed for college in just a few years, and Teddy and I don't have any idea where we're going to scrape the tuition from—how do you think it makes us feel, watching you give that kind of money to a museum?"

"I didn't know you felt like that," Zaga said, unwilling to admit how impulsive her gift had been. "The museum was very important to Joel."

"What's important is family," Marianna said. "If you ever came home, you might have some idea what was going on."

"I visited as much as I could," Zaga said. But she knew that this was not precisely true. Within a few years of her marriage to Joel, the row houses and narrow streets of her family's neighborhood in northeast Philadelphia had come to seem unpleasant. Christmas days they had spent with Joel's family, but on Christmas Eves they went to her parents' house, where all her relatives gathered. Each year she'd been more uncomfortable turning off Roosevelt Boulevard and heading into the blocks where she'd grown up. Reindeer and sleds on the shabby roofs, shrubs wound with colored bulbs and children everywhere. The contrast with Merion, where her neighbors hung small wreaths on their front doors and framed trees between half-drawn curtains in front of picture windows, had made her queasy. Joel had never mentioned the garish decorations or been less than courteous to her family, but she had always imagined that he suppressed his distaste only out of kindness. Rob and Alicia had sometimes giggled out loud.

Abashed, Zaga promised her sister that the next time she felt like giving money away she would keep her family in mind.

Zaga would not have said she knew Dr. Sepulveda well: during their afternoons in the hotel lounge she learned only the barest facts of his life. He was a widower, he had three grown sons. He had an apartment in Santiago and, during the ski season, a suite of rooms at the Hotel Portillo, which he received in exchange for his services as hotel doctor. He didn't ski but he loved the mountains, and he said he enjoyed the hotel's cosmopolitan clientele.

He didn't ask Zaga any more questions about her life and he seldom talked about himself, but he was a pleasant companion, full of interesting tales. In 1835, he told her, his great-great-grandfather had shown Darwin around what existed of Santiago and had helped with arrangements for Darwin's journey over the Portillo pass. "They were friends," he said. "These stories have come down through my family. I still have first editions of the journals Darwin published." The last Darwin story he told her, on the day before the blizzard ended, was the most unusual.

"I've never been able to get this story out of my mind," he said. As he spoke he took a small black camera from his leather bag. On the *Beagle*, he said, the ship that had carried Darwin and his companions around South America, "—on that ship were three Fuegians, natives of Tierra del Fuego who'd been away from their home for years."

FitzRoy, the *Beagle's* commander, had made an earlier visit to Tierra del Fuego, during which some Fuegians had stolen a whaleboat from him. In retaliation, FitzRoy had taken two men and a young girl hostage. Later he added a little boy, whom he bought from his family for the price of a pearl button. The Fuegians seemed happy aboard the ship, and FitzRoy took the four of them back to England with him.

Dr. Sepulveda cradled the camera in his left hand as he explained how one of the men had died of smallpox while the other, whom FitzRoy had named York Minster, survived. The girl, named Fuegia Basket, thrived, and so did the boy, called

Jemmy Button after his purchase price. "They learned a good deal of English," the doctor said. "They adopted English dress and were quite the wonder of London for a while. The queen met them and gave Fuegia Basket a ring."

But the Fuegians weren't happy, the doctor said, and Fitz-Roy was no longer sure that he'd done the right thing in taking them from their native land. And so when he set off on his second voyage—the one on which Darwin was present—he carried the Fuegians with him, along with a missionary and a huge store of goods donated by a missionary society. He had hopes that Jemmy and Fuegia and York might teach their tribes to welcome Englishmen. Then a shipwrecked sailor or a passing stranger might not have to fear for his life.

"Darwin was quite a young man then," the doctor said. "Your age, maybe a little younger—twenty-three, twenty-four. He found the Fuegians very interesting and was particularly fond of Jemmy Button, whom he describes as sweet-tempered and amusing. He expected a great reunion when they finally came on Jemmy's tribe, but the tribe was hostile and unwelcoming. Jemmy, who had forgotten how to speak his own language, had changed so much that his family hardly recognized him.

"FitzRoy's crew unloaded the gifts of the missionary society and showed the members of Jemmy's tribe how to use a shovel and a hoe," Dr. Sepulveda said. "Then they packed up and went off to do some botanizing. They left Jemmy behind, along with the missionary and York and Fuegia. A few weeks later they returned to find the gifts demolished and scattered among the tribe. York and Fuegia were all right, but Jemmy was miserable and the missionary, who was terrified, gave up his plans and sailed off with the *Beagle* when it left again."

The story made Zaga restless, as did the camera glinting darkly in Dr. Sepulveda's hand, but he seemed compelled to go on talking. In his journal, the doctor said, Darwin recorded his suspicions that Jemmy would have been glad to rejoin the ship along with the missionary. He'd been civilized, he noted; perhaps he would have liked to retain his new habits.

A year later, when the *Beagle* returned to the area, a canoe headed out to greet the ship. A long-haired man wearing nothing but a scrap of sealskin was washing the paint from his face while a woman paddled. No one recognized the man until he hailed FitzRoy and Darwin, and then they saw that this ragged stranger was the Jemmy they'd left, plump and clean and clothed, all those months ago.

He still remembered the English he'd learned and he told FitzRoy and Darwin that he was very happy now. He had plenty to eat, he had found a wife, he liked his family. And although York and Fuegia had run away with the few belongings his tribe hadn't already taken, he claimed to be content.

Jemmy gave FitzRoy an otter skin and Darwin a pair of spearheads. Then he returned to his canoe and paddled away. When he reached the shore he lit a bonfire. The last sign Darwin saw of him was the long and wistful column of smoke outlined against the horizon.

Dr. Sepulveda paused and sipped his coffee. In the Andes, he explained, Darwin had mused on the story of Jemmy Button, and so had he. Before Zaga could smile, he held the camera in front of his face and clicked the shutter. "For your baby," he said. He gestured toward her waist and spoke a few words in Spanish; perhaps he addressed her child. Then he said, "Think of that. Jemmy Button: captured, exiled, re-educated; then returned, abused by his family, finally re-accepted. Was he happy? Or was he saying that as a way to spite his captors? Darwin never knew."

Zaga imagined how she might look through his lens, surrounded by wealthy skiers from France and Spain, California and Brazil. Small, slight, insignificant. Ill-bred and poorly educated. "Are *you* happy?" she asked the doctor. He replied, "Are you?"

. . .

Despite her promise to Marianna, Zaga continued to give money away. It was a fever that came over her. It was a burning in her fingertips, which could only be relieved by writing checks. She gave money to the Girl Scouts, the Boy Scouts, the Shriners, Kiwanis. Her money seemed like a dead skin, and the more she shed the better she felt. "Visit lawyer," she wrote on her list of things to do. "Set up college funds for the kids." But meanwhile she gave to political candidates, medical research foundations, slim girls in jeans begging funds to save the whales. Her list was still by the phone when Rob called. It was the first time she'd heard from either him or Alicia since her move.

"How are you doing?" he asked her. "How do you like your new place?" As if her efforts to mother him had worked, as if they were actually close. He told her how his job was going and then said he had a friend who very much wanted to meet her. His name was Nicholas Bennett; Joel had known him and had thought the world of him. Nicholas had something he wanted to discuss with Zaga. Would she see him? She said she would.

A week later she met Nicholas for lunch in the museum café. He was tall, as he'd said over the phone, and lean and dark-haired; he was younger than Zaga, with interesting planes between his cheekbones and the crisp line of his jaw. When she spotted him at his table in the corner he rose to greet her.

Over a salad of ripe pears and Roquefurt he offered his condolences and told her how much he'd admired Joel. For an hour she waited to learn why he'd wanted to speak to her, but instead the conversation eddied pleasantly around Joel and common acquaintances and the situation at the museum. "You were right," Nicholas told her. "To give them the funds. Joel would have wanted those paintings hung properly." Zaga had two glasses of Chardonnay and when Nicholas asked her about her family she told him more or less the story she'd told Dr. Sepulveda years ago.

Nicholas said, "Really?" and smiled at her. His teeth were white and charmingly uneven. By the time he finally, casually, mentioned what must have been his real purpose in seeing her, she had entirely lost sight of the fact that he wanted something. The light coming in through the high, arched windows was gentle and everyone else had left the café. Nicholas was absurdly young, he was barely thirty. She was not so much attracted to him as she was warmed and flattered by the image of her younger self she saw in his eyes. He explained how he'd recently purchased the rights to an excellent new drug.

He was starting up a company to market it, he said. A few people, some savvy investors, would be helping him get started; once the drug hit the market and the stock went public the profits would be staggering. As she listened to him, she thought how she still had too much money sitting in dead investments instead of building something new and vital. By the time the first tired museum-goers had wandered in for afternoon tea, she had convinced Nicholas to let her invest with him.

"I couldn't let you do that," he said at first. "There's some risk involved, I'm not sure Joel would have approved." He was bashful, reluctant; he dragged his feet and nearly blushed.

"Joel's dead," she said. "It's my decision." Even then, she may have understood what was bound to happen.

He brushed her hand and said, "I wouldn't feel right."

"Please," she said. "I insist."

That night, alone in her clean bed, she dreamed of Dr. Sepulveda. In his white shirt and silk scarf and elegant pleated pants he led her outside the hotel and around the lake, where they met three mules loaded with blankets and food and cooking utensils and hardware. There was a mare with a bell around her neck, but she was not for riding: she was the *madrina*, Dr. Sepulveda explained, the steady mother who led the mules. Dr. Sepulveda wrapped Zaga's feet in enormous boots and then led her to a pass between the peaks.

The two of them stepped quietly in the wake of the sure-footed mules, the mules followed the horse with the bell, the horse followed a silent man whom Dr. Sepulveda did not intro-duce. Up they went, and up and up, moving effortlessly through the lightly falling snow. They crossed a snowfield interrupted by columns of ice, and they passed a horse frozen head down in one of those columns with its hind legs stretched stiffly skyward. From behind the column, dressed in the hide of an animal, Jemmy Button appeared. Three condors dotted the sky between him and Aconcagua.

The horse represented her inheritance, Zaga decided when she woke. Frozen, useless; she had done the right thing in freeing it up. Dr. Sepulveda had told her a story of how Darwin had seen such a horse and described it in his journal, but she could no longer remember how the horse had come to its fate.

Six months later, when Nicholas's company went under, Zaga was left with so little that she could no longer afford the maintenance fees for her lovely condominium. "I was investing the money for the children," she told her siblings. "I wanted them to have more for college." If they knew she was lying, they didn't call her on it. By then they were treating her as carefully as if she were sick.

She rented her condominium to a pair of brokers she could hardly tell apart, and she moved into the first floor of a three-story row house within walking distance of two of her brothers and not far from the house where she'd grown up. Marianna, after her initial rage, found the apartment for Zaga; she also found Zaga a job as a receptionist for a pediatric dental practice.

The waiting room there was always full and Zaga learned that she was good with children—much better than she would have thought after her experiences with Rob and Alicia. The children called her by her first name and drew stars on her hands with felt-tipped pens. She hung the drawings they made for her on the wall above her desk.

At night, when the office emptied and the dentists drove off in their new cars toward the area she'd abandoned after nineteen years, she walked home through the crowded neighborhood. Her family began, slowly and tentatively, to invite her to Sunday dinners and birthday parties and confirmations and school plays. When they took her aside, one by one, they all asked the same questions.

"How did you lose Joel's money?" they asked. "What could you have been thinking?"

She could not explain that it had nothing to do with thought. It was the buzz, the rush, the antic joy of flinging her old life to the winds. She was abashed by her final loss, adrift and up-set—and yet there was also the fact that she had not felt so content in years. Every trace of the life Joel had given her was gone, and she had nothing left to live on but her wits. She knew that what her family really longed to know was why she couldn't have given the money to them. *I would have*, she wanted to say. *If I'd known what I was doing.* But even their resentment could not shatter her sense of relief. Even her stepchildren couldn't make her regret what she had done.

Rob and Alicia came to visit her four months after she'd moved into her new apartment. It took them that long to agree on a day when they could both find the time, and when they arrived they were hot and exasperated and two hours late.

"We got *so* lost," Alicia said as she flounced in the door. "Unbelievable, these streets—how does anyone find their way around here?"

She was thirty-four, still flamboyant, now completely blond. She set down her purse and walked through Zaga's rooms, which ran in a row from front to back: the kitchen just inside the door, then the living room, then the bedroom. The bathroom was off the kitchen and had no shower, only an old, deep tub with a rubber nozzle that Zaga used for rinsing her hair. Alicia stared at everything in the three small rooms—weighing, Zaga thought. Judging, as she always had—and said, "Do you really have to live like this?"

"Alicia," Rob said, but Alicia would not be stopped. She wandered across the linoleum, from the old gas stove to the window propped open by a book, and when she looked at Zaga her puzzlement seemed genuine. "What happened to all the good furniture?" she said. "What happened to everything?"

Zaga explained that she'd sold much of it and left the rest in the condominium for her tenants, but she could tell that Alicia did not believe her.

"Are you living like this just to make us feel guilty?" Alicia said.

"*Alicia,*" Rob said again. But then he looked around glumly and added, "You ought to sue that bastard."

Zaga refrained from reminding him that he had sent Nicholas her way, and that, after she'd given Nicholas the first check, Rob had called her and had seemed pleased and horrified in approximately equal parts. Now he said, "I wish you hadn't trusted him so much."

He had, Zaga knew, lost a fair amount with Nicholas himself. But in his eyes she read his conviction that she had lost everything. In his townhouse he hid his TV and VCR in a nineteenth-century French armoire that had passed to him through more generations of family than she could bear to remember. He was searching the room for some trace of his father and failing to find the smallest thing, and she couldn't explain to him that the objects she'd shed were no more meaningful than the donations the British missionary society had sent to Tierra del

Fuego with Jemmy Button and his companions. Still, occasionally, she thought about the equation Dr. Sepulveda had seemed to suggest between Jemmy's life and her own.

Beaver hats and white tablecloths and soup tureens and pants; a complete set of dishes painted with flowers and little trays for tea. How FitzRoy's crew had laughed when they'd opened those crates on Tierra del Fuego! And how strange it had been, Dr. Sepulveda said, when the boat's crew returned to visit Jemmy the first time. The dishes were smashed, the vegetable garden trodden into the mud. The fancy clothes had been torn into strips that waved gaily from heads and wrists.

"I heard you're working," Alicia said.

"For some dentists," Zaga replied. She offered nothing more. She had planned to bring them with her to a family barbecue, but after a few more minutes of awkward conversation they exchanged a glance and then made excuses and left. She changed her clothes and went to Marianna's by herself.

"They got to my place late," she explained to Marianna. "Then they had to leave early."

Marianna was holding Timothy's youngest daughter in her lap, watching the rest of the children spread mustard on sausages and potato salad on paper plates. "Why'd they bother coming at all?" she asked.

Zaga remembered how miserable she had been in Portillo, caught in the hot beam of Rob's and Alicia's eyes. What had she expected to find in that place? Ease and elegance, manners and wisdom, a past she could share with her husband. She had never considered how isolated she would be. But Joel had been out on the slopes with his children, and when he returned he alternated between describing their thrilling runs and pressing Zaga to come outside. She didn't feel well enough, she'd said. Whenever she'd alluded to her pregnancy, Rob and Alicia had looked at the walls, the floor, the snow.

"It's good that you're pregnant," Dr. Sepulveda had said. Was that the afternoon he took the picture, or another, earlier one when she asked about his wife and he said quietly that she was dead? In the lounge, when she'd been driven to ask him her last question and he'd responded with one of his own, she'd refused to answer him. She'd risen and said goodbye and left the hotel without seeing him again. But before that, he had said, "A baby with Joel's money and your looks and character, born into Joel's world—a child like that might do anything."

But she had lost the baby. Afterwards, she had wanted to move; her grief had been outrageous, excessive, and she'd told Joel that the sight of the house where she'd lost their child was unbearable to her. She had been hysterical. She had blamed the long flights, the altitude of Portillo, the injections with which Dr. Sepulveda had cured her of *soroche*. She had blamed Joel for the pleasure he'd taken in skiing and Rob and Alicia for the way they'd stared at her barely thickened waist.

She had written to Dr. Sepulveda, remembering his pointed tales but forgetting the image of her he held captive in his camera. *What did you mean by those stories?* she'd scrawled. *What am I supposed to do?*

He never answered, or she believed that he'd never answered. For years she'd imagined him baffled by her failure to understand that the link between her and Jemmy Button was specious, only a surface resemblance: Jemmy had had no choice. But she had always seen that, as clearly as she could see her lost child in the toddler Marianna held in her lap. She had simply not known what to do with the knowledge.

Marianna, still annoyed about Rob and Alicia's absence, said, "Why do you even bother with them when they treat you like this?"

Zaga watched her youngest brother put together a kite for his son and then struggle to launch it. "I don't know," she answered. "Joel would have wanted me to." It seemed impossible to admit that all the years she'd spent with them had not forged a connection strong enough to survive Joel's death.

Joel had led her through their house after she lost their baby, pointing out the peach curtains she'd hung in Alicia's room, the built-in desk she'd had made for Rob. The children's mother was staying in France, he said. She wasn't coming back. Then he asked her if she couldn't be happy raising Rob and Alicia as their own. "It's too late," he said. "I'm too old to go through this again." Tired and heartsore she'd bent to his wish, the way one of her grandmothers might have bent to life in her new country. No one had consulted Alicia or Rob.

The kite had a body of lightweight blue nylon and a red tail that spun like a pinwheel. "Bird," said the baby in Marianna's lap, pointing at the kite as it rose. A string of children trailed Zaga's brother, his two grade-schoolers mingled with the toddlers produced by her oldest brother's son. It seemed impossible that she should have a brother who was a grandfather. Impossible that everyone in this family had children but her and that all of them could grow up without her help.

Birds with No Feet

There was no breeze that night. The sea, lit by the full moon, shone smooth and silver; the Southern Cross turned above the ship and below it squid slipped invisibly through the depths. Between sky and sea lay Alec Carrière, sprawled like a starfish in his hammock and imagining how the treasures packed in the holds were about to change his life.

Beetles and butterflies and spiders and moths, bird skins and snakeskins and bones: these were what he'd collected along the Amazon and then guarded against the omnivorous ants. Mr. Barton, his agent back home in Philadelphia, had sold Alec's first specimens for a good price, and Alec expected this shipment would finally set him free to pursue his studies in peace. He was a few months shy of twenty-one, and dreaming a young man's dreams.

Until he'd sailed for the Amazon, he'd worked in a shop making leather valises, not far from the tavern his parents ran in Germantown. But like the young English collector he'd met in Barra, near the flooded islands of the Rio Negro, he'd been saved from a squalid and unremarkable life by a few kind men and a book. With his uncle's ornithology text in his pocket he'd wandered the banks of the Wissahickon, teaching himself the names of birds and imagining wild places. His brother Frank had taught him to shoot, and behind the outhouse he'd prepared his first clumsy skins and mounts. Even then he'd known that other naturalists had taught themselves their trade. Others had risen from just such humble beginnings, and he'd seen nothing extraordinary in his ambitions.

Once every few months he went into downtown Philadelphia to visit the Academy of Natural Sciences, where a few of the members corrected his malformed preparations and taught him what they could. His interests spread from birds to other species. Titian Peale showed him an excellent way to pin and display his moths. Two of the Wells brothers, Copernicus and Erasmus, taught him how to prepare skeletons. All this gave Alec great pleasure but annoyed his father; by the time he was sixteen his father was pressing him to abandon this childish hobby and take his work more seriously. He almost gave up. But in 1850 Peale made him a gift of William Edwards's small and wonderful book, *A Voyage Up the River Amazon.*

When Alec read it a door seemed to open. What was there to keep him in Philadelphia? Edwards had been only a few years older than him when he'd set off; Alec was strong and healthy and his three brothers could look after their parents. And he had a most earnest desire to behold the luxuriant life of the tropics. Mr. Barton, a natural history auctioneer whom he'd met at the Academy, assured him that all of northern Brazil was little known, that Edwards had brought back only small collections, and that Alec might easily pay the expenses of his trip by gathering birds, small mammals, land-shells, and all the orders of insects. Among the wealthy, Mr. Barton said, glass cases filled with tropical creatures arranged by genus or poised in tableaux were wildly fashionable. And so few specimens had reached North America from the Amazon that high prices were guaranteed.

With the brashness of youth Alec wrote to Mr. Edwards

himself, who provided him with letters of introduction to several traders. Then he packed his things and used his small savings to book passage on a merchant ship. His father was angry with him; his mother wept. But he saw miracles.

The mouth of the Amazon was like a sea, and could be distinguished from the ocean only by its extraordinary deep-yellow color. The Rio Negro was as black as the river Styx. Jet-black jaguars and massive turtle's nests, agoutis and giant serpents; below Baião, a crowd of Indians gathered, laughing and curious, to watch Alec skinning parrots. Driven to gather as much as he could, Alec shrugged off the heat and the poor food and the fevers that plagued him intermittently. His persistence was rewarded in Barra, where Alfred Wallace greeted him like a brother.

Wallace wasn't famous then. Except for the light that burned in him and lit a similar flame in Alec, he was just another collector, exceedingly tall, with a thatch of yellow hair and clothes as shabby as Alec's own. On the day they met the sun dropped like a shot bird, and in the sudden tropical night they compared skins and guns.

Alec was lonely, and glad for the company after months among Indians whose language he couldn't speak. He talked too much the night he met Wallace, he knew he did. But although Wallace was a decade older, wracked with fever and ready to leave for home after three hard years in the jungle, he never laughed at Alec's chatter or made him feel less than an equal. He showed Alec the blow-pipes his Indian hunters used, and the bitter vegetable oil with which he coated the ropes of his specimen-drying racks. Alec showed him the glorious umbrella-birds he'd captured in the flooded forest of the *igapo*. Standing by the side of this long, lean, wasted man, Alec took pleasure in his own youth and compact sturdiness; how his hands, next to Wallace's fine bones, were all broad palm and spatulate thumb. Around them the toucans yelped and the parrots chattered and the palms went *swish*, *swish* in the evening breeze. They ate fish and farinha and turtle. Later they traded stories about the books that had saved them. When Alec learned that Wallace was no gentleman scientist but was, like Alec himself, solely dependent on selling specimens to pay his way, he felt an immediate bond.

After they parted, Alec collected with even more fervor. Now the results lay snugly packed below him, and as the ship rocked sluggishly he was imagining how he'd drive up to his parents' tavern, dressed in a new suit and laden with more money than they'd ever seen.

They would be thrilled, Alec thought. As would everyone who'd helped him. How surprised the Wells brothers and Titian Peale would be, when Alec made them gifts of the especially amazing butterflies he'd set aside for them! And then the hush inside the Academy, as he lectured to the men who'd taught him. Holding up a perfect skin from one of those rare umbrella-birds, he would point out the glossy blue tufts on the crest-feathers. "When the bird is resting," he would say, "the raised crest forms a deep blue dome, which completely hides the head and beak." The men would give him a desk, Alec thought, where he might catalogue his treasures. And he might marry, were he to meet someone appealing.

He was happy; he was half-asleep. Then the cabin-boy ran up to Alec's hammock and shook him and said, "Mr. Carrière! The captain says to come immediately. There seems to be a fire!" And Alec, still dreaming of his wonderful future, stumbled from his cabin with only the most recent volume of his journal and the clothes on his back.

The scene on deck was pure chaos: smoke rising through the masts, a sheet of flame shooting up from the galley, crew members hurling water along the deck and onto the sails. Captain Longwood was shouting orders and several of the men were unlashing the boats and preparing to lower them, while others hurriedly gathered casks of water and biscuit.

"What's happened?" Alec shouted. "What can I do?"

"Save what you can!" Captain Longwood shouted back. "I fear we may lose the ship."

Even as Alec headed for the forecastle, he could not believe this was happening. Some months after his meeting with Wallace, he'd heard that the brig carrying Wallace home had burned to the waterline, destroying all his collections and casting him adrift on the sea for several weeks. This news had filled Alec with genuine horror. Yet at the same time he'd also felt a small, mean sense of superstitious relief: such a disaster, having happened once, could surely never happen again. Although Alec's own collections were not insured, since he could not afford the fees, Wallace's bad luck had seemed to guarantee Alec's safe passage home.

All this passed through his mind as he fought his way forward. Then every thought but panic was driven away when he saw the plight of his animals.

In the holds below him was a fortune in things dead and preserved—but in the forecastle was the living menagerie he was also bringing home. His sweet sloth, no bigger than a rabbit, with his charming habit of hanging upside down on the back of a chair and his melancholy expression; the parrots and parakeets and the forest-dog; the toucans; the monkeys: already they were calling through the smoke. And before Alec could reach them a spout of flame rose like a wall through the hatchway in front of him.

Wallace's ship, he knew, had caught fire through the spontaneous combustion of kegs of balsam-capivi, but their own fire had no such exotic cause. The cook had knocked over a lamp, which had ignited a keg of grease, which had dripped, burning, through the floorboards and set fire to the cargo of rubber and lumber just below. From there the fire licked forward, downward, upward; and when the hatches were opened the draft made the fire jump and sing.

Alec was driven back to the quarterdeck and stood there, helpless, while the men prepared the boats and hurriedly gathered spars and oars and sails. The captain flew by, still shouting, his hands bristling with charts and compasses; they were five days out of Para and no longer within sight of land. The skylight exploded with a great roar, and the burning berths crackled below them. Terrible noises rose from the bow where the animals were confined. His lovely purple-breasted cotingas, roasting; the handsome pair of big-bellied monkeys, which the Brazilians called *barraidugo*—his entire life, until that moment, had contained nothing so distressing.

For a moment he thought the birds at least might be saved. One of the men dropped from his perch on the cross-trees and smashed in the forecastle door with an axe. Then the toucans, kept unconfined, flew out, and also a flock of parakeets. The cloud of birds seemed to head for the cloud of smoke but then swooped low and settled on the bowsprit, as far from the fire as they could get. They were joined by the sloth, who had magically crept up the ironwork. But meanwhile the mate was shouting, "Go! *Now!*" and hands were pushing against Alec's back, men were tumbling over the stern and he tumbled with them, falling into one of the leaky boats. Someone thrust a dipper into his hands and he began to bale, while men he had never noticed before barked and struggled to fit the oars in the oarlocks. The man pressed against his knee dripped blood from a scratch on his cheek and gagged, as did Alec, on the smoke from the rubber seething in the wreck.

The shrouds and sails burned briskly; then the masts began to catch. Soon enough the main-mast toppled and the moon-lit water filled with charred remains.

"Please," Alec begged Captain Longwood. "Can we row toward the bow? Can we try to save some of them?" His animals were lined along the last scrap of solid wood.

Captain Longwood hesitated, but then agreed. "Two minutes," he said sternly.

But when they approached the bow Alec found that the creatures would not abandon their perches. As the flames advanced, the birds seemed to dive into them, disappearing in sudden brilliant puffs that hung like stars. Only the sloth escaped; and he only because the section of bowsprit from which he hung upside down burned at the base and plopped into the water. When Alec picked him up, his feet still clung to the wood.

They were three days drifting in their leaky boats before they saw a sail in the distance: the *Alexandra*, headed for New Orleans. A fortunate rescue. Alec was grateful. But a year and a half of hard work, on which his whole future depended, was destroyed; as was the sloth, who died on the voyage. Alec reached home in one piece, but with hardly more to his name than when he'd left. As a souvenir he was given nightmares, in which the smell of singeing feathers filled his nostrils and his sloth curled smaller and smaller, and closed his eyes, and died again and again.

In November, recuperating at his uncle's house as his father would not have him at his, Alec learned that his acquaintance from Barra had written two books, one about his travels and the other about the exotic palms. Alec read both and liked them very much. They had shared a rare and terrible thing, Alec thought: all they'd gathered of the astonishing fauna of the Amazon, both quick and dead, turned into ash on the sea. Alec wrote to him, in England.

Dear Mr. Wallace: I expect you will not remember me, but we passed a pleasant evening together in Barra in September 1851. I was the young American man heading up the Rio Negro in search of specimens. I write both to express my

*admiration for your recent books, and to record an
astonishing coincidence. You will hardly believe what
happened to me on my journey home. . . . .*

Wallace wrote back.

*Dear Alec: My sympathies on the distressing loss of your
collections. No one who has not been through this himself
can understand. Beyond the horrors of the fire itself, the
terrible loss of animal life, and the substantial financial blow
is this fact, so difficult to explain: That each specimen lost
represents a double death. Our hunting always had a point;
each bird we shot and butterfly we netted was in the service
of science. But burnt, they now serve no one. It is very hard.
I thank you for your kind words about my books. I plan to
head, this coming spring, for the Malay Archipelago: an area
hardly explored at all, which should prove extremely rich for
our purposes. Perhaps you might like to consider this
yourself?*

Alec's mother, who had faithfully written to him during his
absence, without understanding that he would get her letters
only in one great batch when he returned to Para, was during
this hard time very kind to him. She visited Alec weekly at his
uncle's. And when he told her what he planned to do next, she
encouraged him and secretly bought him two suits of clothes.

[*Ague—1855*]

It was not as if Wallace and Alec traveled together throughout
the Malay Archipelago, nor as if Wallace took Alec under his
wing in any practical way. Alec was in Macassar when Wallace
was in Bali; Wallace was in Lombok when Alec was in Timor;
they both visited the Aru Islands, but in different years. And
their situations were no longer as similar as they'd been in the

Amazon. Wallace was still strapped for money, but his books had made him a reputation and the Royal Geographical Society had paid his first-class passage to Singapore aboard a fast steamer. Alec made a slow and uncomfortable voyage on three merchant ships and a filthy whaler. Wallace had with him an assistant, 16-year-old Charles, who helped capture, preserve, and catalog specimens, whereas Alec was all alone, and often overcome by details.

During the wet season of 1855, Alec was in Sarawak, in northwestern Borneo. He'd heard tales of a lively Christmas house-party at the bungalow of Sir John Brooke, the English Rajah of the territory—all the Europeans in the out-stations being invited to enjoy the Rajah's fabled hospitality, and so forth. But he had not been asked to join the party, and he never suspected that Wallace was there. Over that Christmas, and into January, Alec was miles east of the Rajah's bungalow, collecting beetles and hunting orangutans in the swamps along the Sadong River.

For some weeks he'd been blessed with astonishing luck. Moving through the dense foliage he would hear a rustling overhead, then glimpse one of the reddish-brown apes swinging. Branch to branch, tree to tree, never touching the ground. His desire for possession seemed to carve a line in the air between his gun and his target; he aimed and a moment later the orangutan was his. Retrieving the body was more difficult, but here the native Dyaks helped him. As the orangutans fed on the fruit of the durian tree, of which the Dyaks were very fond, the Dyaks were happy to guide Alec to them and then, after the shooting, to fell the trees in which the bodies were trapped, or climb the trunks and lower the bodies down. With their help Alec obtained four full-grown males, three females, and several juveniles. Just before the ague hit again, he also shot another female high in a giant tree. While lashing the body to the carrying poles, one of his Dyak hunters found the orangutan's little infant face-down in the swamp, crying piteously.

This orphan Alec brought back to camp with him. He could

not feel guilty about shooting the infant's mother; this was part of his work, what he was meant to do. But neither could he abandon the small creature who'd become his responsibility. While he lay on his cot, alternately burning and chilled, the infant orangutan clung to his clothes and beard and sucked on his fingers as he might at his mother's breast. For a long time no one had touched Alec. He gave the infant sugar-water and rice-water and coconut milk through a quill, and later offered bits of fruit and sweet potato. The orangutan insisted on clinging to some part of his body at all times. And Alec found this peculiarly touching, despite the weakness and lassitude brought on by his fever. When a pair of strangers walked into his hut, he was flat on his back, in a violent sweat, with the infant curled like a cap around his head.

Wallace, Alec learned from the strangers, had been at the Rajah's bungalow this whole time, staying on alone but for Charles and a Malay cook after the holidays had passed and the Rajah and his entourage had left. Having heard of Alec's plight through some visiting Dyaks, Wallace had sent these two back to fetch him. The pair carried Alec through the swamp and the forest, on a litter made of bamboo poles. Some of his helpers followed with his belongings, including all his crates of insect specimens and the skins and skeletons of the orangutans. The infant rode on his chest.

Wallace had the ague as well. When Alec arrived at the Rajah's bungalow, and first caught sight of the veranda and the huge teak beams, the wicker chairs and the spacious library, Wallace was desperately ill, and in bed. A few days later, when Wallace could get up, Alec was delirious. For ten days the men alternated bouts of fever as if they were playing lawn-tennis, but then finally, after large doses of quinine, both were well at the same time. In their weakened state they sat on the veranda, sipping arrack from narrow bamboos and talking. Wallace claimed that the bouts of ague stimulated his brain.

"Aren't these beetles astonishing?" Alec said, pawing through the box at his feet. His clothes and person were clean, he had had a good dinner, he'd slept on a real bed. He felt wonderful. This Brooke, he thought, truly lived like a king. And even though the Rajah had welcomed Wallace and not Alec, Alec was consoled by the beautiful things he had to show for his isolation.

"In two weeks I collected more than 600 different kinds, sometimes a dozen new species a day—it's bewildering," Alec said. He held out a beetle with horns twice the length of its body. "Have you come across this one? And what do you make of the remarkable multitude of species here?"

Wallace smiled and turned the beetle delicately on its back. He said, "I have several of these; they're charming. I do not see how a reasonable man can believe any longer in the permanence of species. All species, as you have seen yourself, constantly produce varieties. If this process goes on indefinitely, the varieties must move farther and farther from the original species, and some of these *must*, in time, develop into new species—but how and when does this happen? What is the method by which species undergo a natural process of gradual extinction and creation?"

"The method?" Alec said. Wallace passed the beetle back to Alec and Alec held it cupped in his palm. Since his first day in the archipelago he'd been haunted, vaguely, by the question Wallace now posed clearly: where had all these creatures come from? But Alec had had no time to theorize, caught up as he was in the urgency of trying to capture and name everything he saw.

"There must be a *mechanism*," Wallace said.

The rain was falling steadily. From the trees three Dyaks emerged and joined the men on the veranda; Wallace produced a piece of string and tried to show them how to play the child's game of cat's cradle. Much to Alec's astonishment the Dyaks knew it better than he did. The three of them stood in a close circle, weaving figures he'd never seen before on each other's hands and passing the cradle back and forth. When Alec joined them they netted his fingers together.

Later Wallace showed Alec the lone specimen he'd found of a huge new butterfly, which had brilliant green spots arrayed against the black velvet of its wings. "I have named it *Ornithoptera Brookeana*," Wallace said. "After our host." In return Alec showed Wallace how happily his little orangutan, whom he'd named Ali, lay in his arms as he brushed its long brown hair. He tried not to feel jealous when Ali leapt into Wallace's lap and licked his cheek. Wallace was Alec's friend, but also his rival, and sometimes Alec longed for Wallace to have some failing. A certain coldness, say. Or an absent-mindedness, brought on by deep thinking. But it seemed there was no part of their lives in which Wallace could not surpass him.

The ague struck them both again on the following day—and to their great sorrow, it also struck Ali. Wallace, too weak himself to rise from bed, had Charles give the infant castor-oil to cure its diarrhea, but although this worked the other symptoms of fever continued; Ali's head and feet swelled; and then he died. Everyone at the bungalow much regretted the loss of the little pet. When Alec's own strength returned, he wept over Ali's body and then decided to bring the skin and skeleton home with him. Ali was sixteen inches tall, four pounds in weight, with an arm-spread of twenty-four inches. Alec made these measurements, but he shrank from the task of preparing the specimen and thought to have Wallace's Charles help him out. Wallace discouraged that.

"Charles is a nice boy," he said. "But quite incapable—look what he has done with this bird."

He showed Alec a bee-eater Charles had been putting up, which resembled Alec's own first specimens. The head was crooked, a lump of cotton bulged from the breast, and the bird's feet had somehow been twisted soles uppermost. Alec looked at this, sighed, and steeled himself to prepare Ali's remains alone.

Separating the skin from the bone and muscle beneath, he reminded himself that, in so doing, he served science. Was this
science? That night he was unable to sleep. Some hours after the
bungalow had lapsed into silence, he found himself outside, in
the dripping forest, slashing savagely at a tangle of lianas.

Not until later did he learn that somewhere during this long
run of fever-soaked days, Wallace had written a paper on the
possible origin of species by, as he put it, *natural succession and
descent—one species becoming changed either slowly or rapidly
into another. . . . Every species has come into existence coincident
both in time and space with a pre-existing closely allied species.*
His paper caused a stir when it was published in England that
September, bringing him to the notice of such eminent men as
Lyell and Darwin.

What was Alec doing while Wallace was writing? Tossing
on his sweaty bed; mourning his little orangutan as he sorted
and arranged his insect collections. He prepared a shipment for
Mr. Barton, with a long anxious letter about the difficulty of
his finances, and how much he needed to receive a good price
for this batch of specimens. He wrote,

Enclosed please find:

Beetles	*600 species*
Moths	*520 species*
Butterflies	*500 species*
Bees and wasps	*480 species*
Flies	*470 species*
Locusts, etc.	*450 species*
Dragonflies, etc.	*90 species*
Earwigs, etc.	*45 species*

*Total: 3155 species of insects
(note: multiple specimens enclosed of many species)*

Alec never claimed that his financial difficulties kept him from such fruitful speculations as Wallace made; he knew that Wallace, like himself, spent precious hours sorting and crating specimens and was largely dependent on the income from the sale of same. Alec merely noted that Wallace had Charles, however incapable; a bungalow-palace where he might return from time to time to regain his strength; and powerful friends.

[*Theories — 1862*]

Here is one: Two human beings, coincident in time and space, cannot simultaneously think the same thought; one always precedes the other. As Wallace always preceded Alec, except in a single case. For consolation Alec had this: that *he* was the first to bring living specimens of paradise birds to the western world. And he believed he was the first American to see these creatures in their native forests.

Although Alec thought of Wallace often, and longed to see him, the Malay Archipelago is a very big place and they never crossed paths again. Not until the winter of 1860, while Alec was on Sumatra plowing stupefied through a year's accumulation of letters—his mother was ill, or had been the previous May; his brother Frank had married; Mr. Barton had sold his last shipment of insect specimens for a gratifying sum, but had advanced all the money save for a pittance to his father, at his father's request—did he again hear news of Wallace.

In a letter Mr. Barton, who kept up with the natural history journals in both England and America, recounted to Alec how at Ternate, while suffering again from the ague, Wallace had written a further essay on the origin of species and mailed it to Darwin for comments. The essay had caused a sensation, Mr. Barton said, summarizing its main points for Alec. It had been read at a meeting of the Linnaean Society, along with some notes of Darwin's expressing a similar idea.

Genius, Alec thought, sitting stunned on his wooden stool. That's what had come of Wallace's ague. Of his own, which was upon him again, there were only incoherent letters begging to know the true state of his finances. He would not repeat to anyone what he wrote to his family. To Mr. Barton he wrote,

> *Thank you for your last, and for the most interesting news of Wallace's essay. You cannot imagine how tired I am after my last year's voyages. During the recent months, when I might have been resting, I have been cleaning, labeling, arranging and packing the enclosed: some 10,000 insects, shells, birds, and skeletons. Also hiring men and obtaining stores for my trip to Celebes and the Aru Islands—none of this made any easier by the fact that you have sent me hardly enough money to live on. Do not give the proceeds of this shipment to my family, but forward a full statement directly to me.*

Perhaps this is when Alec first wondered why his journal had deteriorated into little more than a tally of species, interspersed with fumbling descriptions of places and people. Why all he'd observed and learned had not crystallized in his mind into some shimmering structure. Certainly he'd never lacked for facts— but he was caught like a fly in the richness around him, drowning in detail, spread too thin. If he were to narrow his gaze, perhaps? Focus on one small group of species, contemplate only them? Then he might make both his reputation and his fortune.

As a boy he'd spent hours in the Philadelphia museum staring at a skin labeled *Magnificent Bird of Paradise*: red wings, dark green breast-plumes, cobalt-blue head, a stunning yellow ruff or mantle, and behind that a second mantle of glossy pure red. Sprouting from the tail were two long spires of steely blue. He had stared not only because the skin was so beautiful, but because it had no wings or feet.

Birds with no feet—could there be such a thing? From a book in the museum's library, he'd learned that Linnaeus had labeled the skin he'd seen *Paradisea apoda*, or the footless paradise bird. A Dutch naturalist wrote that the paradise birds, wingless and footless, were buoyed up by the beams of the sun and never touched the earth till they died. How tantalizing, Alec thought now, looking up from his papers and crates. They were elusive, irresistible; and their skins were so rare as to be very valuable. Money crossed his mind, as it always had. Nearly penniless, and still without a wife or any possibility of supporting one, he seized on the prospect that the paradise birds might save him. Had Wallace married yet? He thought not. Once more he gathered the necessary supplies and prepared to disappear from sight.

After a long journey in a native *prau* from Celebes, during which his life was often in grave danger, he arrived in the Aru Islands. He shut his eyes to the fabulous trees, the astonishing moths and ants, and sought singlemindedly the Great Paradise Bird, with its dense tufts of long golden plumes raised to hide the whole body; the King Paradise Bird, so small and red, with its beautiful, emerald-green, spiral disks lifted high on slender paired shafts. The islanders with whom he was staying took him to see the *sacaleli*, or dancing-party, of the Great Paradise Birds.

In a huge tree, deep in the forest, he saw several dozen gather together. They raised their wings, they arched their necks, they lifted their long, flowing plumes and shivered them as if to music, darting now and then between the branches in great excitement. Their beauty and strangeness beggared even that of the lyre-tailed drongo-shrike or the Amazonian umbrella-bird. Above the crouching, glossy bodies the plumes formed golden fans. The islanders taught Alec to use a bow, and arrows tipped with blunt knobs. He sat in the trees, dazed by the beauty surrounding him, and shot strongly, so as to stun the birds without rending the skins or staining the plumage with blood. On the ground below him, boys wrung the birds' necks as they fell.

And of course they had feet, strong and pink and sturdy. The theories about them, Alec learned, had only been misinformation. He was one of the first to see how the islanders, preparing skins for traders, cut off the wings and feet, skinned the body up to the beak and removed the skull, then wrapped the skin around a sturdy stick and a stuffing of leaves and smoked the whole over a fire. This shrank the head and body very much and made the flowing plumage more prominent. Alec prepared his own specimens differently, so that the natural characteristics were preserved. And this absorbed him so completely that only in brief moments, as he fell into sleep, would he wonder about such things as how the golden plumes were related to the emerald disks.

Rain, fungus, aggressive ants, and the ever-ravenous dogs of the region all plagued him. Still, before the fever overcame him and he had to declare his journey at an end, he salvaged four crates of excellent skins and also captured three living specimens. He might not have an hypothesis about the divergence of species, but he knew how these birds lived. At the Smithsonian Institution, where he thought to donate them, he could point to their sturdy pink feet and say, "Look. *I* was the first to bring these back."

As he hop-scotched his way across the archipelago to Singapore, he easily found fruit and insects his birds would eat. Little figs they particularly enjoyed, also grasshoppers, locusts, and caterpillars. From Singapore to Bombay he fed the birds boiled rice and bananas, but they drooped in the absence of insect food and after Bombay even the fruit ran out. It was Alec's good fortune to discover they savored cockroaches, and for him to be aboard a battered old barkentine that swarmed with them. Each morning he scoured the hold and the store-rooms until he'd filled several biscuit-tins, and during the afternoon and evening he doled them out to the birds, a dozen at a time. As the ship headed south to round the Cape he worried that the increasing cold would bother them, but they did fine.

And if, as he learned after being back in Philadelphia for only a month, Wallace had been making his way to England simultaneously, carrying his own birds of paradise; and if Wallace's trip was shaped by the same quest for cockroaches—what did that matter? Wallace had traveled once more on a comfortable British steamer, aboard which cockroaches were rare; from his forced stops to gather them on land he made amusing anecdotes. But *I* was the one, Alec thought, who first solved the problem of keeping the birds alive.

From a London paper Alec learned that Wallace had returned to fame, as a result of his Ternate essay. His birds had taken up residence in the Zoological Gardens, where they were much admired. Meanwhile Alec had himself returned, unknown, to a country at war. To a half-country, he thought, which might soon be at war with England. His crates of skins lay uncatalogued at the Academy of Sciences. And the curators at the Smithsonian seemed less than grateful for his beautiful birds. No one had time to look at birds, their eyes were fixed on battles.

Alec wrote to Wallace once more—inappropriately, he knew; their stations had altered, their friendship had lapsed. Still he felt closer to Wallace than to anyone else in the world, and he could not keep from trying to explain himself to this man he'd meant to emulate. After giving the details of his voyage, of his birds and their fate, he wrote:

All of this may be blamed on the war. I cannot explain how bewildering it has been to return, after my long absence, to see what's become of my country. My mother died during my journey home. All three of my brothers have married, and my father has gone to live with my brother Frank,

*having lost through improvidence both the tavern and much
of the money rightfully mine, which he obtained through
trickery from Mr. Barton. Mr. Barton himself is gone,
enlisted in the Army. The weather is cold and grey; the
streets swarm with pallid people lost in their clothes; the air
rings with boys shouting newspaper headlines, over and over
again. In the Dyak longhouses, the heads of their enemies
hung from the rafters, turning gently as we ate: and I felt
more at home with them than here. Do you feel this? When
you walk into a drawing-room, do you not feel yourself a
stranger?*

    *What I meant to do, what I wanted to do, was to visit
Mr. Edwards, whose book sent me off on my life's work. He
is no great thinker himself; only a man who traveled, like
me, and described what he saw as I have failed to do. I
thought he might help me gather some of my impressions
into a book. But now I find that what I must do is abandon
my collections, leave home once more, and enlist. The
Potomac swarms with a great armada, ready to transport
100,000 men for an attack on Richmond.*

As he mailed his letter, he thought about the legend that
seemed—even before he left—to be growing up around his presence in the Aru Islands. He'd learned some of the islanders'
language, and had occasionally entertained his companions by
lighting fires with a hand-lens, or picking up bits of iron with
a magnet, which acts they regarded as magic. And because he
asked questions, even laughable questions, about the birds with
no feet before he ever saw them; because he knew where beetles
might be found and how to lure butterflies to a bit of dried
dung; and most of all because he walked alone through the
forests, for hours and days, and was comfortable there, and at
peace, the islanders ascribed mystical powers to him. The birds,
they claimed, came down from the trees to meet him.

    One of the boys he hunted with said, "You know everything.
You know our birds and animals as well as we do, and the ways
of the forest. You are not afraid to walk alone at night. We

believe that all the animals you kill and keep will come to life again."

Alec denied this strenuously. "These animals are *dead*," he said, pointing at a cluster of ants preserved in spirits. "Truly, truly dead."

The boy looked serenely into a golden glade dense with fallen trees. "They will rise," he said. "When the forest is empty and needs new animals."

Alec remembers staring at him; how the jar of ants dropped from his hand and rolled into the leafy litter. The suggestion seemed, in that moment, no more likely or unlikely than what Wallace had proposed for the origin of species: another theory of evolution; another theory. In that instant a line from Wallace's first letter to him returned and pierced like a bamboo shaft through his heart: *Each bird we shot and butterfly we netted was in the service of science.*

But this was only ever true for Wallace, not for him, he thinks; he has never been the scientist he'd believed himself to be, perhaps is no scientist at all. And that legend is as false as the moment, on the first leg of his first voyage home, when he hung suspended in joy. All the animals he's collected, sure that more would spring forth from the earth, are gone and will not rise. But as he packs his bags and readies himself for another murderous journey, they are what he thinks of now. The objects of his desire along the Amazon, in Borneo and Sumatra and Celebes, on the Aru Islands; his sloth, his orangutan, his birds with no feet.

$\mathcal{T}he$ $\mathcal{M}arburg$ $\mathcal{S}isters$

[*1. History*]

The girls' mother told them stories: how their grandfather Leo had grafted French vines onto North American roots with his German-Russian hands, finding the western New York winters easy to manage after the Ukraine. At the head of the lake the Couperins, who ran a rival winery, had laughed at Leo's cultivation practices, but in 1957, when Bianca was born, Leo had his revenge. That winter's violent cold spell left the Marburgs' earth-shrouded vines untouched when everyone else's were killed, and Walter Couperin lost all his hybrid vines and switched back to Concords in a fury.

Leo smiled and kept his secrets and established acres of *gewurztraminer*, which Couperin couldn't grow, and *rkaziteli*, a Russian grape temperamental for everyone but him. The girls grew up hearing words like these: *foxy, oaky, tannic, thin*. Like all children, they knew more than they knew that they knew.

In the fall the cold air slipping down from the hills hung white and even below the trellises. Leo's winery thrived, and his oldest son—Theo, the girls' father—threw himself into the business with a great and happy passion. Peter Couperin, Walter's heir, field-grafted Seyvals onto half his Concord stock, and still Theo outdid him.

The girls' mother, Suky, told them this, along with much else; she was herself the daughter of another winemaking family. When the girls were still quite small, she said, "Your father named you red and white, like girls from a fairy tale."

So they were Rose and Bianca, Bianca and Rose: inseparable. Or so they thought. In the white house in Hammondsport, on the western shore of Keuka Lake, their names formed a single word in their mother's mouth, like the name of one of Leo's grapes. *RoseandBianca*, they heard, as she called them in for dinner. "You were lucky," Suky said, "that you weren't named Merlot and Chardonnay or Cabernet and Aurore."

In other ways they were not so lucky. When Rose was ten and Bianca almost nine, a tourist speeding down the lakeshore road struck their strolling mother and killed her instantly. *Suky Marburg*, the headstone read. *Beloved wife of Theo; cherished daughter of Alice and Charles; adored niece of Agnes, Marion, Caroline, and Elaine.* Nothing about "Missed Mother of," and they were thought too young to attend the funeral. Yet who could miss her more?

After that they were wild girls, in a place that seemed like wilderness. Suky's Aunt Agnes came to care for them; a loving woman, but soon she took sick and spent her days perched on the porch glider while her mind disintegrated. When she called the girls she said, *Rose? Bianca?*, the long pause between the two names another bewildered question. Meanwhile the girls' teachers called them holy terrors and the neighbors referred to them as "the Marburg sisters," which term connoted nothing so kind as their mother's fusing of their first names. Even before her death they'd been unusually close. Afterwards they seemed like the two sides of a coin, easy to distinguish but impossible to split. Much of what they did together is best passed over.

Despite their disgraceful scrapes, they whizzed through school at a frightening pace. A strange rivalry drove them, darker and more serious than the one between the wineries—some sort of competition for the scraps of their father's attention. When he allowed it, they helped him out in the winery. Most often he ignored them and they worked on their own projects. A chemistry set appeared one Christmas, along with this information: yeast enzymes, he said, were the proteins made by yeast, which made winemaking possible. The girls made wine from grapes and honey and different flowers and once from rhubarb, for a lark.

From a book full of mysterious pictures, they learned about the uses of hair and eggshells and feces and worms, herbs and the blood of a red-haired man. They painted black the walls of their room and then hung pictures they snipped from their books; alchemists' labs juxtaposed with models of DNA and the three-dimensional structure of hemoglobin. Their father turned dirt and sunlight into wine; was that alchemy, or chemistry? Either one might turn their isolation into freedom.

And so of course they studied biochemistry in college, first Rose and then Bianca right behind her. Both of them gawky and geeky and barely sixteen when they entered. And of course they were entranced by the equipment and the theories, which made their earlier experiments seem childish. They never dreamed that they wouldn't work together.

In college they shared lovers and books. In graduate school, before Bianca dropped out, they wrote two papers together. Now Rose studies enzyme structure and kinetics at a research institute outside Boston; she has several grants and two technicians, although she's still younger than some of her graduate students. A whole section of her address book is devoted to Bianca—San Diego, Vancouver, Alaska, Hawaii. All places Rose has never been. Bianca does different things, which vary from year to year and are hard to explain.

. . .

That's the short version, the dry version—of course the details differ, depending on which of us tells it. Still, anyone could tell that version of our history to a stranger in a bar, and both of us have done so. *Oh, look*, in effect we say wryly. *A dead mother, a crazy great-aunt, a distant father. But here we are.* All the shameful details buried, all the juicy parts elided; both of us grown now, no big deal.

Good enough for strangers. But once we were closer than twins, and there were times, with the width of a street or a country between us, when we wondered why this version of our history didn't account for how we drifted so far apart. The drift was far from steady, but it was persistent.

On an August night in 1980, we made a fumbling attempt to find our way back to each other. Our evening included drugs and drink and voices and visions, a lot of water and a dog. Later, we'd look back on it as a time of preparation that failed in most ways but succeeded in a few, which helped us endure the loss to come. The story of this night forms a sort of pendant to our early history.

[*2. Alchemy*]

As Bianca drove from state to state while meaning only to reach Boston, she'd been thinking about the dead. The road beyond the cone of her headlights had been as black as a lake, and from the corner of one eye she had seen faces: Suky, Agnes—almost as if Rose had been beside her in the car. This had suggested a plan to her, for which she needed Rose's help. By the time she arrived at the institute's low white building, she was bursting with things to say. But before she could reach her sister, a man in a uniform stopped her in the lobby.

"Miss?" he said politely. "Miss?"

He blocked her with his body. "I'm sorry," he said. "Visitors must be accompanied past this point. May I ring someone's office for you?"

"My sister," Bianca said.

"And your sister would be?"

"*Rose,*" Bianca said huffily. When he still waited she said, "Rose *Marburg.*"

The man took her name and repeated it into the phone. A few minutes later a pair of doors opened with a hermetic sigh and Rose appeared in the lobby. Her dark hair was cut very short; her hands were in the pockets of her long white coat and she had a nametag pinned to her chest. For a minute Bianca wasn't sure who she was.

Rose, who'd run from the lab to the lobby as soon as she got the call, suspected trouble right away. "What is it with that guy?" Bianca said. "How come he couldn't see we were sisters?" Then, as they passed dark labs and offices, Bianca described how she'd been brooding about Suky and the accident and their lumpy impossible childhood.

That old story, which Rose already knew. At the moment all she wanted to do was fend off Bianca's rush of words.

"Isn't it obvious?" Bianca said. Although she was tall and fair and Rose was dark and slight, she couldn't understand why that man at the door hadn't seen their resemblance at once.

"Wally," Rose said to her babbling sister. "His name is Wally. He was just doing his job."

"Wally, schmally," Bianca said. "He should have known who I was. When did you cut your hair so short?"

Rose led Bianca into her lab. Gleaming benches and rows of glassware; a tidy office in which a computer screen glowed. She didn't stop to show Bianca all the gadgets in the lab; Bianca had been here before and knew how to use them as well as Rose did herself. In her office she guided Bianca to a chair. "I wasn't expecting you," she said, interrupting Bianca mid-sentence. "Is everything all right?"

"Fine," Bianca said. "A little ragged, a little jagged. I almost got arrested but that was last night. You have any coffee?"

Rose poured her a cup, noting the fine tremor in Bianca's hands and the way her pale hair stuck out in all directions. Rings beneath her eyes, a stain on the front of her shirt; a general air of funky poverty. For the last few months she'd been supporting herself by proofreading organic gardening articles for a magazine in Vermont. Rose suspected that Bianca needed another loan.

Bianca rose from her chair and paced the small room. "What a drive," she said again.

Rose tried to shape the cloud of her sister's words into a plot as linear as the graph on her computer screen. "When did you leave?"

"Last night—seven o'clock? Maybe eight?"

"From *Brattleboro*?"

Somehow Bianca had been on the road for almost twenty-four hours. Rose had driven twice to the house Bianca had shared for the last year with two potters, a fiber artist, a disk jockey for an alternative radio station, and an herbalist—a three-hour drive, no more, up Route 91 to a tiny road that led back into the hills. In the middle of nowhere stood a fussy Victorian with porches and peculiar windows. There were chickens in the yard, and two tethered goats and a mound of firewood as big as a shed. Rural, and yet nothing like Hammondsport. In the vegetable garden off to the side was a good-sized patch of marijuana, chastely surrounded by tasseled corn. Inside, dope plants hung in the stairwell like dead men, drying upside down.

Bianca stuck both hands into her mass of hair with her fingers outspread like rakes. "I didn't drive *straight*," she said impatiently.

When Rose raised an eyebrow Bianca laughed. "Not straight through," she said. "Not straight, either. We were having a little party at the house, checking out the new weed. And then I got this idea to visit you, and I got in the car but when I hit Brattleboro I remembered I hadn't seen Tommy in a while. I told you about him. So I drove over to North Conway and woke him up, and he was crabby at first but we had some drinks and did a few numbers and then we got to talking about Margie and Don—you remember, my friends from Vancouver?—and Tommy said they'd moved to Maine so I thought I'd just buzz over and see them but when I got there they weren't home and so I decided to swing by Keene and see another friend but halfway there this cop stopped me and . . ."

"Bianca," Rose said quietly. "When's the last time you slept?"

"Tuesday?" Bianca said. "I think." It was Thursday now.

Rose stared at the data she'd been plotting and then turned her computer off. Bianca said, "I think I called Dad last night."

"You did?" Rose said. She'd had a rule for some time, which was one of the things that stood like a wall between her and Bianca; she forbade herself to dwell on their past. At the moment she was also forbidding herself to think of their father, who had recently announced that he was getting married and was considering selling the winery.

"I'm not sure. I think I might have. From a phone booth— New Hampshire? Maine? I don't know, I don't remember what I said to him. I think I was stupid."

Bianca in a phone booth in the middle of the night, babbling at their father the way she was babbling now; it was more than Rose could bear to contemplate. If she'd known how to do so, she would have cut her past away with a knife. "How about I take you home?" she said. "I'll make you some dinner, you can have my bed. I'll sleep on the couch."

"No, no, no," Bianca said. "Here. I'll sleep here. On the floor—I don't want to be in your way, I don't want to be any trouble. And I brought food and stuff to drink—everything for a picnic." She had this plan, which she'd hatched in the car and would not reveal to her sister yet. It depended on them staying in the lab.

She reached into her knapsack and took out a bottle of Jim Beam and another of tequila; lemons, salt, tortilla chips, two cans of bean dip, and a jar of salsa; then a loaf of dill-and-wheatberry bread and an ounce of dope, a chunk of hash, some papers, and a pipe. "This cop?" she said. "Last night, when he stopped me, I was sure he was going to look in here. He asked me why I was driving so late, and . . ."

"Okay," Rose said. "I get the picture." She shut the office door.

"Relax," Bianca said. "Who's here? You're the only one who keeps such wacky hours."

She pushed the door open again and Rose let it stay that way. Bianca was right: no one else would be in the building except a few security guards and the night cleaning staff. Perhaps a handful of graduate students, running experiments or crunching numbers—but no one like Rose, none of the senior staff. They'd all be safely back in Newton or Concord, having dinner with families and dogs. She didn't socialize with them. She was single, she lived by herself in a studio with a broken-down couch and a wall of books and no TV. She had no friends, no pets, at the moment no lover. The lab was cheery and well-lit, the only place in the world where she felt at home. Her sister was here.

Bianca said, "So?" and Rose said, "Well. We could camp out here, I guess."

We demolished almost everything in the pack. Bianca gave Rose a bracelet she'd picked up in Maine and Rose clasped the heavy metal around her wrist. After midnight it started to rain, and we opened the window in Rose's office and stuck our heads out to catch the falling water. This felt so good that we exchanged a glance and then dropped through the window to the empty ground below. We were as high as kites, as high as Denali, which Bianca had once climbed but which Rose had never seen. Bianca was perfectly comfortable, but Rose felt like she'd lost her mind.

We ran across the wet grass until we reached the fringe of woods at the edge of the grounds. A creek wound between the trees, and Bianca was the first to shed her clothes and flop down in the shallow water. We were both soaked to the skin already, and so Rose didn't resist when Bianca grabbed her ankle and pulled her in. The rain was cool but not cold, the night was warm but not hot. The water flowing through the creek seemed to have no temperature at all.

Rose leaned against a boulder with her legs floating in the creek and watched the stars swirl and dance above her head. One star blazed red and then crossed the path of another. It might have been a satellite, or perhaps it was only a plane. Her sense of time was so deranged that she couldn't judge its speed. Against the sky she saw substrates and binding sites, inhibitors and antagonists. She said to Bianca, "Don't you miss doing science?"

Bianca, rolling happily in the mud on the bank, said, "Don't you miss this?" Her white skin was painted brown. She meant, not the mud specifically, but the fact that it was late, that we were alone, that our minds were shattered almost completely, and that we were doing something forbidden. This was the state in which, as girls, we'd held at bay our mother's loss and the taunting of our schoolmates. This was the state in which the rivalry between us dissolved. We couldn't mention the dissolution because we seldom admitted the rivalry. How could we have admitted that we eyed each other's lives and work with envy?

"I do," Rose said. "I miss it something awful. But I'd miss work more if I couldn't do it."

We did not talk about the scene that had led Bianca to abandon science: a moment, in Bianca's third year of graduate school, when we had fought bitterly over the interpretation of some data for a paper we were writing together. It was not the argument that had sundered us but Rose's refusal to join Bianca in a certain ritual during which we might have asked our dead mother for advice. Rose had firmly turned her back on this.

A dog came bounding down the creek, flashed white before us, and then disappeared. Of course this wasn't our father's dog; that dog lived in another place and wouldn't be important to us for years. But this dog, even then, made Rose think of our father. We had not had a dog when we were young, because our father had claimed to be allergic. Recently his allergies had disappeared, and from phone calls Rose had learned that he'd acquired first one dog and then another. First dogs and soon a wife. Both of us were troubled by this possibility. Bianca, although Rose didn't know it then, had in mind a consultation with Suky, which might have told us how to feel about our father's decision.

"Conformation and catalysis," she said, waving a muddy arm over her head. "Specificity and inhibition, protein architecture and gel chromatography. It makes me tired. Where's the excitement? Where's the fun?"

"The job part isn't so fun anymore," Rose admitted, thinking how biochemistry had seemed like magic when she and Bianca were young. The white dog reappeared and floated over the field to them. "I can't explain it," Rose said to Bianca. She held out her hand to the dog but the dog ran off again. "The experimenting part, the real part—it's still fun for me."

Bianca said, "I'll show you something fun," and pushed herself up from the muddy bank.

Back into our wet clothes, back across the dark lawn, back through the narrow window and into Rose's laboratory. Rose's lab, not Bianca's; Rose's name was on the door and on all the papers and awards. Both of us knew this to be unfair; the name was only half a name.

Bianca rummaged in the pack and found some chocolates, which she and Rose shared. Then she led Rose into the lab and swiftly arranged tubing and glassware into an elaborate array. She spread a white cloth over the bench and set down a handful of mushrooms.

"Where did you get those?" Rose asked.

"Out there," Bianca said, pointing towards the creek. "From the trees."

Rose could not remember gathering any mushrooms, nor any time when Bianca might have slipped away and gathered them herself. She sat on the floor with her back against the spectrophotometer and watched, half in a dream, as Bianca took over the lab.

What was Bianca saying? A long stream of words, only some of which made sense. "I'm losing you," Bianca said. And then something about how she believed she could see our futures and that they looked like this: Rose would grow drier, thinner, sharper, more famous; Rose would win prizes and buy a small house of her own, in which every room would be cool and clean. Bianca would drift from state to state: Wyoming, Idaho, Maine, Hawaii; panic, detachment, elation. Most of what she said that night would not come true, but she believed it and feared it. In one important way her fear was justified.

As Bianca spoke she minced the mushrooms very fine, ground them in a mortar and soaked them in water and then in ethanol. She squeezed and extracted, strained and heated, stirred and cooled. Then she set up a fractionating column and let the vapor from the distilling flask rise gently through the wisps of glass wool. Fluid dripped into the receiving flasks, a drop or two at a time. One fraction, quite aromatic, was as clear and bright as rubies.

Fire, water, earth, and air, she mumbled while Rose listened.

Cinnabar, hartshorn, verdigris, tartar. Cinnabar, she reminded Rose, was once called dragon's blood and was thought to be the blood of a serpent crushed to death by a dying elephant. She pipetted a sample of ruby fluid and released it on her tongue: bitter, she said. So bitter. Musky, alkaline, faintly salt. "Outlaw pharmaceuticals," she said. "Every biochemist's province."

Rose closed her eyes; when she opened them again she saw bundles of herbs and retorts. The athanor, the furnace of transmutation, was shaped like a giant egg. Suky said, *Would you girls like to go for a sail?* and Bianca said to Rose, "Did you hear that?" It was not possible that her sister could deny it.

"Mom?" Rose said. Suddenly our mother seemed to be speaking inside her head.

Bianca nodded, relieved. When school was out and the weather was good, she and Rose had sometimes sailed Suky's small green Comet and tried to make sense of the sheets and lines. The wind, bouncing off the hills, had come from all directions at once and made the sailing difficult.

A bubble rose slowly in one of the flasks and broke with a sigh. A few minutes later we heard our great-aunt Agnes say, *Dear, could you rub my back? I have this pain in my side.* Rose shifted on the floor and moved her hand along her ribs. "That was strange," she said.

"I don't know," Bianca said, almost absentmindedly. "I hear Aunt Agnes all the time. I think this is almost done."

Bianca removed her clothes for the second time that night and sat cross-legged and naked on the floor, not far from sleepy Rose. She tore a tiny strip from a piece of filter paper and held it, hardly more than a hair, to the corner of Rose's eye. Rose tried not to blink. A bit of moisture crept up the paper and turned it dark. Bianca dropped the paper into the flask and then added a bead of her own saliva.

She was talking, still. Rose tried to concentrate on her words. In Hilo, Bianca said, she had swum the harbor in the dead of night, secretly boarding the boat where she lived alone and illegally. In Alaska she had had visions in a tent by a lake so wild she saw no one for weeks at a stretch.

"All of it's slipping away," she said. "Do you know what I mean?" Rose nodded, although most days Bianca's life seemed utterly foreign to her. "All the people I meet now, they're like radios that only get two or three stations while the news from the rest of the universe slips by. No one's listening. I can't stand it."

"That's not what I'm like," Rose said. "That's only part of me."

But Bianca shook her head. Rose would see this evening as an aberration, she declared; come morning, she'd be ashamed of herself. The world was spinning in such a way that soon everything that had once seemed important would be declared an error or a dream. All Bianca wanted to do was to keep her sister in touch with a part of the world she persistently denied.

The rest of that night is mostly lost to us now, but we remember a handful of things. Sometime before dawn we either did or didn't call our father, waking him to beg him not to sell the winery. But why would we have done this, if we did it? Rose would not have wanted to echo the phone call Bianca claimed to have made the night before, and even if she'd forgotten that, the winery was not a place we ever visited. Nonetheless, Rose believes that Bianca woke her after a brief, shared nap; that we made this call; that during it our father invited us to his wedding and we both said we were busy that day. Childish, childish. Rose is still ashamed of this, but Bianca claims that Rose dreamed the entire conversation. It's true, though, that neither of us took part in the festivities.

The next morning, Rose woke after eight with a stiff neck and a numb foot. Bianca was nowhere to be seen. Rose, hungover and tired, believed that Bianca might be seducing a janitor in a closet or making a fool of herself in the cafeteria or driving back to Vermont by way of Labrador. She always had a tendency to believe the worst of Bianca. But Bianca's pack was still on the floor and the office was strewn with bottles and damp shoes and half-smoked joints.

Quickly, guiltily, Rose disposed of the evidence. She flung open the window, praying that the sweet, heavy odor might dissipate before anyone dropped by. In the mud below the window she saw deep footprints, which led away from the building and into the grass and looked exactly as if two people had leapt from the lab and escaped.

When Bianca walked through the door, her hair brushed and her clothes changed and her hands full of paper bags from the fake-French bakery down the street, Rose couldn't keep from leaping on her. "How did you get out?" she said. "How'd you get back in? Did you sleep?"

"Explain the obscure by the more obscure," Bianca said. "The unknown by the more unknown."

There was a time when Rose would have understood exactly what she meant. Suky had taught us a secret technique, which had to do with water and the faces of the dead and could not be talked about. Nor could it be explored alone—we'd both tried it separately and failed. When we were young, though, and together, we had made it work.

Bianca set her offerings on the desk: steaming coffee and rolls and butter and jam. From another bag she pulled two new wineglasses, still with price tags on their feet, and a bottle of organic cranberry-raspberry juice. She poured juice into the glasses, disappeared into the lab with them, and returned.

"Cheers," Bianca said, holding one out to Rose and raising the other to her lips.

Ruby fluid: magic potion; we knew better than that. Rose has never acknowledged that she knew what Bianca added to the glasses. But she did know, as she also knew what it was meant to do: fuse our vision back together, the way Suky had fused our names. But we didn't call on Suky that day, because Rose continued to resist the idea as if it, not the potion, were poison. And so nothing changed between us, although we were reminded of how much we loved each other.

We stop here, usually, or actually a little before this: If one of us is telling tales to a stranger we stop with the raised glasses and the toast. As we do with our history, we try to maintain a light tone when we talk about that night. We try to make it sound like a tale of youthful excess, pharmaceutical madness; a last gasp from the seventies. The sort of escapade someone older and wiser can look back on with a smile.

Time passed. Lots of things happened to both of us, some important and some not. We met now and then, when Bianca passed through Boston on the tail end of some journey, but after that night we met casually, mimicking the interaction of any pair of sisters. Mostly we talked on the phone.

Our lives continued like this for almost a decade, until our father got sick and we went to Hammondsport to see him. During the time of his dying we saw each other intensely, intently, but where it counted we were as separate as stones and it seemed clearer than ever that the ruby fluid had failed us.

A year after that, though, we returned to Hammondsport for the first anniversary of our father's death. What happened then is not a part of our history. We swore we'd never tell anyone and still can hardly mention it between us.

[3. *Speaking with Suky*]

You said, "Look down into the water. A hole will open if
you spin the surface with your hand or a stick, and you will
see what you need at the base of the hole." We're sure that's
what you said. Under clear skies, on a hot day, in a green-
painted Comet with natural trim, during a summer when we
were still children and you were still around. We spun the
water beside the boat with an extra paddle, twirling and twirling until a vortex formed. Looking down, into the hole that
seemed to lead to the bottom of the lake, we saw grandpa
Leo's face.

And today?

Today we spun the water and found you.

Why did you wait so long?

It's only been a year. It took us that long to get ready. We were
drowning in memories of the last time we'd seen our father.

    When we met here that time, we slept downstairs on a large
piece of furniture not quite either sofa or bed. The upholstery
was smooth to the touch, except for the spots where the dogs
had shredded it. There were arms and backs and edges, which
made it like a sofa; then big stretches of ambiguous flatness the
size of a bed. We were sleeping there, in the basement, because
there was no other place for us. Your house—his house, our
house—was gone, and the acres of vines and the stone buildings,
the casks, the vats, and all the equipment, all the wine. We had
never seen the place our father had rented after his wife had
made him sell our house. Both of us lived elsewhere, with other
men.

We had never shared a bed with each other, and except for a night in a lab in Boston we had not slept in the same room since we were little girls. We felt uncomfortable lying next to each other and so we moved until we were lying head to foot and foot to head, toes near each other's ears. In that position, with the glass doors letting in moonlight and shadows and the sound of the water at the edge of the lawn, we rested and talked. The painting of you had been moved from the living room in the old house to the hallway between the half-finished basement room and the extra toilet.

Who has it now?

The painting?

The painting.

We don't know. It's gone. We had rushed to Hammondsport after his phone calls to find him alone except for the two huge dogs in a filthy and uncomfortable house. The dogs followed our father everywhere. They slept on his bed, laid their heads on his knees, looked at him imploringly. He was weak and could no longer walk them, but although they were frantic with restlessness they would not leave his side. They growled and lunged at us at first, and even after several days they leapt from our father's bed and barked each time we moved from room to room or even from chair to chair. At night we willed ourselves not to stir and wake them. In the mornings we watched as our father groomed them with the last of his energy. One had white hair, very long, which flew out with the strokes of the comb. The other had hair that was shorter and brown. Our father's arms and legs had grown very thin but his middle bulged from the tumors in his liver.

And what has happened to these dogs?

The dogs are gone; it's a long story and you don't want to know. On the first night we were home we fed them biscuits and then rubbed a chicken with oil and garlic and herbs and roasted it in a hot oven for an hour and forty-five minutes. Our father's hands began to shake as the smell filled the house. "I have no appetite," he said, but this turned out not to be true. He had no energy with which to cook or shop, and the foods he managed to make for himself were in no way appetizing. His wife was there but not there, present but absent; she had taken a job and an apartment in Syracuse and came home only on weekends then. As there was no one around to cook for him, he had convinced himself that the feeling he felt wasn't hunger. But when we sat him down and placed the food in front of him water came into his eyes and his mouth. His head was hardly higher than the surface of the table. When he lifted his fork he was so anxious to greet the food that his neck craned and his mouth thrust forward. He ate very fast, smearing his mouth with fat and dropping fragments onto his shirt. His irises were pale blue against a field of yellow shot with red. His hands were heavily wrinkled, dry-skinned, swollen, and discolored. Earlier, one of the dogs had rested a paw on his forearm and left behind a trail of bruises.

What did he look like?

Didn't we just say? Dry, pale, shrunken, shriveled. Not the way you remember him. The top of his head came below the chin of one of us, below the nose of the other. His hair was thin and gray and the skin on his forehead was mottled. When he walked his legs were unsteady and splayed. His hands shook until he'd had the first two or three drinks of the day. After they steadied, he cut apples in half and tossed them at the dogs, who adored them. The dogs also liked grapes, he said, but in July, when we visited him, the grapes here were only wishes.

Were you frightened?

Not frightened, exactly. Years ago, when Aunt Agnes was sick, we had taken turns nursing her. Our father wasn't around very much; the winery was flourishing and he was busy becoming rich. During the time when we were alone with her, we had learned about the relentless disintegration of the body. Perhaps you're familiar with this—the drying and thinning of the skin, until the slightest blow or scratch leaves blood behind. The rubbing together of fleshless bones, the sores and bruises and rashes and welts, the loosening teeth and the bleeding gums, the clumps of hair coming out in the comb, and the alternating waves of hunger and nausea. All of this was familiar to us; none of what was happening to our father was unexpected. Although we were, of course, surprised that he was still drinking so heavily. And the first night we stayed in the house, before we became used to it, we were surprised to find the two huge dogs in bed with him, their heads on pillows and their paws thrown across his body.

Tell me what you left behind.

Men. Several men, for one of us; for the other a lover with jet-black hair and narrow feet, who had ended a long dry spell in Boston like a flow of cool water. The skin over this man's ankles was pale and so thin that the blue veins were visible, and this seemed lovely until the day we had to bathe our father's feet and saw the same veins over the ankle, beneath the dry and fragile skin. Our father wore baggy boxer shorts that gaped at the fly when he bent to pat one of the dogs or pick up a bone or a brush. He had always done this, but we had not lived with him for many years and had forgotten how disturbing it was. The men with whom we share our beds wear narrow pants that cling closely to their bodies.

And what did she leave?

The wife?

Her.

She took off so fast she left half of what she owned behind. We weren't sorry to see her go. There had been several women since your departure and she was the worst of them. We disliked her voice, which was affected and loud. She left behind a blue hassock embroidered with swans, several sets of expensive sheets, a cabinet full of cosmetics, and a refrigerator full of food. She had cooked for our father; all of them did.

She'd begged him to sell the house and the winery, so they could be free to travel. It was time, she said. After half a century of being tied to that piece of land. We think she also hoped, in the back of her mind, that by freeing himself of the property he might free himself from you. For a while he kept your portrait over their bed in the rented house, although she objected. After their first trip, to the Grand Canyon, she came home and moved your portrait to the basement. The second trip, the one to Bordeaux, went badly as well. What could she have been thinking? That the chateaux and the acres of vines on the stony soil would not remind our father of what he'd given up for her? It was then, we think, around this time, that she realized the house and the land and the vines had been a large part of what had attracted her to him. She was forty-five and on good days looked younger. She bought some clothes and went off to Syracuse and found a job, from which she returned to the rented house on weekends.

Halfway present, halfway absent. In her absence, our father seemed unable to feed himself.

Where did the money go?

We don't know. Grapes were down, and so was the price of land, and he didn't get what he should have for the property. Then there were trips, and bad investments; probably she took the rest. Who can say? When we arrived, we cleaned out the refrigerator. We found a red enamel pot containing the remnants of a barley mushroom casserole, part of a pork roast gone slimy and slick, four half-empty cartons of milk, liquefied broccoli, rotten lettuce, three-quarters of a red pepper, a container of instant pancake batter, old bacon, stale bread, moldy cheese, dead fruit. On the porch were large boxes full of old vegetables, which our father said had come from the produce stall in the village and would otherwise have been thrown out. Much of the money had disappeared in the year before he got sick, but he refused to talk about this with us. On the porch, where we sat for an hour in the warm sun while our father was taking a nap, we looked at the lake and the fallen trees and the expensive lawn furniture now rusted and worn, and one of us said to the other, "This is a different way of being poor."

We had a problem, we knew: the problem of our father, who could not feed himself, and the dogs, who could not feed either themselves or our father and also could not walk themselves. We had lives of our own, elsewhere, and soon we would have to go. In those other lives, in our real lives, we sank down at night into beds with men who were precious to us, who had strong thighs, strong arms. But during this visit we slept with no men. We slept with each other, on the bed that was not a bed, and when we rose we fixed our father breakfast and then went to the market and bought more food and then came home and fixed him lunch and fed the dogs as well. We walked the dogs in the marsh south of the lake. The largest dog, the white one, every day pushed his way through the weeds to the rim of black mud and sank down to his shoulders. When we came home, we wiped him off with a cloth. Always, before we were done, he tore himself from us and bounded into our father's room and leapt up on the bed and curled himself next to his master.

You were jealous of the dogs?

Our father said, "They are all I have. They are the only ones who treat me affectionately." He was talking about the dogs, not us. We were cleaning and cooking and shopping and wondering what to do; we couldn't agree about anything. We argued about what we should do for him and how we should do it. One of us would want to peel fruit for him at the same moment the other decided he needed meat, a roast. Sun or shade, hammock or bed, hot tea or cold juice—always chaos, always conflict. We quarreled one night, when he said he'd like ice cream: which of us should be the one to fetch it and which the one to stay behind with him, for a private moment when we might be redeemed. We wore him out, and for all that, neither could feel like his favorite.

Our father sat on one of those wrought-iron chairs that had served as decoration in the summer-room of our old house, but which here had become the sole, inadequate kitchen furniture. A moth flew against the window over the sink and then fell into the standing water and drowned. Our father had always been a small man, but we had never noticed it before. After he ate he felt tired and went back to bed. The white dog lay like a person beside him.

His head on the pillow?

On two pillows, turned to face our father. We went to the store. We bought spinach fettucine and fish and grated hard cheese and butter and muffins and coffee and cream, and when we came home we washed the kitchen floor, which was suddenly, mysteriously, covered with small ants. Against the baseboards were drifts of dog hair. A doctor called and then another; appointments were made. In our houses, we told each other, the counters shone in the sun. At night we undressed in darkness and avoided looking at each other's bodies. You know how differently we are built—one tall and rounded, one short and spare—but in the light of our father's disintegration we seemed identical in our health and smoothness. Our father told us a story about your mother, our grandmother, and how she and Agnes and your other aunts were raised by their mother after their father died and left them the vineyard and no men to cultivate it. In the Ukraine, he said, at about the same time, his father, our grandfather Leo, was struggling to establish vineyards for Stalin. He said our family had been drawn together by forces that felt like fate. Later he mentioned that he had borrowed heavily against his life insurance and had not been able to pay the money back.

Do you wish you'd stayed?

Yes. No. Yes. How could we stay? We had our own lives. But it's true that despite that we thought of staying, talked of staying. On our knees on the kitchen floor, scrubbing the accumulated dirt and dog saliva and ant tracks and juice from a surface that for months had seen only the briefest sweeping, we looked at each other and said, "Anyone could walk into this house and tell there are no women here." And this was a strange thought, for both of us—that much of what had gone wrong had to do with the absence, not only of women, but of women willing to do those things that have always been women's work. Our father's wife was a busy woman, successful in her own way and seldom home. We were busy ourselves, and gone. And so there was no cleanliness, no order, no smells of good food cooked with care and eaten with pleasure, no signs of the raising of children, no curtains ironed, no flowers tended and cut for the tables. No one to relish a clean yellow counter shining in the sun. Our father could not do one thing to make life pleasant or comfortable for himself.

Didn't you do what you could?

We abandoned him.

Didn't he welcome your help?

We abandoned him.

Wasn't he glad to have you there?

He died one August weekend, when we were absent and his wife was present. She was furious with us for coming to visit and then furious that we couldn't stay. She'd moved back to the house for his last weeks, and when we returned for the funeral she opened the door as if to let us in and then started to say something and flushed and slammed the door on us. She couldn't keep us from the church, but she wouldn't let us into the house and so we stayed outside. We drove around the lake, up into the vineyards on the hill near where our old place had been, and when it grew dark we simply stopped the car where we were. There was no one around and the sky was very clear. We took two blankets out of the trunk and spread them on the ground and lay there, talking and holding hands. We slept, we think, toward morning, because we were not awake when the dew fell, and we woke covered with cool water. The sun crept over the hills across the lake, lighting the mist that filled the valley. We thought we sensed you there, but we weren't sure.

After the funeral, we tried once more to come into the house.

We meant to take the dogs, about whom our father had been very worried, and the portrait of you, and a few other small mementos. But again his wife would not let us in. She had already found homes for the dogs, she said. She had already let go of the lease on the house, already arranged for the sale of the few pieces of furniture that were left and the removal of the things she wanted to her new apartment in Syracuse. She had a new life, she said, and she wanted to start it, and that new life didn't include us. So we left.

But last week, one of us said over the phone to the other, "We should go back, it's been a year." So we made arrangements and met each other here, and although there were strangers living in our old house, as there have been for many years, and although of course the house where our father spent his last days had been cleaned and rented to someone else, and although the dogs were gone and everything we'd ever known, we thought we had done the right thing.

We rented this boat at the dock near the post office, and as soon as we'd sailed into deep water, both of us realized you were near. One of us took the tiller and the other handled the sheets.

You were always good sailors.

This is a lake on which it is impossible to get lost. But so much else is gone, all the remnants and relics of our family. The house, of course: but also your mother's rugs and sofas and chairs, and your lamps and bureaus and paintings and knickknacks, and Aunt Agnes's cups, and our old books—everything, really. And when our father's widow disappeared from our lives and disposed of the dogs, it was as if our family had never existed. It was as if we'd imagined our history. All that is left is the shared set of memories we have of our last days with our father in that house that wasn't his house.

He asked after you, during our last day with him. He thought we were back in our old house, and he wanted to look at your picture in the living room. We sneaked downstairs and took the picture from the hall and dusted it and brought it upstairs to him. We told him we'd brought it to him so he wouldn't have to move. We did not have the heart to tell him that there was no living room, filled with books and our family's things, with your picture hanging from its cord.

Was he glad to see me?

Of course he was. Have you seen him since then?

No.

[4. *The White Dog*]

Were we really speaking with Suky? Was Suky really speaking with us? Bianca says yes, absolutely. I say yes, sort of, maybe.

Nothing happened after our sail on the lake—we didn't see our father's ghost or feel his presence or even reach any sort of peace or understanding. We were comforted, of course; Suky's voice fell on us like balm. But I believed that what we'd done was wrong, and even as Bianca couldn't help showing her triumph at having lured me into speaking with Suky, I couldn't help resenting it.

That night we shared a room with two beds in a new motel where no one knew us. We slept uneasily and guiltily, aware that we had left things undone and that there were people in the village whom we should have visited. The next morning I dropped Bianca at the airport and then I drove home.

Now I can't talk to Bianca about what went on then, or

earlier, because Bianca is gone. The stories we've made of our past have come to nothing. A month after we met in Hammondsport for the anniversary of our father's death, she fell in love with a landscape painter our father's age and moved with him to a house on a cliff in Costa Rica, where she has no phone.

I live back here in Hammondsport now. Around the time that Bianca took off I quit my job and decided to move; Boston, where I'd lived for more than a decade, suddenly seemed like a place where I'd set no roots. When my colleagues pressed for reasons for my decision, I told them I'd inherited something from my father that required my attention. Quite quickly I learned that any mention of his death would stop the conversation. No one will pass the screen thrown up by that word, I've learned. Behind it I could and did—still do—conceal my confusion.

Only Bianca felt entitled to pry. When I told her my plans, she told me I was making a big mistake; this, after all the complaining she'd done about my job. The last time we spoke, I was in my lab in Boston and she was at the Houston airport. She said, "You're crazy. There's nothing in that place for you."

"It's what I want to do," I said. "Why is it any stranger than moving to Costa Rica with someone you hardly know?"

"Because it *is*," she said. "Those people—you'll always be who you used to be, for them. Is that what you want?"

This, like the predictions she'd made in Boston, would turn out not to be true. But even then, not knowing that, I said, "Would that be so bad? Is that worse than being with people who don't know anything about us?"

"Oscar knows me," Bianca said. "He knows what I want him to know." Meaning, I think, that he understood her in terms of the stories we'd manufactured together.

For a minute we were silent, listening to the low roar of airport noise and the hum and whisper of the instruments in my lab. "Come with me," Bianca said finally. "I'm all for your getting out of that lab, but it's stupid to go back home. Oscar wouldn't mind if you came to stay with us."

"Maybe next year," I said. "Maybe I'll come for a visit, once I figure out what I'm doing."

"Maybe I won't be here by then," Bianca said.

We promised to write and hung up, disappointed with each other. Honestly I think we have felt this way since our last conversation with Suky. Hallucination, perhaps; but if it was we shared it. Since then, though, we have found it almost impossible to share anything.

I moved back here after that phone call and rented an apartment that I only kept for a little while. Then I did two things even more distasteful to Bianca: I got a job teaching chemistry to sophomores and juniors at the school Bianca and I had attended, and I moved into a house in the village, with Harry Mazzullo and the white dog.

Harry is, was, my father's lawyer. The white dog is not the one Bianca and I saw by the creek in Boston but one of the dogs my father cherished. The other dog is dead; when I tracked down the family who'd taken him from the pound, they told me he'd barked uncontrollably until they'd had to put him down. But one day, shortly after I moved back, I found the white dog by accident as I was walking through the village. He was sprawled on a broad porch, looking completely at home, and when I knocked on the door of that house Harry opened it and greeted me as if he knew me.

"Rose?" he said. "Rose Marburg?"

When I nodded he said we'd been introduced at my father's funeral. I didn't remember this; I remembered almost nothing of that day. Bianca and I had been in the back of the church, as if we were guests and not daughters, while our father's widow had accepted condolences up front. At the cemetery we had stood at a distance, talking to no one, and then we had left. When could Harry have met me?

But he swore he had. And when I said, "How did you get that dog?" he said he'd had it for more than a year. "Your father's wife," he said. "After the funeral she was so . . . confused. She was making a lot of decisions very fast, and I was worried about the dogs—your father was very attached to them."

"I know," I said.

"They'd gone to the pound. I'm sure she didn't mean to do that, but she was under a lot of pressure. By the time I got there the brown one was gone, but no one wanted this one and so I took him home myself."

All this time, it turned out, the dog had been safely with Harry. Harry took me out to dinner that night, and a week later he took me sailing. Cool water, a gentle breeze, a bottle of wine. This is where the shameful part comes in. Already I had sketched our history for him, and I'd told him the story of the wild night Bianca and I once shared in Boston. But while we were out on the lake, while I was relaxed, a little drunk, almost hypnotized by the water, I told him about the vision Bianca and I had had, which in different ways had caused both of us to move.

Harry sat quite still and listened, only his hands moving on the tiller and the sheets. I told the story just as I remembered it, a dialogue in which I played both parts. My mother's questions I rendered high and thin and soft; our responses lower, slower, doubled. Two sisters speaking simultaneously with one voice.

Harry didn't shrug or make a face or look at me as if I were crazy. How calm he was, how cool. Perhaps his years as a lawyer have exposed him to stranger things. He said, "That's interesting. I knew your mother a little, when I was a boy. She was quite a woman. So were your great-aunts, for that matter. That was one of your great-aunts, wasn't it? The woman who moved in with you?"

"It was," I said. "She took care of us." We were not, apparently, going to pass judgment on either the scene with Suky or the way I'd rendered it.

"I remember," Harry said. "And when she was sick, I remember that you and Bianca took care of her."

A few months later, he asked me to move into his house and I accepted. I live with Harry because of the way he absorbed my story; because he was good to my father near the end; because he tells me tales about my father's last days that I would otherwise have no way of knowing. Tit for tat, my secrets for his. It's not much of an excuse to say that perhaps I sensed this was what I'd gain.

Five weeks passed between the time Bianca and I last saw our father and the time we returned for his funeral. During those weeks I was back in Boston and Bianca was in Dixon, New Mexico, where she was working on a garlic farm. During those weeks, Harry said, some strange things happened.

Bianca and I had envisioned our father the way we'd last seen him—how could we imagine anything else? Guilty, horrified, we'd imagined him alone. On a Friday night, we had left that house together: both afraid, it seems to me now, that the one left behind would never find the strength to leave again. Or maybe both afraid that the one left behind might somehow gain the upper hand. And then there was also, beyond these fears, the problem of our father's wife.

Leaving, we had told ourselves that she was due home within the hour. By then we'd realized that our father wanted her, not us; our fussing and cleaning and cooking only tired him, and none of it led to what he wanted. He welcomed the filth, we had come to see, and the signs of his abandonment. He believed these signs would sway his wife and bind her to his side for his remaining days. Each night of our visit she'd called, and the change in his voice when he talked to her had been unbearable to us. By the time we left, we almost understood that all our efforts had only postponed the moment when he might have his wish. The clean house we left behind meant his wife could feel free to leave again come Monday.

But we'd buried that thought beneath our need to feel that we'd done some good; in our departure, finally, we acted with one mind. Only back in our own worlds could we see the ambiguous nature of what we'd given him. *Alone*, we said to each other, when we learned she'd disappeared again. *How could we leave him alone?* But while it's true that his wife left after that weekend visit and didn't return for good until three weeks later, the fact is that even then he wasn't alone. There was a nurse with him for several hours each day: I spoke with her frequently on the phone and always felt relieved after hearing her voice. She was strong and practical and had a nice laugh. She bathed our father, and washed his sheets and changed his bed and cooked some meals.

Bianca and I thought his wife had hired the nurse, meaning by this to prove that she was capable and we weren't needed. But Harry told me a group of our father's old friends had been responsible.

"What friends?" I said. We had not known that our father was that close to anyone. He golfed with a group of men: other winemakers from the valley, a doctor, a dentist, a broker. They had never seemed like more than drinking buddies.

But Harry said they'd rallied when it became clear that my father was dying. They hired the nurse, he said. They rented a gadget that would buzz in their homes if my father pressed a button for help. And they paid, Harry said, for my father's funeral. Harry claims that Peter Couperin—the same Couperin who'd figured in our mother's stories as our father's greatest rival, but who'd been hardly more than a name for us—organized the other men, and that together they did what they could to ease our father's last days.

Perhaps he was more than a name. I remembered Couperin, vaguely, as a red-faced man who spoke too loudly. When Bianca and I were young he used to visit our house sometimes; always, after he left, our father would make fun of him and his pink Catawba. They'd had an argument when Bianca and I were in college, over some land that Couperin had sold to a real-estate developer. I wasn't aware that they'd seen each other much after that.

But Harry said that the last few years had brought hard times to Couperin as well. He had developed a bone disease that was eating its way through his spine; he was in a wheelchair and his head was held upright by a brace that stretched from his shoulders alongside his ears to end in a metal halo pinned to his skull. One son had died; a daughter was in a drug-rehabilitation clinic. Harry, who was Couperin's lawyer as well as my father's, says that when he brought the news of my father's illness to Couperin, Couperin had first laughed and then cried and finally said, "Look at us two old buzzards—after all these years, the both of us sick and alone."

Harry, at Couperin's request, brought my father to Couperin's house for a reconciliation. It was something, he said: those two old, beaten men, their families lost or scattered, one in a wheelchair and wearing a halo and the other frail and in pain, perched on chairs in front of Couperin's fireplace and getting drunk on Couperin's oldest brandy. Harry was there, sitting in the background. He says Couperin said, "What are we saving it for?" He also says the two men talked some about their children.

When Harry told me that I didn't ask him anything; I suppose I was afraid to know. But later, after I'd slept on that story for a couple of days, I asked him if he could tell me what they'd said.

"I'm your father's lawyer," Harry said. "You know the things he told me have to stay private."

"You weren't at that conversation as a lawyer," I said. "Were you? You were there as my father's friend."

Harry admitted that this was so, but all he would do was answer me in generalities. Couperin had said something nasty about my father's daughters, who couldn't find the time to take care of him, and my father had said that we had visited just recently and that we planned to come back again soon. We were good girls, he said.

"He said that?" I asked Harry. "Did he say anything specific about either of us?" I couldn't help asking that. Harry gave me a skeptical look. Then he said, "Your father told Couperin that you had a great job and that he was very proud of you."

"And Bianca?"

"He loved to tell stories about her adventures."

"Hawaii, you mean? Alaska? The climbing stuff?"

"All that." All the things I hadn't done. Harry wouldn't tell me if my father's pleasure in Bianca's adventures outweighed his pride in my accomplishments. Instead, he told me other stories about my father's friends.

They brought food, some of them—not one of them had a wife left, all their wives had died or abandoned them, but they cooked clumsy meals and brought them to my father. They planted a chaise in the front lawn and on sunny days guided my father out there for some air. They drove him to the doctor. They talked to the nurse. They brought Scotch and wine and sat on the end of my father's bed, refreshing their drinks and telling bawdy anecdotes from their shared youth. Harry said they made my father laugh.

These stories give me such a pain. Because women had come and gone from our father's life with some frequency before his second marriage, and because he never seemed to miss any of them any more than he missed us, Bianca and I had labored under the impression that he had no emotional life. And yet this turned out to be untrue. Our father had an emotional life, although it was not one we could recognize. It was centered, while he waited for his wife, on his dogs and on this group of men.

Now, when I see these men in the village, they are quite cool to me. They judge me harshly, and rightly so, for not sharing my father's last days. But everyone else treats me as if nothing has happened. In the high school there are still a few teachers left from the time when Bianca and I were students: Mrs. Komnetz, who teaches English; Mr. Baker, who teaches biology. And of course there are plenty of other people in town who remember me and Bianca as girls. When I first moved back here, and even more when I first got my job, I wondered all the time what these people thought of me. They remember me and Bianca, but they remember us as if we were different people.

"You were such bright girls," Mrs. Komnetz says. "So spunky, so talented. We all knew you had a future. What is your sister doing these days?"

"Painting," I say, although Bianca is not painting but only living with a painter. But everyone accepts this, as if we are only doing what they expected. They're a little surprised to find me back here, but happily surprised, pleased. They have no knowledge of anything Bianca and I did after we left this town, and what they remember of our girlhood here is sanitized and wrapped in a shroud of nostalgia. No one mentions the times we were suspended from school, the endless notes sent home to our father, the policemen showing up at our house at night after certain acts of vandalism that pointed unfailingly to us. In their revision of our history, we are local girls who made good. They act as if they're grateful that I came back, and they are so tactful they never ask if I mind the cut in salary or if I miss being called "Professor" or "Doctor" instead of plain "Ms. Marburg."

Of our visit to our father before his death, they remember that we came and cooked and cleaned; they forget that we left. Of the funeral, what they seem to remember is two young women struck speechless by loss. No one knows that we slept on that hill; no one wonders, or not out loud, why we were never seen with our father's widow. If they remember anything strange about that time, they tend to blame it on her. She was not a local woman.

Instead of talking about those things, they tell me stories about our grandfather and our great-aunts as if they were still alive. "You look like Agnes," they say to me, or "Did you know you have Leo's nose?" They've forgiven or forgotten everything, especially now that I live with Harry and his white dog.

This dog and I share a secret: our pasts are lost to everyone but us. I remember who I was as a girl, but everyone seems to have entered into a conspiracy to deny that that girl was me, as they deny their knowledge of what I did while my father was dying. As for the dog—who knows what the dog remembers? People treat him like Harry's dog: ancient, arthritic, harmless. I think he remembers each of my father's last days.

Since my arrival, this dog has attached himself to me. He sleeps on the floor beside me, within reach of my dangling arm. When I'm absent he pulls my dirty clothes from the hamper and gathers them patiently into a heap, on which he turns and turns and turns before flopping down. At night, when I sit grading my students' exams in the room that Harry has turned into my study, the dog lies groaning and scratching the floor as he dreams his way through our past. If I wake him up too suddenly, he jerks stiffly to his feet and then barks at the portrait of Suky, which turned up at a flea market in Ithaca after I thought it was lost forever. If dogs could talk, I believe this one could list each moment where I failed.

· · ·

What am I to make of all this? I've tried to describe much of it in my letters to Bianca—always leaving out the most important part, which is that I've shared our deepest secret with Harry. Bianca suspects this, I believe; she didn't reply the first two times I wrote. But a month ago, after I wrote describing Couperin's involvement in our father's last days, and the recovery of our father's dog, she wrote back to me.

"Why are you telling me these things?" she wrote. "I bet you don't remember Couperin any better than I do. But I'm glad you have Dad's dog and that he's all right. Are you happy with this Harry? Please tell me you're not with him because of that dog."

Harry is kind. Harry helps me understand. But I'm not in love with him, and Bianca knows it. She writes that yes, she finds it odd that our father's widow has vanished from our lives without a trace. And yes, she thinks of our old life sometimes, and of our father and his last days, and of the talk we did or didn't have with Suky. But she doesn't think about these things often, she says. Not very often at all. In her new life, in her new country, she never speaks about our past.

Do I believe her? Sometimes; sometimes not. Often I wonder if she hasn't told Oscar all I've told Harry and more; if she doesn't lie tangled in sheets at night, talking the darkness away. But all the rest of Bianca's letter was about her daily life. Oscar paints her nude, she writes. In their house on a cliff in Costa Rica, both their old lives left behind, he poses her on white sheets strewn with flowers and then works furiously on a gigantic canvas. It's steamy, she says. Impossibly sexy. The things he says, the things he does; she has never had such wonderful sex, she has never been so in love. Around them are orchids, iguanas, bananas and parrots, howler monkeys and coatimundis and frogs the size of salad plates.

At night, she writes, they make love outside, in the jungle, in the rain. *The here and now, the moment,* she says. This, when for years she chided me for leaving our history behind. I can hear her voice in my study, as clear as an equation. *Why dwell on the past?*

Ship Fever

January 27, 1847
Skibbereen, County Cork

Dear Lauchlin:
  Does this find you well, my friend? For myself I am well
enough in body but sick at heart: small excuse for not
writing sooner. All has been confusion since our arrival. I
have been traveling from county to county with two Quaker
relief workers, an American philanthropist, a journalist from
London, and various local authorities. Matters are worse
than I expected.
  At Arranmore, in County Donegal, the streets swarm
with famished men begging for work on the roads. At
Louisburgh, in County Mayo, the local newspaper reports
between ten and twenty deaths a day, and I myself saw
bodies lying unburied, for want of anyone to dig a grave. In
a hut that had been quiet for many days we found on the
mud floor four frozen corpses, partly eaten by rats. That
same day, a dispensary doctor told me he'd seen a woman
drag from her hovel the corpse of her naked daughter. She
tried to cover the body with stones.
  Does this give you some idea? Here at Skibbereen, I
saw in one cabin a man, his wife, and two of their children,
all emaciated beyond belief, sitting around a tiny fire and

mourning a young child dead in her cradle, for whom they had no way to provide a coffin. In some places, men have constructed coffins with movable bottoms, in which the dead may be conveyed to the churchyard and there unceremoniously dropped. Those lucky enough to be buried at all have no mourners, often no more than a handful of straw for a shroud.

I see no hope of this situation changing; the British Government continue their benighted policies and say they've spent vast sums. Yet we hear reports that the people, having eaten their seed potatoes and cattle and horses, are reduced to eating frogs and foxes and the leaves and bark of trees. Dysentery rages among those who eat the unground Indian corn passed out so grudgingly by the Relief Commission. To the complaints of Parliament, that the land lies unworked and that the lazy Irish refuse to fend for themselves, I would only ask that they visit here and see with their own eyes the terrible apathy brought on by starvation and despair. Or let them hear the horrifying silence lying over this land. We travel for miles and never hear a pig's squeal, a dog's bark, a chicken's cluck, or a crow's caw.

As you might imagine, I've been writing articles, the first of which I am sending to the Mercury *by this same post. The American with whom I travel has also undertaken to arrange publication of some of these in the* New York *papers. Anything to counteract the London papers, which are enough to drive one mad. Yesterday I read a column stating that the cause of the "potato murrain" is a sort of dropsy. Others contend that the rot arises from static electricity generated in the air by the puffs of smoke from locomotives, or from miasmas rising from blind volcanoes in the interior of the earth. Always the potatoes; not a word about the ships that sail daily for England with Ireland's produce, which might have been used to feed the starving.*

I wonder what you would make of all this? You are busy, I imagine. But I know you are keeping an eye on Susannah, as promised. Do try to visit when you can, and keep her in good spirits; I expect she is lonely but I cannot

be both here and there and I know you will help her
understand this. With luck I will leave here in April, but it
is possible I may go to London and do what I can to
influence matters there. There will be a vast emigration this
spring, for which you should prepare yourselves. Forgive my
haste and this scattered letter.

AA

Dr. Lauchlin Grant paused, after reading most of this letter out loud to Susannah Rowley. They were in the Rowleys' handsome house on Palace Street, in the city of Quebec, behind a door carved with a pair of As intertwined with an S. Susannah's husband, Arthur Adam Rowley, had built the house and arranged for the decoration of that door. So confident was he of his place in the world that he signed everything, even his newspaper articles, solely with those initials.

But even Arthur Adam could not control the weather, and his sitting-room, with its windows still sealed against the Quebec winter, was overheated on this unexpectedly warm day. It was April already; winter had delayed the mail even longer than usual. The letter increased Lauchlin's discomfort, and he removed his jacket as he finished reading.

He had not read the lines about watching over Susannah, because they would have infuriated her. Nor had he read the part about the corpses devoured by rats. Now, as he draped his jacket on the chair, he spoke two lines that did not exist: *Please ask Susannah to forgive me for writing so infrequently to her. She is in my mind always, but I cannot bear to subject her to all I've seen.*

Susannah made no response, but Lauchlin felt the sweet, easy mood in which she'd welcomed him disappear. Annie Taggert, the Rowleys' parlormaid, set the tea-tray down on the claw-footed table by the fireplace, and still Susannah said nothing more than, "Thank you." Only after Annie's departure did she turn to Lauchlin to ask, "Do you suppose Annie heard you reading that?"

"Annie?" Lauchlin said. "How could she?"

Susannah shrugged. "She hovers, you know. She stands outside and pretends to dust that cabinet in the hall. She's been with Arthur Adam a long time—I'm still new to her, and she doesn't entirely trust me."

"With . . . me, you mean?" His face grew so hot that he moved toward the sealed window. "Can't we get this *open*?" he said, pushing irritably at the latch. At night he dreamed of women he'd glimpsed during the day, and in his dreams their garments fell away, revealing milky skin. But his dreams were no one's business.

"With anyone, I suppose. She thinks my manners are appalling. She thinks I'll say something that will prove I'm not a lady."

That was all she meant, then. He leaned his forehead against the window, but the glass was hardly cool. Then he said, "I'm sorry about the letter—I shouldn't have read it to you."

"Why not?" she said. "How else would I know what's going on? Maybe he's on his way home already."

As she paced the room, the sun cast the folds of her blue gown into deep shadow and struck silver highlights on her breast and shoulders and back. These glimmers were her only jewels, other than her wedding and engagement rings—although not born a Quaker, she'd been raised by her Quaker aunt and uncle after her parents' deaths, and she still dressed simply. And yet, Lauchlin thought, part of her seemed to miss the glitter of her childhood. When he'd entered this sitting-room earlier, he'd found her kneeling before the tea-table, turning over the contents of her mother's jewel box. The sight of that mahogany box, with its chased silver hinges and rose velvet lining, had frozen his greeting in his mouth. When they were very young, and had lived next door to each other, Susannah's mother had sometimes let them play with the box on rainy days. The string of pearls

Susannah held, and the hatpins—one tipped with cloisonné flowers, the second with an onyx knob—were as familiar to him as his own mother's earrings and brooches.

"Do you want to put it on?" he'd asked, bending over to touch the necklace.

As he did so he'd remembered her, at age seven or eight, parading around her mother's dim dressing room while the rain streamed down the windows. Her parents had gone out and the nursemaid who was supposed to be watching them had fallen asleep. Susannah had stuck the hatpins in her pinafore and, because neither she nor Lauchlin could open the clasp, draped the necklace over one shoulder and around the heads of the pins. She'd smiled broadly and tilted her chin, imitating her mother. Later she'd been given some modest jewelry of her own: a ring with a small ruby, which Lauchlin had watched her unwrap at her tenth birthday party; a dainty gold bracelet. And he had chosen, with his mother's help, a pretty enameled hair-clasp for a Christmas present. Where had those things gone?

"I don't like to wear them," she said, dropping the strand back in the box. "But they're so pretty to look at. . . . remember these?" She held up a dangling pair of coral earrings.

"Of course I do," he said. "Surely you could wear those? They're very plain." Her earlobes were just visible below the wings of her dark hair, which was parted in the center and drawn up in a simple knot. The coral drops would look lovely against her hair and skin, he thought.

She shook her head, but did not object when he crouched across from her and peered into the box. "Your mother dressed so beautifully," he said. "And that whole house looked like her, somehow—those violet drapes, remember those? I used to think she must have picked them to match her eyes."

"She might have," Susannah said. Her own eyes were closer to gray than violet, and were set unusually far apart. They'd made her look oddly adult when she was a girl. Now they made her look girlish. "I wish I could picture her more clearly. Do you ever have times when you can see all the things around your mother, her clothes and jewelry and furniture—but you can't see her face?"

"Sometimes," he said.

Then he'd risen hastily, turned his back on her and the mahogany box, and produced the letter that seemed, suddenly, to have soured the afternoon. All because he couldn't bear to think of the year when Susannah's parents had died within a week of each other, and his own mother's life had been extinguished like a lamp within a room he was not permitted to enter. Afterwards he and Susannah had been separated. She'd gone to her aunt and uncle's house, in the suburb of St. Roch; he'd been shipped off to cousins in Montreal. Throughout those years, and then through his medical training and his postgraduate studies in Paris, he hadn't seen her.

On his return to the city of Quebec two years ago, he had rediscovered her: grown and married to Arthur Adam Rowley. How had this happened? But the answer was obvious. She was intelligent and beautiful; Arthur Adam was tall and wealthy and clever. And although she had no more dowry than her mother's jewel-box, her upbringing set her apart from many of the more frivolous young women in the city. Her seriousness fitted well with Arthur Adam's ambitions. Already he'd made a name for himself as a journalist, despite the fact that he had no need to earn a living. He liked to make crusades in print, and to outrage his peers by taking up the causes dear to Susannah's adoptive family. Older men predicted for him a career in politics.

Lauchlin had grown fond of him, despite twinges of envy. All that energy and enthusiasm, his warm hospitality and vibrant conversation—no, it was impossible that Lauchlin should resist him. And their growing friendship had meant he could see Susannah easily. He could knock on the initialed door, as he had today, and be sure of a welcome. Just now, though, he felt confused. Was it the information contained in the letter that had upset her? Or the fact that the letter had not been written to her?

"His news made me miserable," Lauchlin said: both stating a fact and searching for the source of Susannah's unhappiness. "It's unbearable, what's going on over there. And me here, doing nothing—I should *be* there." He pressed his forehead against the glass, as if he could push through it to the air.

"It's not as though Arthur Adam is actually *doing* anything," Susannah said. "He's watching. He's writing. That's what he does. Why does he write in such detail to you, and not to me?"

"He's writing articles that move people," he said, evading her question. "Move them to send clothes, money, food—that's hardly nothing."

"Anyone could do as much. . . . oh, I don't mean that, I know what he's doing, how important it is—but I *miss* him. All the time." She continued to pace, swishing her skirts against the heavy furniture. "Does he think I wouldn't be interested? Why can't *I* be there?"

"It's no place for a woman."

She spoke as if she hadn't heard him. "Stuck here, sorting old clothes and running bazaars . . . and feeling you watching me all the time. He asked you, didn't he? To keep an eye on me."

"Only the way a friend would ask another friend—to ease his mind, you know. And perhaps to make sure we each have some company in his absence."

"That's how you see yourself? As company?"

Was she mocking him? The room was stifling. He had taken great pains, he thought, not to let her know the depth of his feelings for her. He had been friendly but no more than that; well-mannered, discreet. Although it was true he fussed over his clothes when coming to see her. Now he sneaked a glance at the oval mirror hanging from a cord on the wall. Bushy red hair as neat as a pair of brushes could make it in this weather; a flush spreading from his cheekbones across his freckled, blocky nose. His new shirt was handsome enough, but for all it had cost it still bunched at the collar as if made for a smaller, daintier man. He sat and extracted a fat, prickly cushion from under his elbow. Then he flushed more darkly as he caught Susannah's gaze.

"Vain boy," she said. She settled herself in a low chair and poured the tea.

"I am *not*." But even as he protested he found himself oddly comforted by her tone, which brought back the bickering of their childhood. Once, in the garden behind his family's house, they had argued for hours over a passage in a book.

She shrugged, spilling tea into her saucer. "I was only teasing." Then she let out a small, exasperated sigh. "But here I am. And here you are. Both of us wanting to be over there. I wish you'd stuck with your work at the hospital."

"But the director wouldn't let me *do* anything. . . . bleed, bleed, bleed; that's all he does, and all he wanted me to do." He reached for more sugar. "You know that."

They'd argued before about Lauchlin's unwillingness to continue working at the immigrant hospital supported by Susannah's aunt and uncle. "You're as prejudiced as your father," Susannah had said. In Findlay Grant's eyes, the cholera that had killed his wife in 1832 had come from the Irish immigrants, and since then he'd never had a kind word for anyone or anything Irish. But Lauchlin's defection had nothing to do with his father, only with the limits his own research placed on his time. He studied the nature and uses of alkaloids, those active principles isolated from plants. A substance as useful as atropine or quinine might reveal itself to him, if he were diligent. He'd thought Susannah understood the importance of this. She'd seemed to agree when he explained, after his second hospital visit, how he wasn't really needed there, and how the work disrupted his research.

Now she offered him a biscuit and said, "Of course your own practice keeps you so busy—how is your practice?"

"The same," he said bitterly. "As you know." Why was she being so hard on him? His practice was the least part of his professional life, and the part in which he'd most obviously failed. "Hypochondriacs, asthmatics, rheumatics. And few enough of those. If Dr. Perrault had ever told me that a man with my training would have such a hard time finding patients. . . . "

"Perhaps you ought to pay attention to that," she said. "Perhaps you ought to think about other ways to employ your talents."

Why were they arguing? All the warmth of their moment over the jewel-box had dissolved into this disagreement, which had surfaced several times since Arthur Adam's departure. Where Lauchlin had always believed that his dedication to science would serve the world in large ways, Susannah believed in more immediate good works, embracing the recent flood of immigrants as if by doing so she might bring her parents back. During their honeymoon, she and Arthur Adam had investigated the slums of Paris and Edinburgh, and Arthur Adam claimed she'd contributed to his articles. Since he'd left for Ireland, she'd been helping her aunt and uncle gather food and bedding for the sick. But it was not as if Lauchlin had been idle.

"You've made your point," Lauchlin said. "I notice you don't seem to mind living in this fine house, though. Even if you're too good to wear a necklace."

Immediately he was ashamed of himself; she had lost both parents, where he had lost only one. And the oil portraits in their gilt frames, the piano, and the table with the claw-feet grasping marble spheres were not her choice. Once, when the three of them had been playing whist with another of Arthur Adam's friends, the friend had complimented Susannah on the new Turkey carpet and she had said, "Arthur Adam picks out everything—congratulate *him.*" A silence had fallen across the card-table, but later she and Arthur Adam had stood arm in arm at the front door, waving good-bye to the two single men.

"I'm sorry," Lauchlin said. "I know you wish I was more like your admirable husband."

He'd meant to be sarcastic, but to his horror she didn't disagree. "So *do* something," she said. Her handsome hand, flicking the air in a furious gesture, knocked her cup to the floor.

And at that, so discouraged and disheartened was he by both her attitude and Arthur Adam's letter—Arthur Adam, brave and noble, off doing all that he ought to be doing himself—that he set down his own cup and left, his jacket tossed over his arm and the afternoon completely spoiled.

Annie Taggert watched Lauchlin leave. She had overheard most of this conversation; she had also, as Susannah suspected, listened to him read Arthur Adam's letter. But the letter didn't keep her from wishing the emigrants arriving here would all stay home. They were like Sissy, she thought. She bustled back into the sitting room and swept up the fragments of broken china while her mistress stared out the window. Too pathetic to help themselves, more and more of them flooding this country: like Sissy, whom Mrs. Heagerty had hired last fall in a moment of weakness. Filthy and stupid and good for nothing. Making a mockery of the people already here.

Down the stairs she went to the kitchen, balancing the heavy tray and already anticipating all that Sissy would have done wrong in her absence. Annie had left Ireland almost twenty years ago; she remembered her fellow passengers as poor but respectable. Men who found work immediately, on the docks or in the forest, cutting timber. Women like her, who went into service with a knowledge of what it meant to do their part in keeping up a household. Nothing like the new arrivals. She noted a small puff of slut's wool on the stairs; Sissy, again. And in the kitchen she found Sissy crying as she peeled parsnips.

"What's with her?" Annie asked Mrs. Heagerty, the cook. "What's the girl sniffing about now?"

Mrs. Heagerty was filling and trimming the lamps, which marched across the table in tidy rows. The room was fragrant with the pies cooling on the range. "I went across to see Mrs. Mullaney," Mrs. Heagerty said. "Just for a minute, you understand. And what do I find when I come back? Our lazy girl here, sleeping under the table like a dog."

"What can you expect?" Annie said. She and Mrs. Heagerty had an old and firm bond; they had both worked for Arthur Adam's parents for years, in one of the finest houses in the city, before coming here to set up this new household. They knew how things should be done. "The stairs are a horror, you know. You saw the filth she left in the corners?"

"No," Mrs. Heagerty said. "Really?" They turned to weeping Sissy and shook their heads. Annie piled the crockery near the sink. "Don't you be smashing these when you wash them," she warned Sissy. "Mrs. Rowley's already done enough damage for one afternoon—and the good china, too." She turned to Mrs. Heagerty. "Swept a cup right to the floor, she did. She was that angry at the doctor."

"What was he wanting?" Mrs. Heagerty asked.

"He had a letter," Annie said. "From Mr. Rowley. I heard him read part of it. Terrible goings-on over there. If you could hear the things he writes—a stone would cry."

"*He'll* cry," Mrs. Heagerty said darkly. "When he gets home. If someone doesn't have a word with that wife of his."

"They had a fight," Annie said. "I think that'll be the end of our doctor—you should have heard the tone in her voice."

"He's a useless creature, isn't he? I heard from Mrs. Mullaney that whole days go by when he isn't called to a decent house."

Annie agreed, although she was not sure what it was she wanted the doctor to do. No one could emulate Arthur Adam Rowley, and the idea of the doctor joining in Mrs. Rowley's do-gooding was hardly better. Annie disapproved of her mistress's actions almost entirely. Exposing herself to filth like that, walking through low parts of town with only a Quaker woman for a chaperone—no, it was not appropriate. Although it was just what you might expect from a woman brought up so irregularly. Mr. Rowley's mother would never have done such a thing.

Sissy sniffed. "I heard," she said, in a quavery voice just audible to Annie.

"You heard what?" Annie said sharply. "Speak up."

"I heard," Sissy repeated, "from Margaret—you know, at the Richardsons'—that a patient of his died because of something he did. Mrs. Sewell it was. She had the dropsy. And Dr. Grant wouldn't bleed her, Margaret says. She says Mrs. Sewell swolled up like a great pig and died, because Dr. Grant wouldn't bleed her."

"You *heard*," Annie said angrily. "You heard. You know better than to repeat that sort of gossip." But to Mrs. Heagerty she said, "What can you expect of a man like that? Learning here isn't good enough for him, he has to go to Paris, France. Then he's surprised when he comes back here with his fancy theories and finds no one to welcome him but our generous Mr. Rowley."

Mrs. Heagerty made a sour face and picked up the first pair of lamps. "And his generous wife."

On an evening two weeks later, the only lamps lit at Lauchlin's house were in the kitchen, where he had no place, and in his crowded office. He shared this house with his father in theory, but in fact his father was not around for more than a few weeks a year. In his absence, Lauchlin had let go all the servants but one housemaid and the housekeeper and the housekeeper's nephew, who slept in the stables and did part-time duty as gardener and groom. Lauchlin could hear them laughing downstairs, by the warm range.

His room was cold. He sat on the floor, in front of the fire, with a glass of Bordeaux beside him and a plate of food congealing on the arm of his chair. Slowly, meticulously, he pried the top from a large crate and began to unpack the shipment of books he'd been awaiting all winter. Henle's *General Anatomy*, which he handled reverently and then set on the shelf beside his earlier work, *On Miasmata and Contagion*. Chadwick's *Sanitary Report*, which he placed next to Southwood Smith's *Treatise on Fever*. Thick books bound in smooth calfskin, containing knowledge he'd begun to think he would never use.

In Paris, where he'd studied with the famous Dr. Pierre Louis, he had learned to be suspicious of excessive blood-letting and over-zealous purgation and to seek scientific explanations for disease. He had learned percussion and auscultation and how to use a watch with a second hand for the counting of the pulse. In Paris human dissection was legal; he had not had to rely on demonstrations but had explored scores of bodies himself. Here, though—here the doctors were old-fashioned, even ignorant. Although they'd admitted him to the Quebec Medical Society, no one agreed with his methods and no one sent patients his way. His research had yielded nothing so far and his practice was dead. He might be better employed doing almost anything.

Susannah's right, he thought. I'm useless. Still stinging from her sharp tongue, he'd called a few days after their argument on his father's old friend, Dr. Perrault, and mentioned his desire to find some way of combining his interests in research and preventive medicine with patient care. To his surprise Dr. Perrault had responded enthusiastically, although he hadn't had an immediate solution.

"Public health," Dr. Perrault had said. "It's the emerging

field—think about Mathew Carey's study of yellow fever in Philadelphia. Or Dr. Panum's handling of the measles epidemic last year in the Faroe Islands. In his report he proved beyond doubt the efficacy of quarantine and the fact that measles is not miasmatic but purely contagious in character. The most rigorous, mathematical epidemiology and investigation of underlying cause, combined with patient care and social policy—good science combined with good medicine. Or so it seems to me. You might keep your eyes open to opportunities here for similar work. It's a shame to waste your kind of training."

The conversation had sent him back to his books and, even more than Susannah's apparent scorn, had made him think perhaps he should reconsider his direction. He had not gone to see Susannah these past two weeks; no more evenings playing cribbage, no long talks over tea. Since their argument he had felt himself to be a scuttling little creature: a rodent, say. Or a louse. His desk was piled with unpaid bills and he'd have to draw on his father's account again. The house needed repairs, after this long harsh winter. Gutters needed patching, stonework repointing, the shrubberies were a mess; workmen had to be organized and plans drawn up. He had more than enough time to attend to all this, but the idea filled him with an overwhelming boredom. Surely, surely, this was not how he was meant to spend his life.

He finished shelving his new books and then methodically broke the crate into kindling and stacked the pieces beside the fire. Nothing to do now but face the mail. Bills, a heap of medical journals, some of them from the States; a letter from Bill Gerhard in Philadelphia and one from a Dr. Douglas.

He opened the letter from Gerhard first: the usual list of triumphs and enthusiasms. In Paris, Gerhard had already been established as Dr. Louis's prize student when Lauchlin arrived, and they'd overlapped just long enough to establish a friendship. Since his return to the States, Gerhard seemed to have done everything that Lauchlin wished he'd done himself. An appointment at the prestigious Pennsylvania Hospital; an enormous practice; an investigation into epidemic fevers that resulted in a series of brilliant papers in which he differentiated typhus and typhoid in terms of their distinctive lesions.

Increasingly I lean toward the theories of Henle, Gerhard wrote, after giving the news of his family. *These fevers must be due to some sort of pathogenic microbes; and not, as the miasmatists contend, to noxious exhalations given off by filth. But I have to admit I have had no success in finding these microorganisms.*

Lauchlin skimmed the rest of the letter and then put it down, feeling very tired. His twenty-eighth birthday had passed without anyone noticing it but him; perhaps, as Gerhard had once suggested, he should have settled in New York or Philadelphia upon his return from Paris, instead of coming here. He almost burned the other letter unread. A request for money from one of the newly founded medical schools, or an invitation to a dinner honoring a colleague he did not respect; he could not bear one more reminder of his failure to make his mark in this city.

But it was just possible that the letter was a referral, and so he slit the envelope.

May 2, 1847
Grosse Isle Quarantine Station

Dear Dr. Grant:
   Dr. Perrault has been in touch with me, about your recent inquiry into the possibility of entering the field of public health. I am writing to ask if you might consider assisting me here at the Quarantine Station for the summer months. Every evidence suggests that the coming migration from Ireland will be extraordinarily large this year. We have news that vast numbers of emigrants began leaving Ireland in February, and I believe we may expect them here within

*a few weeks, now that the ice has finally cleared from the
St. Lawrence.*

*No doubt you have read in the newspapers the various
expressions of alarm by the citizens of Quebec and Montreal.
Their alarm is justified, I believe. And likely you are also
aware of the recent harsh legislation in the United States,
which will almost surely have the effect of turning the bulk
of the emigration toward us. However, I have not so far
succeeded in convincing Buchanan of the probable
seriousness of the situation. I have been granted hardly a
tenth of the money I requested for preparations.
Nonetheless, I have been empowered to hire several
physicians to assist me.*

*Dr. Perrault has recommended you most warmly, and I
pray, if your own business is not too pressing, that you
consider joining this important effort. If you can see your
way to doing this, I could use you at your earliest
convenience. Our small steamer, the St. George, arrives at
the King's wharf on Fridays for supplies, departing Saturday,
and is available to convey you. Please let me know your
decision as soon as possible.*

Yours sincerely,

Dr. George Douglas

[*II.*]

The island looked like this at first: low and verdant and beautiful,
covered with turf and trees. The shrubs growing down to the
water's edge were mirrored in the St. Lawrence, so calm that
day that the island seemed to hang suspended above a shadowy
version of itself. A huge white porpoise rose, disturbing the
silver surface, and gulls dove and then emerged with fish writhing
in their beaks. As the *St. George* steamed past the coast, Lauchlin
saw a series of miniature bays, craggy and appealing. Toward

the island's center, where the ground rose, were stands of large trees and a white steepled church. None of these conventional beauties eased the knot in his chest.

He had not called on Susannah to say farewell. Instead he'd sent her a brief, businesslike note, wishing her well in her efforts and telling her his destination. He'd asked that she welcome Arthur Adam home for him, thinking Arthur Adam would be sailing up to the King's wharf any day, but he had not said, though he often thought: "What if I can't do what's asked of me? What if all my training isn't enough?" She believed he was vain, and she might be right. He could not conquer his fierce desire to be recognized as intelligent and competent.

How tired he was of himself! He thought of Arthur Adam across the ocean, wielding his pen on behalf of the people he met, and he tried to set his self-absorption aside and concentrate on what he was seeing. Something that looked like a fort, something else that might have been the hospital—these disappeared in the trees as the *St. George* moved on. The island could not be more than three miles long, and was very much narrower than that. So green, so seductively rural. Brown cows grazed, all of them facing him. Parts of the countryside outside Paris had looked like this, offering the same relief from the sights of the crowded city. The view changed as the steamer rounded a point; a small village, and low white buildings near the water that might be the quarantine station. Beyond the wharf jutting into the river at the foot of the village, eight or ten large ships lay at anchor. A number of small rowing boats bustled among them, but Lauchlin could not determine what they were doing.

As the *St. George* eased alongside the wharf, a slight man in a straw hat came trotting down the planks and prepared to board a boat in which four rowers sat ready. He paused to watch the *St. George* tie up, and to exchange a few words with its pilot. In their conversation, Lauchlin thought he heard his own name. He smoothed his clothes and hair and took several deep breaths, aware that his hands were trembling. A few seconds later, the man cupped his hands to his mouth and shouted, "Dr. Grant! Dr. Lauchlin Grant!"

"Here," Lauchlin said quietly; the man was no more than ten feet away.

"Wonderful!" the man said. "Come, come, come! I'm late already for the afternoon rounds, you'd better come with me and see what we've got. Three more ships came in at noon." As he talked he guided Lauchlin off the steamer, down the wharf, and toward the boat where the rowers waited.

"But my luggage . . ." Lauchlin said. He was tired and hungry and a little queasy, as well as worried about his trunk. In it was everything important to him: his medical books, his lancet and lancet-case, a thermometer, some bandages, and some drugs. Morphine, calomel, ipecacuanha, sulfate of zinc, copper salts, sodium bicarbonate, sweet spirit of nitre, Dover's powder. Some Madeira and brandy, of course, and a few sets of clothing. The man brushed his hesitations aside.

"Leave your trunk here, someone will take it up—Dr. Douglas arranged a room for you in the village. We're delighted you've come. Just sit here, fit yourself in this corner if you can."

If this wasn't Dr. Douglas, who was it? The boat pushed off before Lauchlin had settled himself, and he banged his knees against the seat in front of him. He looked up to find a small, creased hand thrust at his waist. "Dr. Jaques," the man said. "Inspecting physician. Pardon my manners. All this rush—but you'll understand when you see. No one expected this. We're very glad you're here."

"Glad to be here," Lauchlin said.

And for the moment, despite the odd flurry of landing, he was. His last patient, before he closed the office, had been a wealthy neighbor who complained that his liver pained him when he drank more than a bottle of wine at dinner. Clutching the bulging flesh below his ribs, he'd whined like an old man but declined to modify his diet. But here were people, Lauchlin thought, among whom his skills might be useful. Almost surely there'd be dysentery, and perhaps a few cases of ship fever; also all the effects of the long starvation about which Arthur Adam had warned him. He braced himself; this was what he was trained for. Meanwhile he took care to sit with his back straight and his chin set, looking over the shoulders of the men who rowed.

It was several minutes before he noticed the water. No longer clear and blue, it was now streaked with dirty straw in which larger objects were suspended. Something floated past him that looked remarkably like a pillow; then several barrels, a blackened cooking pot afloat like a tiny boat, a mass of rags, and some broken planks. There were corked bottles half-filled with clear yellow fluid the color of urine, and baskets lined with scraps of maggoty food. A soggy bed-tick, still kept afloat by pockets of air in its stuffing, elicited a curse from one of the rowers. Two high-crowned hats spun on the water behind it.

"What *are* these?" Lauchlin asked Dr. Jaques. "These . . . things?"

Dr. Jaques was impatiently directing the rowers; they were nearing one of the ships. On the rigging white banners fluttered. It took Lauchlin a minute to realize the banners were tattered clothes, hanging out to dry.

"That's the way they clean," Dr. Jaques said shortly. "The captains aren't idiots, even though the British ones run their ships like slavers. Before they signal that they're ready for us to come, they tell the passengers that we won't keep them in quarantine if the steerage looks clean. They bully the passengers into throwing all their filthy bedding overboard, all their cooking utensils, the nasty straw: it gets foul down there—have you seen one of these holds? There are no . . . facilities, and the floors fill up with excrement and filth. They shovel the worst of it into buckets and heave it into the river before we arrive." He pushed his hat back on his forehead and rubbed at the damp line there.

"Sometimes they knock out the berths and toss the planks as well. If they're healthy enough, they'll scrub out the place with sand and water, maybe throw on a coat of whitewash. If you didn't know better, you might think they'd sailed over under reasonable conditions. But you'll see for yourself—although if this ship is anything like the ones that came in last week, you won't find much cleaning's been done."

Lauchlin nodded, as if this were no less than what he'd expected. He stared at the floating filth and fought down the bile in his throat.

The next half-hour passed in a flurry that left him dumbfounded. On the deck, and then to the captain's cabin; Dr. Jaques barking out orders and questions. Was there sickness on board? What kind? How many passengers dead and buried at sea? Any dead as yet unburied? How many patients now? The captain, Lauchlin saw, looked as confused as himself. Dr. Jaques had a tablet of paper, on which he scribbled the captain's answers to his questions. He passed the captain a small book: "Directions," he barked. "This will explain our procedures. But you must not expect everything to go as stated here. We have room for 150 patients in the hospital, and already we've 220 there. No beds. No beds, you understand—we're building a shed, but we're dangerously overcrowded already. We'll do what we can. We'll take some, the worst cases. The rest will have to be cared for on board until we make other arrangements. The hold, please."

And then he was trotting back along the deck and down the hatch into the hold, Lauchlin at his heels. The smell was staggering. A single oil-lamp hung from the ceiling, and in the dim light Lauchlin saw the stalls and the narrow passages between them. Within the stalls were rows of bare berths stripped of their bedding and hardly more than shelves. In an open area, scores of unshaven men and emaciated women huddled together, some weeping. Children lay motionless. An old man sat on the floor, leaning his back against a cask and gasping for breath.

Dr. Jaques stopped beside the first berth in which a passenger was lying. "There is sickness here," he said to Lauchlin.

Lauchlin gaped; did the man think him a fool? Dr. Jaques felt the young man's pulse and examined his tongue, then gestured for Lauchlin to do the same. Lauchlin shook his head and stepped back, now seeing as his eyes adjusted to the light all the other people collapsed on the bare boards. They shook with chills, their muscles twitched, some of them muttered deliriously. Others were sunk in a stupor so deep it resembled death. On the chest of a man who had torn off his shirt, Lauchlin could see the characteristic rash; on another, farther along, the dusky coloring of his skin.

"Ship fever," Dr. Jaques said, and headed quickly back up the ladder.

"Typhus," Lauchlin said, behind him. "We'll have to find beds for them at once. . . ."

But Dr. Jaques was thrusting more papers into the hands of the mate, with instructions to have the captain fill them out by the following day. "We'll send a steamer for the healthy," he said. "As soon as we can. I'll be back to inspect them before we load. I'll write an order to admit ten of the patients to the hospital, but the rest will have to stay here for another few days."

Before the mate was finished protesting, Dr. Jaques had returned to his boat, with Lauchlin reluctantly following. "Nothing else to do," Dr. Jaques told Lauchlin. "Nothing. You'll see why when we get back to the island."

The second ship they boarded, a brig, was not quite so bad as the first; the passengers well enough to stand had cleaned and dressed themselves and were waiting on deck to be reviewed.

They were very disappointed to learn that they were not to be carried immediately to Quebec or Montreal.

"Tomorrow," Dr. Jaques told the captain. "Or the next day. We're very short-handed just now."

Meanwhile Lauchlin could see that the water-barrels were nearly empty, and the pig-pens and chicken-coops silent. The passengers' beds had been thrown in the river. He said, "But . . ." and clutched the papers Dr. Jaques had asked him to hold. He said, "I'm sorry," to the sputtering captain; then he said nothing. It was impossible to guess the right things to say or do.

The third ship they visited, a bark, was very much worse. The captain had died four days before reaching Grosse Isle, and the mate who'd brought the bark the rest of the way was sick himself, only capable of responding in broken phrases to Dr. Jaques's questions. They had buried a hundred and seven at sea, he said. Or perhaps it was a hundred and seventy. When they ran out of old sails to use as shrouds they'd slipped the bodies into weighted meal-sacks and tipped them over the bulwarks on hatch-battens. There were many sick below. Along the rails a crowd stood pale and thin, some propped up by their companions but pretending desperately to be well. Two boys caught Lauchlin's eye—still in their teens, dark-haired and gaunt, leaning against each other's shoulders for support. Perhaps they were brothers. When they saw Lauchlin looking at them, they looked at the deck.

He said nothing to them, nor to Dr. Jaques; by now his silence seemed unbreakable. There was no way to make sense of this situation. From the deck he saw the green island, the sun glinting on whitecaps, the hills lolloping gently toward the horizon from the river's edge. And for a moment he thought longingly of his clean, empty office at home.

Into the hold: again, again. Already Lauchlin felt as though he knew that place by heart. The darkness, of course; and the rotting food, and the filth sloshing underfoot. The fetid bedding alive with vermin and everywhere the sick. But a last surprise awaited him here. He inched up to a berth in which two people lay mashed side by side. He leaned over to separate them, for comfort, and found that both were dead.

He vomited into a corner, a place already so filthy he couldn't make it worse. Then he scrambled up the ladder and hung breathing heavily over the rail. It was too much, it was impossible. He would go home at once, on the next steamer out, and when Susannah chided him he would tell her that this was not what he had bargained for: this was madness, he could be of no help. All the instruments he'd learned to use, all his theories and knowledge were worth nothing here. These people needed orderlies and gravediggers and maids and cooks; not physicians, not science. They needed food, sleep, baths, housing, priests.

Dr. Jaques came to fetch him. "Feel better?" he asked, offering a clean handkerchief. "Don't be embarrassed—I did the same thing when I started. Everyone does. Dr. Moorhead fainted six times his first day out on the ships. Up and down like a Jack-in-the-box, you never saw a face that color in your life. You'll be all right. Are you ready?"

He turned and backed down the companionway again, looking expectantly over his shoulder at Lauchlin. Lauchlin spat into the handkerchief one last time and steadied himself. Of course he had to follow Dr. Jaques. He was young, strong, healthy. "You'll get used to it," Dr. Jaques said, as the darkness folded over their heads. "They're not all this bad. This is among the worst we've seen."

Among the worst? What could be worse? Lauchlin turned his eyes from one impossible sight to the next, determined to follow Dr. Jaques's lead. Dr. Jaques gave orders to some sailors behind him, sending one up on deck to recruit more hands and another back to his boat, with instructions to have him gather up whatever other boats were available.

"You men," he said to the sailors who'd reluctantly come to join them. "You'll have to help here—we have to get these bodies off the ship. There's a sovereign in it for each of you who'll do a good hour's work."

Even with that vast sum, there were not so many volunteers; he checked the passengers up on deck, but among them not one was strong enough to help. The remainder hunched in corners or lay on the planks, shivering and dull-eyed. Lauchlin shed his coat and rolled up his shirt sleeves and did as Dr. Jaques directed. He and Dr. Jaques and the sailors formed a chain, as they might to pass buckets of water for a fire. Down the length of the hold, up the ladder, across the deck to the rail.

There were boathooks involved at the ladder, where the bodies had to make a transition from one level to the next, but Lauchlin could not bear to look at them or even admit their existence. No thinking, he told himself. Follow orders, do what's needed. He would not, until this task was done, see the ropes binding bodies into bundles and then lowering them, heads and limbs dangling, down the side of the ship to the boats waiting below. Had he seen that journey's last stage, he might not have been able to move, as he did, from berth to berth, gently turning bodies and closing eyes and lifting shoulders as Dr. Jaques lifted legs.

The eighteenth body he lifted and passed was a young woman, hardly more than a girl, who'd been dead for several days. Her feet were black and twice their normal size. The nineteenth body, almost crushed beneath the eighteenth, was another young woman, perhaps twenty-two or three. Her hair was very long, matted around her face and neck. Lauchlin had to move the hank aside before he could grasp her shoulders. His mother had had hair like this, black and heavy and perfectly straight; for an instant, as he touched it, he could see her face. It took him a second to realize that this woman's flesh was still warm. As his fingers tightened reflexively on her arms, she groaned.

. . .

The woman, whose name was Nora Kynd, heard Lauchlin's voice without at first understanding his words. In her delirious half-sleep, she was reliving the last week of her passage.

She had fallen sick before they reached the Gaspé Peninsula and Anticosti Island, and although she had not taken to her bed at first—there being no bed for her to go to—she had spent the days after they entered the St. Lawrence reeling between the deck and the hold. On deck she'd stared at a cabin passenger, neat and clean and well-fed, sketching the sights on a pad. An impossible figure, a gentleman. From the corner where she huddled, he'd looked like someone who might save her, had he cared to. But he was occupied with other interests.

Whales! she heard him exclaim to the mate. She'd seen them too, a great swirl of water near the side of the ship breaking to show a glossy flank. Beluga whales, the gentlemen said; his pencil moved on his pad. A shark followed in their wake with great constancy, and the gentleman mocked the ship's carpenter who said it was a certain harbinger of death. He pointed out sturgeon, green with white bellies—she saw them too, or thought she did, and that was the name he gave them. Eavesdropping on his conversations, she learned the names for porpoises and eels in the water and the white birds overhead. She needed no help to appreciate the green hills and stony cliffs and farms along the water. They'd been right to come, this was paradise. It was curious, though, that the gentleman never noticed her.

She stayed on deck when the weather allowed, even though she was very ill; anything was better than the crowding and smells below. One of her brothers brought her water, the other what food he could. She knew the younger, Ned, had already been caught once begging extra water from the sailors' scuttle-butt. She worried about them, distantly, and prayed they'd stay healthy. But a deadly calm had come over her, a calm she knew came from her illness. Shivering that swept her body in waves, scarlet spots on her shoulders—she had *fiabhras dubh*, the black fever, like all the people dying below. At home she'd taken care of fever patients, using the tricks she'd learned from her grandmother. But now her tongue had gone quiet in her mouth, she could no longer groan, she could not resist. She was filled with a gentle resignation that, during her brief lucid moments, she recognized as fatal.

Where was it she'd finally collapsed? Near the galley, she thought. Somewhere in that crowded space around the range of cooking fires, hemmed in by the cow-house and the poultry pens and the pigsty and the heap of spare spars. Down she'd gone, with the sky overhead rushing down to greet her. Afterwards came a long stretch of darkness and a tormenting thirst. A weight arrived, pressing and crushing as the ship heaved in what must have been a storm. Feebly, during brief waking moments, she had tried to push the weight aside. The weight was first warm and then cool and then cold and very heavy. She woke when the hatches were open, letting in a pale streak of light, and found herself staring into the open eyes of Julia McCullough. They were filmy, like the eyes of a fish.

She'd tried to push Julia's body away but she had no strength. Her brothers were up on deck where she'd ordered them, knowing her death crouched beyond the bulkhead and unwilling for them to witness it. How they had wailed when she'd said goodbye to them!

But here were sounds, and a sense of the boat motionless beneath her in a way she'd never thought she would feel again. A man spoke above her and then lifted Julia's body away. He touched her hair, gentle hands. She wanted to thank him but was unable. He touched her shoulders, released them suddenly, made a strangled noise she could not interpret, and then brought his face down so close she could feel his breath.

"You're alive!" he said.

With a great effort she opened her eyes. Red hair, blue eyes, a nose like a chunk of granite. Almost like someone from home. "Don't worry," he said. "Don't worry—I'm taking you to the hospital."

Another man appeared behind the first man's shoulder; then both straightened out of sight. She heard the sounds of argument, then nothing. And so when Lauchlin carried her up the ladder himself, she was not aware of Dr. Jaques's angry objections, nor of her brothers who broke into sobs as they saw what they assumed was her body draped across a stranger's arms. She did not hear their joy when they rushed to her and found her miraculously alive, nor their anguish when one of the doctors, red-faced and truculent, pushed them aside and denied them entry to the island.

The two boys who'd staggered over to Lauchlin were the pair who'd first caught his eye upon boarding; they were brothers, Ned and Denis Kynd, and this woman he was carrying was their sister Nora, whom they'd believed dead.

"Let us come with her," Denis begged. "We'll do anything—carpentry, cleaning, tending the animals. You wouldn't have to pay us. We could help take care of her."

Lauchlin started to say, "Of course," but Dr. Jaques stopped him. He looked straight at Lauchlin, ignoring the boys.

"I'll admit her to the hospital," he said. "Even though there's no room—let it be on your head, *you* can find a place for her. I said ten patients from this ship, and I meant it. There are others sicker than her. But I absolutely refuse to let these two on the island. They're almost healthy, except for the dysentery, and they're going on the steamer that leaves for Montreal tomorrow. If they stay here they'll die. If they land on the island, there's no telling what will happen to them."

"How can you separate them?" Lauchlin said. It seemed to

him, just then, that he had never met a more callous man. But all his pleas were no use; in the end Dr. Jaques simply pulled rank. "You're the junior doctor here," he said. "Have you managed an epidemic before? Have you ever seen more than an isolated case of typhus? Do you have any idea what's going on?"

"No," Lauchlin said. "But . . ."

"I didn't think so."

The last thing Lauchlin saw of the bark was the Kynd brothers hanging over the rail and wailing, not at all comforted by the thought that they, almost alone among the bark's passengers, would be on a steamer headed upriver tomorrow. Why hadn't he thought to give them some money? He could not imagine what would happen to them after their journey—although they didn't have fever they were half starved, penniless, hardly more than children and deprived of their sister. He could not imagine what would become of any of these people. Already, despite his fury and confusion, he'd begun to doubt the wisdom of singling out a single patient to save among the hundreds needing help. By now he'd figured out the mission of the other boats plying between the ships and the island.

Some carried the patients lucky enough to be admitted to the hospital by Dr. Jaques's orders. From his own boat, with Nora Kynd unconscious in the bow, Lauchlin could see sailors lifting the helpless patients from other boats, dragging and carrying them over the rocks in the direction of the hospital he still hadn't seen. The remaining boats carried the dead.

The dead from the bark, where there'd been no supplies, were dropped on the nearest beach and corded like firewood to await the men who'd build their coffins. Others, from ships where a few healthy passengers remained, were wrapped in canvas or rudely coffined in boards torn from their berths. The boats carrying those bodies formed a long line, moving around the projecting tip of the island to the burial ground. In some a mourner accompanied the corpses, but in most only the rowers were alive. A lone boat moved in the opposite direction, carrying four priests with their black bags, ready to don their vestments and visit the holds.

They would be more welcome aboard the ships than him, Lauchlin thought; perhaps more use as well. And yet despite his despair, and his first sight of the hospital surrounded by piles of coffins, the tents lurching upright as the sound of hammering filled the air; despite the glimpses he could hardly bear to register of a panic equaling that on the ships; still he could see that the island was as beautiful as his first glimpse had promised. Above the beach a mass of wild roses bloomed furiously.

Nora was taken from him, to the hospital he glimpsed in the distance. A man whose name he didn't know led him, on Dr. Jaques's order, to the place where Dr. Douglas lived. The road from the village wound through a beech grove in full leaf, casting a solid shade that cooled him. Bewildered, exhausted, Lauchlin followed his guide to a green lawn stretching before a cottage perched at the water's edge. A dog rushed from the rhododendrons, barking and barking as if prepared to bite, veering off only when Lauchlin's companion seized a stone and threw it. Lauchlin brushed his clothes off as best as he could while his companion knocked on the cottage door. A small man, tidy despite his shirtsleeves, opened it. His hands were full of papers and more littered the table behind him and towered in stacks on the chairs.

"Dr. Douglas," said the nameless guide. "I've brought you Dr. Grant."

Dr. Douglas said, "Where have you been?"

[*III.*]

June 2, 1847. The weather continues terrible; today it rained again. The men finished building the first of the new sheds but the hammering continues: coffins, sheds, more coffins. I have not been sleeping well. Already the hives that occasionally plagued me in Paris, when I was overworked, have broken out along my upper arms. Another letter from Arthur Adam arrived, dated March 4 and forwarded from the city—he includes this news, which I suppose he meant as a warning:

> There is a great deal of fever here now. We see two types: the so-called yellow fever, which the natives call fiabhras buidhe and some of the doctors call relapsing fever; and black fever—fiabhras dubh—which you will know as typhus. You might warn your colleagues who see this class of patient that they should expect to see some cases among the emigrants headed your way. Yesterday I heard a story, which I could not confirm, that the emigrant ship 'Ceylon,' sailing with 257 steerage passengers, lost 117 to fever on the voyage. Have you any evidence yet of this?

One of his articles appeared in the *Mercury* a few days ago. Lots of details, very elegantly written.

Three days after my arrival, another seventeen ships anchored. All of them had fever. By May 26 there were thirty ships, and by the twenty-ninth, thirty-six: a total of some 13,000 emigrants, many of them sick. Yesterday I stood on the wharf and counted forty vessels stretching down a St. Lawrence so befouled I could hardly see the water. We have in excess of a thousand fever patients on the island: more than 300 jammed in the hospital, the rest in sheds normally used to detain passengers during their quarantine, in tents, and even in rows in our little church. More than this number lie sick in their ships, waiting for help we are helpless to provide. At the far end of the island, the quarantine camp for the "healthy" is in fact also full of the sick. Yesterday a boy died there, without ever having seen one of us. First name Sean, last name Porlack? Pallrick?

June 8, 1847. Muggy and hot. Dr. Douglas is a good man, but nothing he does makes more than a dent in this situation. There are more than 12,000 people on this island now, many without shelter and almost all short of food. Dr. Douglas has applied to the government for a detachment of troops to be stationed here, to preserve order. Buchanan, the chief emigration officer, has obtained some tents from the army. These are not much comfort during the rain and hot weather. My feet are swollen and the skin is peeling between my toes.

This day Dr. Douglas sent an official notice to the authorities in Quebec and Montreal, warning that an epidemic is bound to occur in both cities. Any reasonable quarantine procedures, as the medical profession would recognize them, have become impossible to enforce.

We now allow the 'healthy' to perform their quarantine on board, as there is no room for them on the island. They are detained aboard for fifteen days, after which they are shipped upriver. We released over 4,000 last Sunday—truthfully, many were already sick, and many more carry the seeds of contagion. We received word yesterday that three ships loaded with emigrants and bound for this port were wrecked in a late snowstorm along the Cape des Rosiers. All aboard were lost.

Some eighty vessels have now made their way to us. Several among them fly their ensigns at half-mast: captain, chief mate, or other officer having succumbed to fever. Deaths among the passengers are almost past counting. I see I have not yet mentioned the death of Dr. Benson. Arrived here from Dublin on May 21, just before me, he volunteered his services in hospital. After contracting typhus, he died May 28: a kindly, thoughtful man. We are fourteen now, on the medical staff. Twice our number would hardly be enough.

I have hardly seen Dr. Jaques since my arrival. He spends every minute shuttling among the ships. The sick he can do little for—many lie for days without any medical attention. The ships' captains, crew, and passengers despise him for his failures, but I can no longer do so. He—we, I—separate the sick from the healthy without regard for family ties; we have no choice. Yesterday a young Anglican clergyman, newly arrived, chided me for dismissing a fully recovered young man from the hospital while detaining his still fevered wife. "Where is that man to go?" he said indignantly. "You know they're sleeping on the beaches now, without any covering. Do you expect him to go upriver without his wife?"

"Where would you have me put him?" I asked. "He's well, and the ships are full of sick who need the beds here." Of course I heard the echo of Dr. Jaques's rebuke to me in my words. And on the clergyman's face I saw an expression that must have once been on my own.

Why, then, does Dr. Jaques continue so unfriendly toward me? Three young doctors from Montreal assist him at his task, but I am not allowed to join them and he never looks at me squarely. Dr. Douglas says I am needed here on the island more than on the ships; he is courteous to me, but not much warmer than Dr. Jaques, and I cannot help believing that I am under some sort of suspicion because of my behavior that first day. Not because I vomited or fled the hold: Dr. Jaques told the truth there, every new doctor responds this way. But because I argued with Dr. Jaques about the disposition of the Kynd brothers, because I insisted on bringing Nora here . . . was it what I said? Or only that I raised my voice to say it, that I shouted and showed myself to be excited?

I have not once since then left a patient's side when I was needed. I have not once raised my voice in anger. Mrs. Caldwell burned the cuff of my last good shirt, and I said nothing.

The days pass swiftly, each worse than the one before. Already those here to help the patients begin to turn into patients themselves. More Catholic priests have arrived, from Quebec and Montreal. They travel among the ships with Dr. Jaques, giving what comfort they can. Mostly they administer last rites. One, who returned to the village this evening for dinner, looks to be on the verge of fever himself. The miasma arising from the holds of the ships is so dense that he swears it is visible as a stream of tainted air flowing from the hatches like a fog.

June 14, 1847. The weather continues extremely hot. Nora Kynd is recovering—a miracle that anyone should get better under these conditions.

We have almost no equipment. The hospital was over-crowded even before my arrival; we were given, to meet the influx of thousands, exactly fifty new bedsteads and double the quantity of straw used in former years. The new sheds are no more than shacks and what bedding there is has been placed directly on the ground, as there are no planks on which to lay it. Within days it becomes soaked and foul. The old passenger sheds are the worst of all. Here the berths are arranged in two tiers; several patients are jammed in each berth and invariably it seems to happen that the top berths are given to patients with dysentery. The filth and stench are indescribable.

We have very few nurses—how could this surprise anyone? For three shillings a day they are obliged to sleep amongst the sick and have no private rooms where they may rest or change their clothes. They receive the same food as the emigrants, and are granted no time in which to consume it; I see them crowded outside the sheds at mealtime, gobbling on their feet. It will be a wonder if they do not all succumb to fever. Dr. Douglas asked one of the priests to try to persuade some of the healthy passengers to volunteer their services. Even with the enticement of high wages, very few came forward.

Buchanan has issued an order compelling all the servants at present on the island to remain, until and unless they can provide substitutes for themselves. They are surly, nearly useless, re-tained as they are against their will; they taunt us, trying by outright misbehavior to provoke us into dismissing them. The woman whose job it is to bring afternoon tea to me and my assistants yesterday spilled it deliberately. She looked me right in the eye as she let the tray tip, the teapot slide forward and crash to the ground. Her name is Millie. If I dismiss her, there will be no replacement. There is talk of freeing prisoners from the city jail and bringing them here to care for the sick. Meanwhile the police appointed to maintain order wander the streets drunkenly.

On occasion I have longed to join them. I long for many things. Privacy, quiet, sleep, decent food. Susannah. I wonder how she is. If it were not for her and my own fear of appearing weak, I might run away.

Nora is in the little church, which has turned out to be the best of our makeshift hospitals—the bedding stays dry because of the floor, and the large windows allow for good ventilation. Last night, when I stopped by to see her, her skin was cool, her pulse almost normal. She asked me where her brothers were and I told her they were fine. What use would there be in telling her that they have already been carried against their will at least as far away as Montreal? In fact they may be much farther, as we hear that the residents of that city are in an uproar about the condition of the emigrants, and have insisted on pushing many on to Kingston and Toronto.

When I woke this morning, I could not at first remember where I was. I heard hammering—a sound one never escapes from here—and the sounds of carts rattling down the streets, and for a moment I was back at home during the season my mother died. Then I heard the bustle of Mrs. Caldwell below, fixing breakfast for the crowd of us. Besides Dr. Stephenson and Dr. Holmes and Dr. Black, with whom I have been working and who share the second floor with me, we were joined two days ago by Dr. Pinet of Varennes, Dr. Malhiot of Vercheres, and Dr. Jameson of Montreal—a quiet, well-bred man with a passion for bees and some real understanding of physiology. Mrs. Caldwell has arranged makeshift beds for them in the attic above me. Rapidly, this is coming less to resemble a boarding house and more one of the sheds where our patients lie. The other physicians are similarly lodged, the attendants and servants lodged much worse. Food is becoming a problem for us, as it is for the passengers. The beef and mutton Mrs. Caldwell can obtain are sometimes inedible. She bakes, and so we usually have bread except on the days when the local storekeeper runs out of flour. We hear that the bread his wife turns out in large batches is purchased at exorbitant prices by the ships' crews, who are running low on provisions.

June 19, 1847. Still hot; thunderstorms. Today, after finally obtaining Dr. Douglas's grudging permission, I moved my books and supplies to this closet at the front of the church we've converted into one of the hospitals. I will continue to sleep at Mrs. Caldwell's, and have left most of my clothes there. But now I have one small space where I may read and write in relative silence, without the snores and sighs and throat-clearings of Mrs. Caldwell's.

A number of my patients are arrayed in rows in the main chapel. Nora Kynd lies among them; she continues to improve. Last night she felt well enough to walk about, and as she begged for some fresh air I escorted her out to the porch, bringing two chairs from inside. She regrets the loss of her hair, which had to be cut during the worst of her sickness.

She is from a rural area in the west of Ireland, not far from where Arthur Adam traveled. In the years just before the murrain struck, when the potato crops were so abundant that no one knew what to do with the surplus, potatoes were stacked in heaps in ditches and fields, buried in huge pits and never used, fed to animals, plowed back into the fields. The famine is a punishment, she believes, a scourge come from God to punish her people for waste. I was not able to convince her that this was a superstitious view, that the blight is a biological phenomenon and unrelated to the earlier surplus.

Most of her family is dead now; only she and the two brothers I saw on the bark survive. Her account of their passage differs in detail but not in substance from the stories I've heard again and again this month. Later she backtracked and spoke of fever in her village. She sometimes refers to the fever as *an droch-thinneas*, which she tells me means "the bad sickness"; sometimes she refers to it by the name Arthur Adam used, *fiabhras dubh*. Of course it's difficult for me to be sure, but based on her description of symptoms I would guess that in most cases her neighbors suffered from typhus, as defined by Gerhard and Wood. Some clearly had famine dysentery as well—she described the ground outside the huts of the sick being marked by clots of blood. Her grandmother was an Irish nurse—"nurse *Gaelacha*," Nora called her; a local woman with some knowledge of traditional remedies. She seems to have practiced something very close to the quarantine procedures we've tried and failed to employ here.

At first I tried to stop Nora from speaking of this time, but she wouldn't stop and I came to believe it was of some help to let her talk. I found it interesting to hear how the disease process manifests itself elsewhere.

"There were houses in the district next to us in which first one person died and then another and another, and all were so weak and sick that none could do anything until the last person died," she said. "The bodies lay in the houses and the dogs came. When the fever passed by, those neighbors who had come to themselves a bit would go to the houses where everyone had died and find nothing but bones lying there on the floor. The neighbors would gather the bones and bury them and then burn the houses to the ground, so as to burn the sickness out."

She wept quietly for a while; I went inside and returned with a note pad, a handkerchief, and a small glass of brandy, which choked her when she sipped it but brought a little color to her face. Her skin is remarkably white; I still can't tell whether this is the result of her illness, or her natural color. Around the irises of her eyes is a fine line which appears bronze in some lights, dark brown in others—normal?

"In my village half the people died, including my parents, two brothers and a sister, my mother's brother and sister, and many of my cousins. My grandparents, too. But others were spared, because my grandmother on my mother's side helped them before she got sick herself."

This is what I drew as she spoke. Lines of writing, little arrows and crosses; as she watched me draw she said it looked like a misshapen tree hung with apples:

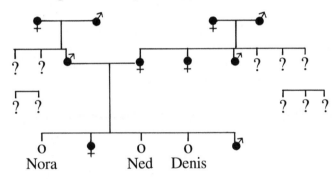

The circles with the small crosses beneath indicate the women in her family; those with the arrows are the men. Each generation on a separate line. Those darkened represent the dead—grandparents, parents, her aunt and uncle on her mother's side, her brothers. When I had explained the figure to her, she took the pen from my hand and added to the bottom row an apple I'd missed; then she darkened it. Robbie, the youngest. She found it hard to say his name.

Here is the rest of her story, or as much as I could scribble while she spoke:

"I helped my grandmother after my parents died. Ned and Denis helped too. When we could we took the sick from their houses and put them into huts—*bracai*, we called them—we made by thatching brambles and rushes over poles against a sheltered ditch. We kept those people separate from the healthy. My grandmother would go into the hut with the sick people, and we would wall up the door with turf and then pass food in through the window, on the blade of a long shovel. Never would we touch the empty vessels she passed back out through the window.

"My grandmother could see the sickness on someone, as good as any doctor could; she knew it was *an droch-thinneas* by the color of their urine. She did not give the sick a mouthful to eat, but she gave plenty to drink, as much as we could gather and pass through the window. Two-milk whey she gave, when we could get it—very light and sustaining. To make it we boiled new milk and then added skim milk to it. The sick would drink this and also eat the curd. Also she gave the juice of cress and wild garlic, and sheep's blood if it could be found. When the color of the urine lightened, she would give a single toasted potato. We saved what few good potatoes there were for this use; ourselves, we were eating ferns and dandelion roots and pig-nuts and cresses. My grandmother did not come out of the fever-hut, nor let anyone in, until her patients were completely well."

When I asked her how she and Ned and Denis avoided the sickness themselves, she said that before they first touched the patients and carried them to the fever-huts, and also before they burned the huts of the dead, they washed their hands and faces in their own urine, to protect them.

"Would you say, then," I asked, "that you attribute your relative health in Ireland to the strict isolation procedures taught you by this grandmother?"

"Isolation," she said. When she raised her hand to smooth

her hair, it slipped off the shorn ends. "That means making someone to be alone?"

June 20, 1847. Rain, which does not alleviate the heat. Two nurses died yesterday. In hospital we have 1,935 sick, according to Dr. Douglas's count. Several hundred more sick remain on board their ships, infecting the well.

No sleep at all last night. This morning I saw a dog by the wharf and thought it was a wolf. Why would anyone allow dogs on this island? I have brought blankets from Mrs. Caldwell's and plan this night to make a pallet here on the floor. The patients cannot be noisier than my fellow medical officers. A number of those working here now have been recruited from the army, and their manner is disagreeably matter-of-fact and hearty.

Nora's story continues to haunt me. Henle makes the distinction between miasma—the disease substance that invades an organism from the outside; and contagium—the disease substance believed to be generated in the sick organism, which spreads the disease by contact. He argues that the pathogenic matter must be animated, although he has as yet no proof for this. Southwood Smith, in his *Treatise on Fever*, discounts the theory of contagion in favor of noxious exhalations, or miasmas, given off by filth. Chadwick, Smith's follower, says dirt is the nurse of disease, if not the mother.

It's true that on the filthy ships the passengers sickened quickly. Here, the disease seems to spread somewhat slower in those places where the beds are less closely crowded, and the ventilation is better.

But Nora says fresh air has nothing to do with it; she spent all the time she could on the deck of the bark and still sickened. In one of the books Gerhard sent to me is a discussion of an old paper by Dr. Lind, physician to the Royal Navy. Lind contended that typhus is carried not only on the bodies of the sick, but upon their clothes and other materials they touch: beds, chairs, floors. In defense of his views, he cites the death of many men employed in the refitting of old tents in which typhus patients had been cared for. He advocates fumigation (camphorated vinegar, burning gunpowder, charcoal); also a thorough scouring of patient quarters and destruction of bedding and clothing. Additionally he recommends that physicians and attendants change their clothing when leaving the hospital.

This may be worth trying here. Now that we must quarantine passengers aboard their ships, Dr. Douglas has given orders that the passengers be removed to the island temporarily, and that the holds be thoroughly washed and aired before their return. Stern and bow ports are opened, allowing a stream of air to pass through the hold and flush out the miasma. On many of the more recently arrived ships, however, passengers are no longer required by the captains to discard all their bedding before inspection; word has spread that the ships will be detained here regardless, and no one wants to cause extra suffering. So the passengers return to the clean holds with their filthy clothes and blankets and belongings. Wood's *Practice of Medicine* notes that the disease "appears even to be capable of being conveyed in clothing, to which the poison has been said to adhere for the space of three months. . . . It is thought that the poison can act but a few feet from the point of emanation; and attendants upon the sick often escape, if great care is taken to ventilate the apartment, and observe perfect cleanliness." Interesting advice, if true. But what use is it? Not one thing on this island is clean. Throughout the sheds and tents, as well as the hospital, we have an infestation of lice. This in itself seems like reason to divest the passengers of their rags and provide them with new.

Nora appears to be making a full recovery. Tonight she asked me again about her brothers and this time I told her the truth: that when last seen they appeared well, but they were carried off on a steamer bound for Quebec and Montreal on May 24 and may now be anywhere. Her face turned very pale. She went outside for a while, and when she returned she asked that she be allowed to work here as an attendant. As she cannot catch the fever again, I agreed. We are desperately short-handed.

Three of my fellow physicians have fallen sick; also two Catholic priests and the same Anglican clergymen who chided me early on. At least six of the attendants are also sick.

The remainder so fear contagion that we have caught them standing outside the tents or in the open doorways of the sheds, hurling the patients' bread rations at their beds rather than approach them. Gray bread flying through gray air.

June 27, 1847. Unbearably hot. Seven out of fourteen physicians are now ill. Of the six Anglican clergymen recently arrived, four are sick: Forrest, Anderson, Morris, Lonsdell. Our death-register now shows deceased 487 persons whose names we cannot ascertain. 116 ships so far. The backs of my hands are completely covered with hives.

Last night I stole a brief hour of conversation with Dr. John Jameson. Over a glass of brandy, and without meaning to, I complained that Dr. Jaques never talks to me if he can avoid it. John, who continues good-humored despite the lack of sleep and the working conditions, said, "You must not take this so hard. This island is a government installation, under military supervision—of course everyone's concerned with discipline, the chain of command, the appearance of propriety. Dr. Jaques perhaps a bit more than the others. This is a political situation, at least as much as it's a medical emergency."

Of course it's politics, as he said; Arthur Adam has maintained all along that the famine in Ireland is political, not agricultural, and so by extension our situation here has at least as much to do with government policy as with fever. I have not, apparently, been behaving in a sufficiently 'military' manner. And it's true that John gives an appearance of going along, not asking questions or making comments when one of the superintendents tells him to do something. He smiles and nods. Then as soon as they're gone, he does what needs doing, the way he sees fit to do it.

Am I such a troublemaker?

John said, "In the staff meetings, you ask quite a few questions. Sometimes you want to know why you can't be reassigned here or there, why you can't try this or that, why they can't get better food for the patients, why the servants don't behave better—this isn't a situation where questions are welcomed. And then this place"—he waved his hand around my makeshift office and sleeping quarters, touching two of the walls as he did so— "What do you think it looks like, you unwilling to sleep at Mrs. Caldwell's with the rest of us? You hardly talk at dinner, you bolt your food and run back here . . . some of the staff say you think you're better than the rest of us."

Me—who worries all the time that I'm not holding up my end. Then he brought up Nora and her work with the patients. I have given her too much responsibility, he says. I talk with her too freely.

"It's a question of maintaining our positions here," he said. "Where would we be if the emigrants started questioning the authority of the administration? Tens of thousands of them. And on our side a few hundred of us, an old fort, a handful of guns, a small detachment of troops—not much to keep them from ignoring us altogether and continuing upriver in any fashion they want."

Suddenly I could not like him so much anymore. "You see this as a war?" I asked sharply. "These poor sick people as our enemies?"

"I see that we have a responsibility to our own citizens."

We parted stiffly and I wonder if we will share our precious leisure time again. Now he will be against me as well—but I too have sometimes seen this not as a war against fever but as a war against the emigrants who carry it. Doesn't it come down to the same thing, the way we're forced to run this island? Susannah was right: hidden in myself was the capacity to view the poor as the enemy.

June 29, 1847. I saw four dogs yesterday, slinking along the streets; there can no longer be any doubt of what goes on in the burial ground. The graves are not sufficiently deep; the coffins are laid one above the other, with no more than a foot of earth to cover them. Although we do not speak of it among ourselves, we are all aware of the army of rats come ashore from the fever ships and swarming through the trenches. Six men are now employed full time, digging fresh graves and reburying those disturbed.

Another letter from Arthur Adam, dated April 14th. The usual woe to report, with one bit of good news: the U.S. sloop-of-war *Jamestown*, loaded with food contributed by charitable Americans, landed in Cork earlier that week. He reports that every inch below the gun decks, including water tanks, store-houses, and the ward room, was filled with provisions. The food vanished into the gathered crowd like water spilled on dry ground; yet it was something, he says. Very much something, and more help than those people get from Parliament.

This day the husband of a woman recently deceased on a brig from Limerick set off to bury her in a small boat granted him for that purpose by the brig's captain. Two sailors attended him and rowed. As they were unable to find the burial ground, they dug a grave among the trees at that tip of the island which is cut off from the rest at high tide. In this act they were discovered, and forced to leave. Rowing back to the brig, they came upon the usual line of boats making their grim journey to the burial ground and, joining this line, finally arrived at the right place. The grave was dug without incident, but after it was filled the grieving husband seized one of the shovels and struck the nearest sailor a blow with it. The sailor remains unconscious and we fear for his life. The husband disappeared into the woods and has not been found.

. . .

July 3, 1847. Too busy to attend to this, although every night I mean to. Prisoners from the city jail arrived two days ago, to act as gravediggers, carters, and attendants. More than 2,500 sick now on the island; more physicians have arrived but two have fled in disgust and nine are themselves sick. Father O'Reilly, who visits the tents at the eastern end of the island where the "healthy" are quarantined, claims that he has in two weeks given last rites to fifty who were dying. When I return I mean to go with him, if there are by then any other medical officers well enough to cover here. Dr. Malhiot is pale and weak but swears it is only exhaustion.

Tomorrow I go to Quebec, at Dr. Douglas's request: he cannot spare me, he says, he cannot spare anyone, but someone must go on this errand and he claims that I am "persuasive" and thus will be of much use. We need food, medicine, tents, bedding, everything; he begs me to report in person to members of the Board of Health and press our case. Secretly I wonder if by "persuasive" Dr. Douglas does not mean "pushing" or "argumentative" or both. But I am trying to follow John Jameson's advice and accept my orders without question.

I hope to see Susannah. And Arthur Adam as well, who must surely have returned home by now.

I carry also a message from Nora, which she begs me to run as an advertisement in both the *Mercury* and the *Montreal Transcript*:

"Information wanted of Ned Kynd, aged 12 years, and Denis Kynd, aged 17 years, from county Clare, Ireland, who arrived in Quebec or Montreal about five weeks ago, aboard the steamer *Queen*—their sister having been detained at Grosse Isle. Any information respecting them will be thankfully received at this office."

[*IV.*]

Lauchlin was so tired on his second journey aboard the *St. George* that the landscape passed before him in a kaleidoscopic blur. He dozed and woke and dozed again, each time opening his eyes to sights that no longer seemed familiar. Cape Tourmente and Mount St. Anne, then the orchards and vineyards of Orléans Island, and Montmorency Falls tumbling white and foamy between the firs—how was it these places could look so untouched?

The steamer arrived at the mouth of the St. Charles in the middle of the afternoon. Canoes and pilot boats bustled around the large ships anchored in the harbor. Men streamed along the wharves and timber ponds, carrying out the work by which Lauchlin's father had made his fortune. Before his mother's death, before his father grew so fierce and distant, Lauchlin had often accompanied him here. Then, as now, a fleet of bateaux with great white sails had carried lumber from Findlay Grant's sawmill at Montmorency Falls to the ships lined up along the coves.

Amazing, how the roar and bustle of riverside commerce continued in the midst of this crisis. The confusion in the yards and wharves had alternately bored and frightened Lauchlin when he was a boy, and he'd found the London Coffee House, where his father liked to gossip with the Ottawa lumbermen and ship captains, hot and squalid. His father's disappointment with him had been evident here, as elsewhere. That he did not like to hunt plover and partridge in the Bijou swamp, that he did not much care to shoot caribou near Cape Tourmente, or join the snowshoe races across the ice in winter—all these things had widened the rift between them.

But this summer Findlay Grant was doing business out west,

alone but for his crews among the pines and basswoods and maples, and of no more use to Lauchlin than he had ever been. Lauchlin turned his back on the forest of masts and made his way through the Lower Town and then up to the city crowning the cliff. The long sets of stairs swarmed with people. A woman hurrying down cracked his elbow with a basket and one of the hens inside opened her beak so wide in protest that Lauchlin could see down her gullet. The woman pressed on, leaving Lauchlin with a painful bruise.

In his pocket he had Nora's advertisement, and although he had other duties he went directly to the office of the *Mercury*. The street outside was crowded with emigrants, most of them pale and in tattered clothes, and for a moment as he pushed his way through it was as if he were back on the island. Inside, he had to fight his way to the counter. A boy whirled to speak to someone behind him, banging his bony wrist against Lauchlin's bruised elbow. "Excuse me," Lauchlin said, with growing exasperation. "*Excuse* me." A woman in the corner was wailing, collapsed on the floor with another woman bending over her. A clerk leaned over the counter and beckoned to Lauchlin, ignoring the men who were shouting at him from both sides.

"May I help you, sir?" the clerk said. He had a large mole near the corner of his eye, which moved as he spoke.

The men grumbled but stepped back. "I have an advertisement I'd like to place," Lauchlin said. He handed over the page on which he'd written Nora's message. "I'd also like to arrange for a copy to run in the Montreal paper. Can you take care of that for me?"

The clerk read the message, his face expressionless. "Certainly," he said. "Certainly, if that's what you wish. You'll be picking up any responses here?"

"Yes," Lauchlin said. "Or I'll arrange to have them forwarded to me."

The clerk calculated the charges and Lauchlin paid his bill. "You know the responses to these have been small?" the clerk said, handing him his change.

"These?"

The clerk gestured at the room. "All these people," he said. "All placing the same sort of advertisement, looking for family they've misplaced. I wish you good luck in your search."

As Lauchlin turned to leave, an elderly man bumbled into him and then pulled himself upright, clutching a fistful of Lauchlin's coat. "Your pardon," the man said. "Would a fine gentleman like yourself have a minute to help?"

Lauchlin gently detached himself. The man's fingers had left marks on his coat. "What's the problem?"

"I'm searching for my daughter," the man said. "If you could just spare a minute, to help me write out an advertisement. . . ."

Lauchlin penned the man's message, and then he fled. Throughout the cities along the great waterway he imagined this scene repeated: those left behind here searching for those shipped to Montreal; those left in Montreal searching for those shipped farther inland. Nora's brothers were gone.

One fruitless call after another ate up the afternoon; the members of the Board of Health were more angry than sympathetic, and more concerned with the outbreak of fever in the city than with conditions on Grosse Isle. Sewell was furious and blamed Dr. Douglas; Henderson and Phillips could spare only minutes for him. At Phillips's office he learned that the clothing and provisions gathered by the Quebec Ladies' Protestant Relief Society, and meant for the sick on Grosse Isle, had been diverted to the sick here in the city. But here, in the heart of the city's best neighborhood, the sick were not evident. The clerks bustling around with their papers were remarkably sleek and plump. The physicians' coats were clean and brushed, the servants were well turned-out, the horses stood calmly before their carriages, occasionally twitching away the flies, and the stone steps he trudged up and down were freshly scrubbed.

In and out of offices, through and back out pairs of weighty doors. Grave faces, cups of tea, hurried half-hearted promises, or outright refusals; yes on a little extra bedding, yes on some extra funds, but not now; no on an emergency shipment of flour and milk, there were already shortages in the city. The fever here was already serious, he heard again and again. A tall official said, "The only good news is that so far most of the victims are emigrants—there are upwards of 800 of them at the Marine and Emigrant Hospital and the newly erected fever sheds nearby. We have no medicine to spare at present." Lauchlin stared at this man's shoes as he spoke; they were expensive, and very well shined. Two doors down and a cup of tea later, Jackson told him that the residents of St. Roch, near the emigrant hospital, had torn down the first set of fever sheds in a fury of opposition. "We have had to post guards over the second set at night."

He called at Dr. Perrault's office, but Dr. Perrault, whom he had particularly wanted to see, could not be found. Later a young physician told him that a hundred beds had been equipped for the sick in the cavalry barracks on the Plains of Abraham, and that Dr. Perrault was thought to be out there. Someone promised some corn and barley; another official promised a donation of blankets from the army. No more physicians could be spared, he was told. And nurses were not to be found for any wage.

Defeated, and obscurely ashamed, Lauchlin went to Susannah's house when he finished his rounds, rather than to his own. It was almost dusk and he could not bear to face what he knew awaited him at home. Mail and repairs and the complaints of his servants; what could he do about any of that? In the back of his mind he was hoping, too, that Arthur Adam and Susannah might invite him to dinner. He'd forgotten what real food tasted like, away from the smell of death.

He stood outside the Rowleys' door, thin and exhausted and out of breath. It was Annie Taggert who greeted him, as he'd expected. But he did not expected her news.

"I'm sorry," she said. "Mr. Rowley is still abroad."

"I didn't know," he said. Even Annie looked plump to him. Her apron and cap were starched, so clean. "Is he all right?"

"Of course. He's in London now. We expect him back next month."

Susannah had been alone, then. All this time. He had written her only twice from Grosse Isle: the most perfunctory of notes, not wanting to worry her in the happiness of her reunion. He had written simply to say that he continued well. He said, "Might I see Mrs. Rowley, then?"

Still Annie did not open the door. "Mrs. Rowley is out," she said, her voice harsh with disapproval. "Mrs. Rowley is where she always is these days, trotting between the hospital and the fever sheds in St. Roch. It's a horror, it is. What she's doing, the places she goes with no more escort than her friend Mrs. Martin—does she think the sickness will just keep passing her by?"

"I don't know, Annie," Lauchlin said wearily. Who was Mrs. Martin? "But may I come in? It's late, she'll surely be back soon from wherever she is."

Annie looked him up and down. "You look terrible," she said. "If you don't mind my saying so. Have you been home yet?"

It didn't occur to him to lie to her. "No. I came straight from the island."

"Straight from working with the sick, I'll bet."

He thought she would praise him for his good works among her countrymen. "Yes," he said.

"And why would you be thinking I'd let you into this house,

still carrying the sickness on you? Not me, not through this door." She stepped forward and closed the door behind her, carefully avoiding any contact with him. "You follow me," she said. "You want to wait for the mistress, you'll do what I make her do every night, when she comes home from those filthy places."

Lauchlin was too weary to argue. Around the house she led him, past the hedges and flower beds and the kitchen garden. "Don't you touch a thing," she said, as she led him through the kitchen door. A dirty scullery maid looked up as he passed; Annie said to her, "Dr. Grant's come from tending the sick. Don't you go near him." In an unused storeroom off the kitchen she stopped.

"You go in there," she said. "That's where I make Mrs. Rowley clean herself every night. You take off every stitch of those clothes and push them out through the back window. I'll bring some hot water and a sponge."

He stood, numb and confused, after she closed the door behind her. What was going on in this house, where the servants now gave orders? What was Susannah doing, and why was Arthur Adam still absent? The room was clean and bare and smelled faintly of nutmeg and flour. There was not even a chair where he might sit.

He was still standing when Annie knocked at the door. "Yes?"

"Here's your hot water," she said. "And some soap and a sponge, and a blanket to cover you when you're done. Get those clothes off you, now."

He looked down at his filthy pants and his stained, worn shirt and coat, unable to argue with Annie's caution. "I will," he said. "I'll do that right now. Thank you. But could you bring me something of Mr. Rowley's to put on when I'm done? Even a dressing gown would be fine."

Annie drew herself up. "That would not be possible," she said. "We have put all his clothes in storage, against the moth."

"But Annie—I can't see Mrs. Rowley wrapped in a blanket, now can I?"

Annie sighed. "You tell me what you'd like from your house," she said. "I'll go over there and get what clothes you'd like from your housekeeper."

"That seems foolish. All I need are a few things."

He started to argue that Arthur Adam surely wouldn't mind the loan, but Annie cut him off. "Mr. Rowley's things are not available," she said stiffly. "But it would be no trouble for me to fetch something from your house."

Lauchlin looked down at the cooling water. "Fine," he said. He gave her instructions and then, as soon as she'd gone, tore off his clothes and tossed them out the window to the ground below. Then he began to bathe. Against his skin, the warm water felt heavenly. The storeroom was almost dark, except for the rectangle of dusky sky let into the rear wall; in the kitchen the scullery maid hummed to herself as if she'd forgotten about him.

Annie set off for Lauchlin's house but turned back a few yards down the street. The doctor would be wanting supper, she knew. Mrs. Rowley would come home late, as always, and would bathe and change her clothes in the storeroom, the way Annie had trained her: then she'd discover her waiting doctor friend and offer to feed him, with no thought as to where that food might come from. It was Mrs. Heagerty's day off. Annie, knowing Mrs. Rowley would only pick at some little scrap on her return, had not fixed anything more than a chicken pie, which she'd expected would be more than enough for her and Sissy and the other servants after Mrs. Rowley had taken her two bites.

She ducked back into the kitchen and seized a basket. Sissy cringed. "It's nothing to do with you," Annie snapped. "You finish cleaning that silver before I'm back." Then she was off again; first the market and then the doctor's house.

At the market, in the square facing the Basilica, she looked through the butchers' stalls. Chickens were shockingly high, and none looked as fresh as she would have liked; geese were even higher and the mutton she examined was distinctly off. She bought some oysters, which were cheap and fresh, and a pair of lively lobsters—an oyster stew, she thought, warm and sustaining; then the lobsters split and broiled. She and Sissy would eat the leftovers tomorrow in a salad. The wild raspberries had a wonderful smell and she bought a large pail, undecided yet as to whether she'd serve them plain with cream, or in a tart. Lettuce, radishes, green onions; cream and butter of course. Because Mrs. Heagerty wasn't around to bake, and because she knew she'd be pressed for time, she allowed herself the luxury of a dozen hot rolls.

Then she set off for the doctor's house. She knew where it was, having carried gifts of preserves and extra produce from the Rowleys' garden there on occasion; Mrs. Rowley was overly generous with the bounty of Mr. Rowley's household. Annie walked past the convent, the courthouse, the livery stable, and two hotels. The hotels appeared to be almost empty, which was no surprise; who would visit this city if they could avoid it, now that the fever had come? Behind her she heard the rattle of a pair of carts, and although she averted her eyes she could not help seeing the coffins they carried.

At Lauchlin's house, she registered the disrepair with surprise. Nasty weeds poking up through the flagstone walk; tall saplings waving arrogantly from the places they'd stolen in the hedge; a stain creeping down the wall where rain had poured through a broken gutter. Ashamed of himself, Annie thought. That's what the doctor should be. She blamed him for letting things fall apart. If he'd been here where he belonged, and not off at that horrid island, his house would look at least partly respectable.

Annie knocked at the door. The Rowleys' house might look like this, were it not for the unceasing efforts of herself and Mrs. Heagerty and the others, all joined to keep the place intact for Mr. Rowley, so that he might not be ashamed when he returned. At night sometimes, lying alone in her small attic room counting Mrs. Rowley's faults, she'd been tempted to let the house crumble in just the way Mrs. Rowley's inattention deserved. But who could bear it? She touched the grimy doorknob with distaste. Still no one came to the door. Then she heard voices, just a few feet away, too ignorant to realize she could hear them.

"*You* get it," a girl said. "It's not my place, it never was."

"Well it's not mine either," a boy said. "I wouldn't be in here at all, if it weren't that I'd come in to eat. You want I should open the door with stable-muck all over my breeches?"

"Don't care. You open that."

"Won't."

Annie rapped sharply on the door. "Whatever are the pair of you doing in there?" she called. It was shocking, how far this household had fallen. "You open this door right now—I've a message from Dr. Grant."

A terrified silence, and then a boy, as dirty as promised and with a wild head of blond hair, pulled the door inward.

"Fetch the housekeeper for me," Annie said to the girl. Tall and poorly dressed, the girl was nearly as sluttish as Sissy but looked to be German or Norwegian. She vanished and returned with a middle-aged woman in tow.

"I'm Mrs. Carlson," the woman said. Portly, suddenly filled with dignity, she drew herself up. "And you would be?"

Annie also stood very tall and identified herself. "Dr. Grant has come to call on us," she continued. "On Mrs. Rowley, that is—Mr. Rowley being still in England, on very important business. Dr. Grant has had a small accident with his clothes, and he requires that you gather a new set for him, from the skin out. I am to bring the items back to him at the Rowleys'."

"Indeed," Mrs. Carlson said. "And how am I to know you're telling the truth? What could the doctor have done to himself, to need everything from linens to a coat?"

Annie swallowed the implied insult in silence; this woman was too far beneath her to argue with. "It's the sickness that's on him," she said, lowering her voice dramatically. "From that island. It's on his clothes, and he doesn't want to bring it into the Rowleys'. When he leaves there tonight he'll be coming here. Perhaps he'll give those old clothes to you then, to have washed."

Mrs. Carlson stared silently for a long minute. Then she indicated a chair where Annie might wait, and vanished up the stairs in the direction of what Annie could only assume was the doctor's dressing room.

In Annie's absence, the other servants at the Rowleys' seemed to forget that Lauchlin was in the house. When he let himself out of the storeroom, he found the kitchen empty. The front hall was empty as well and finally, feeling very embarrassed to be wandering the rooms in a blanket, he slipped into the library and closed the door behind him. The windows were closed and the room was stuffy, smelling faintly of leather and cut flowers left to stand too long. He opened two windows and then gingerly set himself down in one of Arthur Adam's magnificent armchairs and arranged the folds of his blanket for maximum modesty. Warm, soft, clean; all these things were delightful but he was very hungry. When he placed his bare feet on the hassock before him, he saw that his toenails were as broken and ridged as those of an old man. His diet, perhaps. Or simply an utter lack of care. On the elbow poking out of the blanket the skin was loose and dry around his fresh bruise.

Briefly he let himself wonder what he'd look like by the end of the shipping season, should he survive that long. Eight physicians had already died on the island; he put the thought out of his mind.

Annie would be back any minute, he thought, as he closed his eyes. The breeze that blew through the windows was balmy and carried the scent of roses. A cardinal perched in a pyracantha whistled his four-note summons again and again.

When he woke, it was almost dark. The door to the library opened behind him, and he lifted his head with a start. "Annie? Could I have my clothes?"

The figure behind him caught her breath. "Lauchlin?" he heard Susannah say. At first he thought he'd dreamed her voice. "Lauchlin? Is that you? Whatever are you doing here?"

He rose without thinking, his blanket swirling about him like a cloak. There she was before him, a book in her hand, clad almost as lightly as him in a maroon dressing gown. In the instant before he blushed and turned, he registered how little she had on beneath the glossy silk.

"I'm so sorry," he said to the fireplace. "Can you pardon me? When I got here you were out, and Annie took all my clothes and made me wait downstairs while she went to fetch others from my house, and I got so tired of waiting for her that I came up here. I must have fallen asleep . . . what happened to Annie? Why didn't anyone tell you I was here?"

His voice stumbled, caught between his apologies and all he wanted to say and couldn't. That she was beautiful in this dusky light, that he had not seen her hair loose in years and loved it; that he had dreamed of her, again and again, during his weeks at Grosse Isle. If only he hadn't been wrapped in this wretched blanket, he might have allowed himself to turn and gain another glimpse of her. But that would be wrong; she was surely just as embarrassed by her own relative state of undress as by his.

He could hear her backing out of the room, but she was

laughing and didn't seem offended. "Poor Lauchlin! So you ran afoul of Annie's obsession with dirt," she said. "I just got in myself—Annie wasn't in the kitchen when I got home, but I didn't dare skip my ritual wash. I'm the one who should apologize: my servants mistreating you and then me showing up like this. Just give me a minute to get into some proper clothes. Then I'll find Annie and see what's happened to yours."

He turned around again only when he heard the door close. His skin was burning beneath the blanket—never, not even as children, had they shared such an intimate moment. He tried not to imagine how it might be to have her appear like this before him willingly; he tried, and failed, and then sank down in the chair with a groan, more jealous of Arthur Adam than he could stand to admit. When the door opened behind him again, he didn't dare rise or turn.

This time it was truly Annie, who was vexed. "Your clothes," she said. She set the pile on the library table and stood with her hands on her hips. "This whole time I thought you'd disappeared—how was I to know you'd let yourself up here? And then Mrs. Rowley creeping in, without even a word to let me know she was back—an hour I've been back myself, after running all over town, and when I return there's not a sign of you."

Lauchlin sighed and rested his chin in his hands. "Annie," he said. She had grown very forward these past months, but he did not feel it was up to him to correct her. Arthur Adam would straighten her out quickly enough, when he came home. "If you knew what I'd been doing these last weeks, or how tired I was— I just came in here to wait for a bit. Where did you think I'd gone, with only this bit of blanket to cover me?"

"I'm sure I don't know," Annie said. "I'm sure, after seeing the state of your household, that I wouldn't have the least idea what a gentlemen like yourself would be up to. Your Mrs. Carlson sends her apologies about the darned shirt, and says to tell you she couldn't find another clean, she'd packed everything away against your return. Mrs. Rowley will be down directly." But then, as if she'd understood for the first time that he was naked beneath his blanket, she relaxed a bit. "You're looking foolish in that get-up," she said. "Go on—get dressed."

Was that a smile? She shut the door behind her and Lauchlin dressed quickly. By the time Susannah returned, with her hair piled up and her frock demurely buttoned over her shoulders and neck, he was almost respectable himself. "Forgive me for barging in like this," he said.

She swept across the room and seized his hands. "Don't be ridiculous," she said. "I'm so glad to see you—you're well? No trouble, I hope."

He squeezed her hands gently and then pulled away. "No more than what's become a matter of everyday. Dr. Douglas sent me back on some business—I return to the island tomorrow. I was just hoping to see you and Arthur Adam briefly. I had no idea he was still away."

For a minute Susannah occupied herself with the lamps. "Couldn't Annie do that?" he said gently.

"I hate to trouble her."

In the warm glow of the lamplight, she looked almost as lovely as she had in the dusk. Perhaps a little cooler, a little harder, as if her clothes had armored her. Just for a moment he found himself thinking of Nora, whose appearance and manner toward him were always the same. Whose eyes had that mysterious ring around their irises. . . .

"I asked her to bring us some supper, and she's annoyed enough over that. Arthur Adam will be so sorry to have missed you—you know he's in London? Still?"

He didn't want to talk about Arthur Adam. What he wanted was to build a fire and lie down on the rug before it, his head in her lap, and tell her all he'd seen and felt in her absence. He wanted to pull a strand of her hair over her shoulder, against his cheek, but as long as she bustled about like this, and chattered as if this were a social call, all he could do was respond in kind. "Annie said something about that."

Susannah gestured toward one of the armchairs and then seized a folder of papers before settling in a matching chair across from him. "This is what he's been doing," she said, ruffling through the folder and pulling out newspaper clippings. "Quebec, Montreal, Boston, London—there's hardly a first-rate paper he hasn't written for, about the famine and the emigration problem. Now he's calling for wholesale reform of the shipping laws. Look at this."

She pulled out a long column from a London paper. " *'The entire system of conveying these unfortunate Irish emigrants stands in need of revision. Who, if not the Government, will assist and protect these poor people banished by hunger from their native land? We are bound to regulate matters so as to see that too many are not crowded upon one ship, and that their accommodations are decent. We are bound to see that they have sufficient provisions to endure the voyage in good health, and that medical attendants be on board to see to their needs. We are bound'* . . . well, you get the idea."

"I do," Lauchlin said. He grasped both Arthur Adam's efforts and the way this evening was to go, at least until supper had arrived and been eaten and then cleared away. Annie or one of the other servants might pop in here at any moment, and it was surely their looming presence that made Susannah so circumspect. "I couldn't agree with him more, after all I've seen this month. You have to admire him, for setting this all down on paper." He could not help feeling a twinge, as he compared that thick file of articles with his own private scribbles.

"Well, of course," Susannah said. "Now tell me about Grosse Isle. Your letters have been so brief."

He was reluctant at first, but she pressed him and he found himself telling her some of the details he'd otherwise confided only to his diary. "The worst thing," he added, "the worst is sending passengers upriver from the island, knowing—*knowing*—that they'll be sick within a few days, that they'll bring the sickness here."

"It's true," Susannah said simply. "I see it every day at the hospital. Some of the doctors here are very bitter about what's going on at the quarantine station."

"You think we're not?" Lauchlin said, indignant. "You think any of us would choose to practice this way? If we had even the slightest support from the government, if we had anything like adequate space and provisions and an adequate staff— you ought to see what it's like, you'd never blame me."

"*I* don't blame you," Susannah said. "It's only the ignorant who do, and even those who blame anyone blame Dr. Douglas. The worst is this fellow called Dr. Racey—he's set up a private hospital at Beauport, for treating the wealthy unfortunate enough to come down with this pauper's fever. I went there the other day, with my aunt and uncle. It made me so angry. Dr. Racey has two beautiful clean buildings with excellent ventilation and an armload of good nurses, all for less than a hundred patients. Each of them waited on hand and foot, given tepid baths daily, helped to special drinks and food—he trumpets all over town that he's only had two deaths. What he doesn't say is how much he charges."

"No doubt," Lauchlin said. Somehow, despite all Susannah's good will and interest, he was growing very melancholy. His spirits picked up when supper arrived; nothing could counteract the aroma of oysters swimming in hot milk and butter, or of lobsters swelling above their bisected shells.

"You're very kind," he said to Susannah. "I haven't had a good meal in weeks." During the time he was eating, he forgave her for the fact that she didn't love him and never had. It wasn't her fault, he told himself. He had not had the sense to find her before he went to Paris; he had not understood how deeply he was bound to her until she'd reappeared married to someone else.

He finished the oysters, he finished the lobster, he ate three rolls and then Annie reappeared with a beautiful tart. His mood improved and he tried to get Susannah to tell him about her work at the Marine and Emigrant Hospital. She was becomingly, infuriatingly modest. "I just help out where I can," she said. "Whatever the doctors find useful for me to do." When he pressed her, she said, "You know what I see, and what I do. Just think of what your own nurses do." He did, and blushed.

"You know," he said, "As a physician I'm very grateful for all the ways you are helping out. But as your friend, and particularly as Arthur Adam's friend, I have to wonder if he would approve. You put yourself at real risk."

Susannah pushed away her plate of raspberry tart. "Oh, risk," she said. "If Arthur Adam had his way, I'd never leave this house. Too much risk, he says, when I begged to join him in Ireland, or when I beg now to join him in London. Everything I want to do is too much risk. Meanwhile he leaves me here alone for eight months—what does he expect me to do? Shall I tell you something?"

"If you wish," Lauchlin said uneasily.

"I hope he doesn't come home for a few more months. If he were to arrive tomorrow, he'd lock me in here and keep me from going to the hospital—anywhere—and I tell you, I couldn't bear it." She held her hands in front of her, staring into her palms. "He's not like you—you'd let me come to Grosse Isle and help out if I wanted to, wouldn't you?"

"I wouldn't," Lauchlin said quietly. "I never would."

Susannah rose and stood by the window. "You wouldn't," she said. "So you're like him, that way. Even though you'll put yourself in the thick of things, you'd still keep me out."

"Arthur Adam loves you. He only wants to keep you safe."

Annie came in, cleared the plates, and vanished, gazing at Susannah as she closed the door. And now Lauchlin was as miserable as he'd ever been. All evening he and Susannah had been at cross-purposes; every opportunity for a real conversation lost, every real feeling subverted. He could think of nothing to do but to rise and stand beside her and then hesitantly, hesitantly, touch her shoulder.

She did not pull away from him. Rather she leaned into him slightly, so that their hips touched, and their shoulders and their upper arms. They stood there for a long time, gazing out at the garden as a current of warmth flowed between those few connections. How starved he'd been for the slightest human touch! "I'm sorry," he said simply. "I spoke badly. But if you knew how much you mean to me. . . ."

"I know," she said.

Did she? But whether she did or not, his heart lightened. After a few more minutes, already far longer than any touch could be justified, they separated by common consent and moved back to the armchairs. They talked lightly then, of other things; Susannah poured glass after glass of brandy for him and then left him—briefly, she said—to take care of a few details with the servants. Eventually, as he had earlier in the evening, he fell asleep. Who covered him with a crocheted throw he never knew; nor who blew out the lamps or closed the windows. Annie, probably, although just possibly it was Susannah herself. But when he woke at dawn, with the sky pinkening through the windows, it was with an extraordinary sense of well-being de-spite the slight stiffness in his neck and the fact that he'd made no proper farewell to Susannah.

He crept out of the house as carefully, and as full of elation, as if he'd spent the night doing something illicit. Behind the kitchen he found his old clothes, lying where they'd fallen from the storeroom window but now covered with dew: proof that

Annie was not entirely efficient after all. He gathered them in a loose bundle and set off through the empty streets for his own house.

To his surprise he found his housekeeper waiting for him, slumped on a davenport in the front hall. "Mrs. Carlson?" he said, shaking her gently by the shoulder. "Mrs. Carlson? What are you doing out here?"

She rose with a start. "Don't touch me," she shrieked. "Don't come near me with those clothes."

He'd forgotten about the bundle under his arm. She'd been dreaming, he thought. "It's me, Mrs. Carlson. Back from the island. I didn't mean to startle you."

She backed away from him. "I know it's you," she said. "I know all about you. Annie Taggert from the Rowleys' was here yesterday, and she said you were back and that your clothes were full of sickness and you needed clean, which of course I sent although there's hardly a scrap in the house that isn't packed away—those very clothes you're wearing. She said you had brought fever with you, in your clothes—and then you bring that bundle to me, without the slightest consideration. . . ."

He stepped backward, opened his own front door, and threw his clothes in the bushes. Had all the servants in this city gone mad? "Fine," he said. "No more clothes, and you have my apologies. Must you believe everything that Annie Taggert says?"

"I believe this," Mrs. Carlson said. "That you have no consideration for this household. You don't even let us know when you're expecting to be back—how can I arrange things here? We'd no food in the house for you last night, and then I rushed out to shop and cooked a meal and then you never came at all—how can you expect me to work in such an ill-regulated house? If your father was here he would never permit it."

Was it reasonable that he should have to explain his actions to his housekeeper? But there was no one else available, and he had to return to the island; he sighed and set himself to the task of mollifying Mrs. Carlson.

Later that morning he boiled his old clothes in the kitchen himself, as he could get no one else to do it, and after he hung them out to dry and gathered a few more things he settled down with pen and paper. First a quick note to his father: *Please return at your earliest convenience,* he wrote. *Or make arrangements by post for someone to take care of the house in your absence. I must return to Grosse Isle today, and I can no longer be responsible for matters here. By now you are most likely aware of conditions at the quarantine station; they require my full attention.*

Then, after much thought, he wrote a letter to Arthur Adam as well. He praised Arthur Adam's articles; he confirmed Arthur Adam's suspicions that there would be sickness on the emigrant ships; he described conditions at the quarantine station briefly. He would not say outright what Susannah was doing, but finally he added this paragraph:

Of course by now you have heard that there is fever here in the city as well. I am worried about this; I fear very much for Susannah's safety, exposed as she is to contagion. There is much going on here worth writing about, and no one better than you to do it. Perhaps you would consider heading home?

Lastly he wrote to Susannah: the simplest, shortest note of all. *Thank you,* he wrote. *You cannot know what last evening meant to me, nor how it helps to have the memory of you to carry back to Grosse Isle. I will write from there, when I can.*

[*V.*]

Nora hardly recognized Lauchlin when he returned from his trip to the city. When he'd left the island, his thatch of reddish hair, uncut for weeks, had been matted and dry, while his skin had had a greenish tinge. Everything about him had faded: even his eyes, even his beard. The mouse-colored patches beneath his eyes had looked permanent.

But here he was ruddy and smiling, almost sleek, after such a brief stay away. Perhaps he had slept. He fairly ran up to her, where she was bent over a patient. "Nora!" he said. "Nora!"

The way he said her name made her catch her breath, but still she finished dipping her rag in water and wiping the woman's face. Dirty bedclothes, dirty skin, foul breath: Margaret O'Connell. One of the people whom, since she'd been well enough, she'd applied herself to helping. Mostly her help amounted to doing battle with the filth that coated everything. At least Margaret's face was clean. She put down her rag and led Lauchlin away from the pallet. Was it possible he had news of her brothers?

But he said nothing about them. "Nora!" he said yet again.

"What is it? What's happened?" There could be no news yet of Denis and Ned—unless, perhaps, they had made inquiries themselves, and Lauchlin had seen them . . . but he would have said. Perhaps he brought some other good news: more doctors, some nursing nuns, better food.

"Nothing," he said. "Only . . ."

He wanted to tell her something; he was as eager as Ned had once been, on discovering a beetle he wanted to show her. Then his face changed, and she watched him decide to keep whatever it was to himself. He said, "It was so strange there, Nora. In the city. The fever's there too. And I couldn't get anything Dr. Douglas wanted, and then the steamer was so slow coming back, and I saw how many more ships were anchored, and the two big steamers headed upriver: somehow I thought you were on one of them. I thought you'd gone to Montreal. I'm glad you're still here."

He worried about her? Surely he was the kindest man she had ever known; and yet after all he understood so little. "How would I go?" she said. "When my only chance of finding Ned and Denis is to stay right here, and hope they find me. You didn't hear any news of them?"

"Nothing," he said. "But I put in the advertisements, as you asked. There were so many people at the newspaper office, though. So many people looking." He touched her gently on the shoulder.

It was as she'd dreaded, then. Her brothers were adrift in this gigantic, unknowable country, along with a flood of their countrymen. She stood frozen for a moment, trying to absorb what he'd said. And why hadn't he told her this calamitous news before anything else? Other things must be weighing on his mind. He had on different clothes, she saw; a worn, darned shirt with a low collar and a jacket that seemed slightly too large.

"You brought new clothes from home," she said. "A good thing, too. You needed them."

He looked down at his shirt front absently. "Annie made me. Annie has ideas about clothes and sickness, she made me strip and wash and put on clean things. I boiled the others, they're in my grip."

Nora nodded. She'd been very careful with her own clothes, sponging them off each night with a solution of vinegar and warm water and then hanging them outside her window while she slept. No substitute for a full change, but she had nothing more than the dress and undergarments in which she'd been taken from the ship. Her trunk was gone; she liked to think that Ned and Denis had it. Around her the chapel was filled with groaning people, who needed her attention. Margaret seemed slightly better today. Somewhere else, perhaps someone was bending over her brothers. "Who's Annie?" she asked.

"One of Mrs. Rowley's servants, back home." Who was Mrs. Rowley? "She's . . . you don't know her, what am I talking about?" He walked as he talked, moving quickly among the patients and checking a pulse here, a damp forehead there.

George Maloney, Catherine Conran, Matthew Kennedy, Eliza Regan.

Nora could hardly keep up with him. "I don't know," she said uneasily. "What are you talking about?"

"Fever," he said, as if to himself. He turned back blankets, lifted shirts. Francis O'Rourke, Martin Mulrooney. "Thready pulse, shallow respirations; this one's dehydrated, abdominal rash . . ." He was not himself; he was changed. What had happened to him?

That day she saw for the first time the wild energy and obsession that overtook him. He'd worked long hours before, but now he seemed to work all the time. He was with his patients when she arrived in the morning and still with them, or bent over his books, when she left late at night for the small room he'd found for her in one of the village boarding houses. When he was not in the chapel he was at one of the other hospitals, or one of the sheds; when he wasn't there he was down at the tents or out making rounds of the ships or at the shoreline helping land the sick. He was at the cemetery, directing the sanitary arrangements; he was in the kitchens giving the cooks and their helpers instructions about food preparation; he was at Dr. Douglas's cottage, writing up reports.

The ships continued to arrive, the numbers of patients and quarantined passengers continued to rise beyond all reasonable bounds, and she saw Lauchlin—"You must call me Lauchlin," he said at some point. "What's the point of standing on ceremony?"—lose his brief, false flush of health and grow pale and gaunt again. His flesh fell off him as if it belonged to someone else, and had only been borrowed. She believed he had ceased to sleep at all.

During those weeks she and Lauchlin flew past each other like birds, both so busy that they paused only to exchange the most important information. And yet they grew curiously intimate, so that in her mind she carried on long conversations with him. She imagined that he knew just how worried she was about Denis and Ned, and about him. She imagined that she rested her hand on his sleeve and said, "Lauchlin. You must slow down. You must rest. What is it that's driving you so?"

She could not imagine his answer to this question, but she understood, after a week or so, that his utter lack of care for himself was not purely a wish to heal everyone but rather a symptom of a kind of insanity: He believed himself to be invulnerable. She had seen this at home, in Ireland; she had even felt it herself. She knew what it meant. When she couldn't bear to think about Ned and Denis she thought of her father, who had lost his mind before he lost his life.

Last summer, when the blight came, her father had at first reacted like everyone else. One afternoon a chill had come, after days of peculiar sultriness, and then a fog that rolled down the mountains. A great silence followed, in which no birds called; nor was there any other sound. When the wind lifted the fog from the ground, it left a dusting like snow on the leaves and stalks of the potatoes. The dust turned brown and spread. And then the smell came, a stench that filled the valley and made the dogs slink into the ditches and howl. The leaves and stalks of the potatoes turned black; the potatoes, when dug, were slimy and corrupted. Her father had bent his head and wailed like his neighbors.

It had frightened her to see him that way but it was normal: tragedy had come among them, and it was right to mourn. What was wrong and from the devil was the strangeness that came on her father that winter, after her mother and sister and brothers had died. He rose one day from the floor, laughing, cursing, and he drove her and Denis and Ned to the river, searching for cress where every living thing had long since been stripped. "We'll not lie down in this cottage and starve like cattle," he said. Nor would he let them join the crowds around the huge iron boilers where the stirabout was cooked and served by the government relief workers. "The feeding of dogs in a kennel is more orderly," he said bitterly. "They treat us as though we were creatures not made in the image of God."

Up the hill he drove them instead, looking for fiddleheads and dock leaves; down the hill, looking for carrion. He found a dead dog and dove on it exultantly, roasting it over a fire he made right there. For days he was like that, full of a frenetic, useless bustle; then he set off for town, where a crowd had gathered demanding work on the roads. When he was denied he threw a rock at the head of one of the members of the relief committee. He was shot, she heard from the men who carried his body home. Shot dead there in the street, still cursing and demanding.

She'd seen others go the same way, men and women both, though more often men. Pretending courage and strength could save them, when salvation was clearly only a matter of luck. The passive waited for death, which came; the active fought and cursed and railed and death came anyway. It was fate, which could not be defeated. Fate was starvation and fever back home, and humiliation and fever here, and in neither case could fate be fought but only tricked a bit.

That was what she'd learned from her grandmother, during the days they'd cared for the sick together. You ought not lie down and let your fate roll over you, her grandmother taught her; neither ought you stand unbending, as her father had, and wait for fate to lop off your head. There was a bending, weaving, cunning way, in which you appeared to give in but rolled aside just slightly, evading the blow at the last minute. The way of eating whenever there was food to eat, sleeping whenever a stray minute came; never angering anyone stronger nor harming anyone weaker. "Make your mind like a pond," her grandmother had said, when she found Nora weeping at night. "Push away longing and fury and make your mind still, like water."

That's what she'd done when Lauchlin had first brought her

to Dr. Douglas and said he wanted her hired as an attendant. That first minute, when Dr. Douglas had looked her up and down—she'd begun to tremble. And when he'd said, as if she didn't have ears to hear, "Can she follow instructions?" she might have struck him had she not remembered her grandmother's training and stilled her mind until it resembled the lake near her lost home. While Lauchlin had argued on her behalf and reminded Dr. Douglas of their desperate shortage of help, she'd stood calm and quiet, waiting. She had even been able to bob a small curtsy when Dr. Douglas agreed.

Here there was water wherever she looked—and Lauchlin, humming like a sail under too much wind. Frenetic, like her father, though surely not useless. She feared for him. One day, crossing paths on the porch, he seized her arm and said, "Nora. Are you all right? Are you taking care of yourself? I'm so tired I don't know what I'm doing half the time, I forget to ask how you are." His hands were dry and cracked and his knuckles were dotted with blood where the skin had split.

"I'm fine," she told him, although in the last few days her bowels had loosened and she feared she had a mild case of the flux.

He patted her arm and then disappeared. He was admirable, if mad. Dr. Douglas called on Lauchlin one evening, and the two of them holed up in Lauchlin's converted closet. As she bathed the patients and tidied bedclothes she overheard them drafting indignant letters to someone named Buchanan, to someone else named Lord Elgin: Canadian officials, she understood, powerful people who might have sent more help but refused. "A petition," she heard Lauchlin say to Dr. Douglas. "To Earl Grey, Secretary of State for the Colonies—we'll demand he take action to stem the flood of immigration."

"These half-naked, famished paupers," she heard Dr. Douglas dictate. "Sick or aged or too young to work—are you writing this down, Lauchlin?—shipped off to our young country with promises of clothes and food and money on their arrival, when in fact there is no one here to greet them, and no prospect but further starvation or private charity: Where is the humanity in this? Where is our common decency?"

It was her and her kind they were talking about; Nora shivered. Of course she was grateful to them, to everyone working on this island. Yet it was horrible to hear herself described this way: a "pauper," a "half-naked pauper." Before the blight fell on the potatoes, her family had been hard-working and decent; if they had no savings it was only because the landlord took everything in rent. What kind of new world was this, where the rich blamed the poor for their poverty?

But still, the physicians were admirable, even Dr. Douglas; despite his brusqueness he worked very hard, and was fair with her and the other attendants. No one worked like Lauchlin, though. She watched him draw up a list of healthy orphaned children and then sit down with a group of six priests and convince them to divide the orphans among their parishes for adoption. She saw him bathe patients with his own hands, when the attendants were too busy. She saw him carry out armfuls of filthy straw he had no business touching, and make new beds from fresh straw he'd gotten who knew where. And at night she saw him reading and writing, reading and writing, as if in his papers he might find an answer to this nightmare afflicting them all.

July 28, 1847. A break in the weather; three days of blessed coolness and light breezes. No word from Susannah, although I have written her twice. No word from Arthur Adam. Perhaps this is because he's already on his way back.

We have been forced to abandon quarantine entirely. Dr. Jaques is down with fever; his replacement now simply calls at the ships and instructs the passengers to file past him while he looks at their tongues. Those in fever are carried here; those appearing even remotely well are given clean bills of health and transferred immediately to steamers headed for Montreal. The steamers move from ship to ship, collecting their cargo. In the prow of these steamers, fiddlers scrape away with a horrible gaiety.

In this month of July we have entered 941 persons in the death-register under the description of "unknown." Dr. Alfred Malhiot died July 22, of fever. Dr. Alex Pinet died July 24, also of fever. Twelve other physicians are sick, including Dr. Jaques.

At night I write letters to officials of our government; it is as if I've turned into Arthur Adam, but without his skills of persuasion. At night I lie on the pallet in this room for a few hours and listen to the sighs and cries and moans around me, and I wonder how it is I spent my whole life with so little understanding. In Paris, I thought of medicine as a science. I thought that by understanding how the body worked, I might cure it when diseased. What's going on here has nothing to do with science, and everything to do with politics—just what John Jameson tried to tell me. Jameson has the fever now. I look out at the harbor and all I can think is: Stop the ships. Stop the ships. This although I know, from talking to Nora, that to forbid further emigration from Ireland would be to condemn those people absolutely.

I met Nora today by accident, just around suppertime. We stole half an hour and walked to the top of Telegraph Hill, where we shared some bread and cheese. She sang me a song about a woman standing on a cliff in Ireland, waiting for a fishing boat to return. Untrained, uneducated, she has been of more use and shown more dedication than anyone except the Sisters who came this month from Quebec. Two of them have already died. Still no news of Nora's brothers. Four dogs were shot today, found scavenging in the cemetery.

August 3, 1847.   Hot again; 98 degrees where I measured in the tent. New sheds are under construction at the eastern end of the island. I have requested that boilers be built between two of the old sheds; if they can be completed I plan to order the attendants and other visitors to the sheds to remove their clothes immediately upon leaving and soak them in the hot water. Nora is in favor of this; I do not tell her the idea comes partly from Annie and partly from her own stories about her grandmother. But why would I scorn their ideas, when everything I have tried on my own has failed?

I believe I can convince the other physicians to adopt this plan as well: there is precedent in the writings of Lind, whom many respect; also in Wood's new text. Of course we will need tents in which to change—I wonder how many of us have a spare set of clothes? I am down to three changes myself; the remainder are in tatters from the constant scrubbing. I will worry about the details later. The important thing is to take *action*, to do something to stem this flood of deaths among the staff.

Nothing from Susannah. Nothing from Arthur Adam. None of the promised supplies have arrived. Dr. John Jameson died yesterday. Two of the carters engaged to transport the sick and dying and dead are dead themselves. In the woods delirious patients wander, finding the forest less fearful than our hospitals. When they die they are buried where they fall, as their finders are afraid to transport them elsewhere.

August 6, 1847.   Still hot; this weather is insufferable. The river surrounding us looks like soup. A man separated from his wife threw himself over the rail of his ship and sank in this turgid filth. On the beach the sick and dying taken from the ships are dumped without ceremony. As there are no longer enough carts to transport them promptly to the hospitals, nor enough healthy carters, they flop like fish among the mud and rocks as they try to haul themselves to higher ground.

I carried a woman up to some grass beneath a tree, where she might have shade until we could get her to one of the sheds. I carried two boys and a younger girl, aged perhaps five or six, and a man my age reduced to half my weight. Then one of Dr. Douglas's clerks spotted me and came running, irritated and anxious; I was needed at the hospital, I was needed at one of the sheds. And what was I doing down here by the water, lifting bodies like a servant?

I am being torn to pieces. Wherever I am, whatever I do, means only the neglect of someplace else I need to be and something else I ought to be doing. I have given up sleeping almost entirely and no longer miss it.

The new hospital is almost completed. No doubt it will be ready for use just as the emigrants cease to come. Will they ever cease?

Bishop Mountain of Montreal has descended upon us. He demonstrates his concern by making speeches and wrinkling up his fat face. In Dr. Douglas's quarters, where the few of us healthy enough to be presentable had been ordered to gather for a welcoming dinner, we listened to the Bishop wax indignant. He is corpulent; his hands are plump and small-boned. With a wineglass in his hand, with his voice trembling in anger or surprise or both, he told us about the scenes he'd witnessed his first day on the island. Sick people newly brought from the ships, lying outside the church and screaming for water: "They were lying on the *ground*," he said. "It is a sin, what's happening here."

Does he suppose we haven't noticed?

When he calmed down, after several glasses of wine from the last case Dr. Douglas had set aside, he spoke at length of the situation in Montreal. Until just a few days ago, he told us, steamers from this island had been landing emigrants at the old stone wharves there. Absolutely as predicted, many were already in fever on arrival. No one was there to receive them, no arrangements had been made. "They lay on the wharves," the Bishop said. "In the open air, like here. Some of them crawled into an old passenger shed."

I could not help thinking of Nora's poor brothers: can this be what has happened to them? Some of the sick, the Bishop said, were carted off to the hospital. Those apparently healthy but destitute were crowded into the old sheds near the Wellington Bridge, there to await transport further upriver by barge. Many sickened, and despite the ministrations of the Grey Sisters upwards of thirty a day died.

Earlier this week they were transferred to a new site, above the Lachine Canal at Point St. Charles, on a low piece of ground where the Indians once encamped each summer. A better place: and yet, the Bishop says, it is still very bad. Fifteen or twenty die each day, and the crowding is appalling. The barge firms, who promised a wait of only a few hours before the next stage of the journey to Kingston or Toronto, must often leave prospective passengers waiting for days. During that time, many sicken.

Of the Catholic priests from Montreal who have been tending to these emigrants, eight have already died. Some twenty of the Grey Sisters are sick, as is the Vicar-General. It is Bishop Mountain's considered opinion that the sick in Montreal number many thousands. How many sick have we here? he asks.

No one could tell him for sure. Our last count was two days ago; more ships have since arrived, and among the fleet still awaiting transport of the sick to the island is the bark *Larch*, of Sligo, with 150 sick out of 440 embarked; 108 dead during the passage. Also the *Ganges*, from Liverpool, with upwards of 80 sick. And more and more: the *Naparima* from Dublin, the *Trinity* from Limerick, the *Brittania* from Greenock among them.

We know that near 80,000 emigrants have arrived here since May; of these some 2,500 have died in hospital or in the quarantine sheds, and we will without a doubt lose another two or three thousand. Among the nearly 200 attendants and nurses and cooks, almost half have sickened and 22 are dead. Eight policemen have sickened, two have died; all of the 21 stewards have sickened and two so far have died. Six Catholic priests have died here: Fathers Robson, Roy, Paisley, Power, Bardy, and Montminy. Also two Anglican clergymen: Anderson and Morris.

Among us physicians, I said—for it was I who told the Bishop these things; I rose from the table, spilling my wine; I shouted, I could not help myself—he had only to look at the haggard faces around our small table: where at our peak we were twenty-six, four are already dead and eighteen down with fever. There were four of us, only four, at that table. Count us, I said to him. Count us.

Dr. Douglas led me outside; although he might have rebuked me he did not. Nora is nowhere to be found. My hand is shaking so that I can hardly write. What is to become of us?

One minute Lauchlin was rushing between two sheds and the next he was flat on his back, in a room he didn't recognize. Like one of his father's trees he'd been felled, thrown in the river, chained into a raft with the others to begin the long journey downstream.

In fact he was in his converted closet, on a pallet surrounded by his books. Dr. Douglas came by when he could, but by then only he and two other physicians were well enough to work. So it was Nora who tended to Lauchlin, sponging him down with lukewarm water, dripping water into his mouth from a cloth, massaging his legs and feet and hands. She did for him all she wished had been done for her during her illness on the ship. All her brothers had wanted to do but been unable. There had not been enough fresh water on the ship for drinking, never mind for washing; there had been so little food, and no brandy of course, no milk, no clean linen, no space nor privacy. Unlike her brothers, she had access to these things. As soon as Dr.

Douglas heard of Lauchlin's illness, he gave Nora everything she asked for. He had a private stock of supplies, she learned, for treating his sick staff.

She did not resent this; the medical staff on the island were not to blame for what had happened to her and the others on the ships. Perhaps the authorities in Quebec were at fault, for not making better arrangements. Certainly the landlords back home had acted badly, and the passage brokers, the ships' captains, the government in England that had encouraged emigration and then closed its eyes to conditions on the ships.

But these people here, the few remaining physicians and nurses and attendants still well enough to work—weren't they all doing what they could? And if they gathered outside in knots sometimes, smoking and talking bitterly about the filth and poverty of her fellow travelers, their ignorance of the most elementary principles of hygiene and the way their habits contaminated the entire province, certainly they didn't mean for her to overhear them. They were exhausted, she knew. They had no understanding of what the people they treated had been through, no ability to imagine the hardships that still lay before those who survived and tried to make a life in this new country. She overheard one attendant say, both puzzled and outraged, that he had yesterday seen a woman land whose only piece of clothing was made from a scrap of a biscuit bag. And how, he said, could a woman let herself come to that?

But they meant well, and they risked their own lives, and whenever she felt bitter she reminded herself of this. Thirty-six people died on the island the first two days Lauchlin was sick, among them another attendant and three emigrants she'd tended herself in the chapel: Jane Quinn, Peter Hogan, Caspar Fitzpatrick. She grieved for them, as she grieved for everyone. But Lauchlin had raised her from the dead, and while she did not neglect her other duties she bent herself to returning the favor.

Her hands cradled Lauchlin's head, but although he was

vaguely aware of her touch his mind slipped and turned like a
sturgeon in the river. He was in Paris, peering into a microscope
and examining the infusoria he'd scraped from his own tongue.
He turned and he was deep in his first cadaver, dissecting the
muscles and nerves of the upper arm; he turned again and saw
a famous physician demonstrating mediate auscultation with a
stethoscope. Dum-DUM . . . swooosh; dum-DUM . . .
swooosh: the sounds of disease in the heart. In his chest something raced and leapt like a heart gone wild, but it didn't belong
to him. Someone said, in French, a sentence that in English
defined nephritis associated with dropsy and albuminuria as
Bright's disease. As a girl Susannah's face had been severe to the
point of plainness, but he had loved her forehead even then.
Dilatation of the aortic arch was named after Hodgson; transpo-
sition of the great vessels was rare but possible. In a café not far
from the university, he and Gerhard had toasted each other
with rough red wine and eaten omelettes and fried potatoes.
Morphine, strychnine, and quinine were among the first alkaloids isolated; in Ireland, just a few years ago, a doctor had
successfully given morphine by hypodermic needle. Why was it
he had never gone to Ireland? Nora said he looked Irish. He
saw the fingers of his left hand plucking at the sheet that lay
over him; he gathered a fold between two fingers and saw in it
a map.

Nora, watching his fingers twitch, was filled with fear. His
fever was very high; although she sponged him again and again
his skin still burned and the words that burst from his mouth
now and then were not in English, except for a woman's name:
Susannah, he cried. She had boiled some milk, which she'd obtained only at frightful expense, using money Dr. Douglas gave
her himself. She trickled a spoonful of the cooled liquid into
Lauchlin's mouth.

And he thought, I have done something wrong. I have come
here out of envy and wounded vanity and have acted without

understanding. And so of course I am to be punished. Something ran down the back of his throat; he tried to swallow and gagged. Then he saw a woman's face recede from his, as if she'd been lying beneath him, passed through him and risen, and he said to himself: But everything's fine. Somewhere, not far from here, Susannah sits in a chair before an open window, basking in the smell of roses as she bends her head over some sewing. He sighed and turned his head until his right cheek was buried in his pillow. The cloth was cool and clean. In his own bedroom, when he was a child, he had pressed his face all the way into his pillow, folding it up over both cheeks with just a small cleft for his nose and mouth. In that cleft he had hidden the evidence of his grief for his mother. That cloth had felt like this cloth; that sun, which came through his window in a low dusty beam, was like this sun. But this sun burned his eyes and brought tears to them and he had a pain in his head, such a terrible pain, and he was extraordinarily cold. A hand came up before his eyes: his hand? The skin was gray and mottled and damp. Whoever owned this hand had typhus; *tuphos*, a mist. Very clouded was the mental state of such a patient. Once he'd had no patients, and then Susannah had chided him and he had been childish and had gone to a place where he had too many patients. Now all the patients were gone. The face appeared again: Susannah? The features could not be distinguished; he saw a pale oval, dark hair, teeth. Something moist and horrid pressed against his mouth and he pushed his lips out and spluttered and blew, trying to push the object away with his breath.

"Patience," Nora said. "Just a little patience, my dear. I beg you. Take a few drops." Had she ever been so tired? Lauchlin's lips were so dry that they cracked when he pursed them and tried to roll the lower one outward. The faintest stream of air came from between them, no more than a sigh. Was he trying to speak? She held the moistened sponge to his lips again, but he would have none of it. She stripped his shirt, kicked it away from her, and eased his arms into a clean one; she had found his spare clothes, and each night she rinsed out a set for him and hung them to dry in the wind, so that he might have fresh things to sweat through the next day. While the clothing dried she stood at Lauchlin's makeshift desk and piled his books into towers that she then dismantled and built again, moving the books from hand to hand and place to place as if, through handling them, the knowledge contained in the words she couldn't read might be absorbed into her blood.

Very early on the sixth day of Lauchlin's illness, with the sun just up and no one watching, she walked into the forest and gathered herbs resembling those her grandmother had taught her to recognize in Ireland. She steeped them in brandy she begged from Dr. Douglas and hid the bottle behind the books; twice daily she dripped the infusion into Lauchlin's parched mouth. All this time, she believed that Lauchlin recognized her and was grateful for her care.

On the eighth day, Dr. Douglas came by for his morning visit and examined Lauchlin briefly. When he stood his face was grave. "Worse, I'm afraid," he said to Nora. "He has a friend in the city who has been inquiring after him. I must write her."

"Annie?" Nora said, remembering a conversation with Lauchlin that might have taken place a year ago. Somewhere, in the city she had not yet seen and might never reach, he had a life she knew nothing about.

"No," Dr. Douglas said. "Susannah, it was." Nora recognized the name Lauchlin had cried. "Although perhaps that's a nickname for the same person. You've been sponging him?"

"Every hour."

"Good." He gave her a small bottle containing solution of ammonia and cayenne pepper, with instructions to rub it along Lauchlin's legs and spine. "Hot bricks, too," he said. "To help stimulate diaphoresis. If you can find them, if you can find the time . . . I'm so sorry, I have to go."

Outside birds were speaking. Lauchlin was aware that he could no longer move his legs, that his spirit and his body were coming unglued from the feet up, like a pair of black-paper silhouettes separating. But it's all right, he thought. The people moving around him would glue his two parts back together; no harm would come to him because what mattered was not his legs or the lack of feeling in them but all he knew and thought and felt. Of course nothing could happen to him, he loved Susannah and had told her so and she had acknowledged it. That she had never loved him, and never would, mattered not at all. What mattered was that he had understood that he loved her, and also his life and the world; what could happen to him now?

His memory turned and burrowed through the places he had loved. First it brought him the foothills of the Pyrenees, through which he'd tramped with Nicholas Benin one July, during a break in his studies. Then the upper reaches of the Ottawa—oh, he had hated being with his father, hated the business and the noise, but after all the place had been beautiful, the massive rapids and the unclouded sky and the smell, overwhelming and everywhere, of the trees. The white sails in the St. Lawrence, fluttering below the cliffs. His mother's hair, the fragrance of the stables, the lobsters Annie had split and broiled, the market at the height of harvest, the weight and smoothness and promise of books—the cadavers, even, cool and preserved on a slab, slowly yielding the secrets beneath the skin.

What had he been doing these past years? What had he been so worried about? Fussing and struggling to build a practice, continue his research, establish himself—if he died now his life would have been only that, almost nothing, a chain of meaningless accomplishments and struggles. Why had he wasted so much time? When he was a boy, before his mother's death, he had understood the beauty of daily life. Somehow this had slipped his mind, and if he died now—but of course he would not die now, he was very sick but it was all right, he was young and strong and outside the sun shone on the meadows and gulls plunged into the river, emerging with fish in their beaks—if he died now it would be ridiculous, because all these years he had not been living but readying himself to live, stuffing himself with knowledge that would help him live later. All this time he'd been learning to live, and now he was ready to start his life.

He opened his eyes. The room was dusky and no sun streamed through the window; he understood for the first time that these people he'd been caring for were, if not exactly him, extensions of him, as he was an extension of them. It was life, simply life, that they had in common, and if he could have his life back he could be happy with anything. That was Nora bending over him, sweet Nora who had shared a berth with death, and in his imagination he said to her: Isn't it lovely, this life? Didn't you love being on that ship, despite the horrors you endured? Didn't you love the clouds and the sun and the rain, the smooth rolling waves and the leaping dolphins and the sight of the moon at night? From Telegraph Hill, he reminded her, we saw groves of silky white birch.

What was this shadow that lay over him now, if not the shadow that had lain over her and all the others? He smelled his own body, he had a slight erection, he remembered a young woman in Montreal, the grey wall next to him loomed. He became aware of a large, echoing space beyond the small space confining him. That space was filled with other beings, turning, murmuring, plucking their blankets as he plucked his; he knew his hands were doing this, but he could not control them. Those beings dreamed, like him. Count me, he thought, remembering a phrase he had once said in anger to someone he could no longer remember. Count me, count them, count us.

[VI.]

Nora meant to leave the island, but she couldn't seem to find the right moment. Early in September the flood of ships began to slow, and the number of patients to drop, but the staff well enough to care for them diminished correspondingly. There was a flurry of work in mid-September, when the new sheds at the eastern end of the island finally opened—twelve hundred patients to transfer, and so few people to help. For days she traced the muddy streets in carts, struggling to keep a few flaps of blanket over the sick and to cushion their heads against the jolting ride. Then the tents had to be struck, and the old sheds and the church had to be fumigated. Numb and exhausted, she did whatever Dr. Douglas asked.

All through October the number of patients decreased daily, but still there always seemed to be more work than people able to do it. One of the hospitals was closed, and then another; two of the physicians were discharged and with them their staffs. She might have left the island then, but there were children to comfort and old bedding to burn and floors to be scrubbed. The weather grew cold very rapidly; she did what she could to distribute the blankets and cast-off clothes sent by relief committees in the city. Slowly the island emptied. There were 500 patients the first week of October, and only three ships waiting at anchor. By the third week of October, all the convalescents had been sent upriver to Point St. Charles and only 60 patients remained.

The first snow had fallen by then. Dr. Douglas found some extra stockings for her, and a discarded coat, but at night a skim of ice began to form on the St. Lawrence and she was still cold much of the time. In a warehouse near the wharf were hundreds of boxes and trunks left behind by dead emigrants, along with a vast heap of their clothes, but she would not go into that room, she would rather freeze to death than touch those things. It was not fineness of feeling that stopped her, but fear of carrying the contagion. Along with the nurses and other attendants, she guiltlessly appropriated the money she found on the bodies of those who died without relatives. But she swept those shillings and occasional sovereigns into a leather purse with a stick, and before she touched them she boiled them in a saucepan of water.

She got a proper set of warm clothes only on October 30, the day the quarantine station was formally closed. That day a last, late ship limped into anchor; the *Lord Ashburton*, from Sligo, carrying tenants from the estates of Lord Palmerston. She thought she had seen everything by then, but this ship was the worst of all. Dr. Douglas was in a fury over it. Under a stunted pine on shore he stood shouting and waving his hands, arguing with another official she didn't recognize; he had aged terribly in the few months she'd known him and his voice was hoarse and cracked. She had no way to comfort him. He was nothing like Lauchlin and kept her at a distance, although he seemed grateful for her hard work.

Dr. Jaques, who'd finally recovered, returned from his tour of the *Lord Ashburton* to report that over a hundred passengers had died on the voyage. Sixty were sick with fever and the crew was so debilitated that five passengers had worked the ship up the river to Grosse Isle. Had she not kept her grandmother's training firmly in mind, she might have expired with rage and grief over the medical staff's inability to help her fellow travelers. Their supplies were gone and the authorities declared that this last shipload was to be sent directly to Montreal. Among the surviving passengers, all were destitute and half were nearly naked. They could not disembark in any decency until clothes were provided for them.

Dr. Douglas asked Nora to help distribute among them the last shipment of cast-off garments rounded up by the Catholic women of Quebec, and in one of those relief parcels she found a blue woolen dress in surprisingly good shape, which she set aside for herself. Boots turned up as well, and a cloak and a kerchief. On the morning after the long day during which the *Lord Ashburton's* passengers were clothed and sent upriver, Dr. Douglas called her into his office and dismissed her.

"It's time for you to leave," he said. "Where will you go?" Not a word to acknowledge the days they'd spent working side by side. She could almost hear his brain whirring, ticking off all he had yet to do. On his desk, next to the money box, was a long list of what looked like names—attendants and other staff, she guessed, to be paid off and sent on their way. After he counted out her wages he made a small mark by the line that represented her. He was very tired, she knew.

"I can't say yet," she told him. "I'll try to find my brothers, first."

"I wanted to give you something," he said. He reached under his desk. "It's a satchel, for your things."

It was made of heavy carpeting and was quite clean, although not new. Perhaps it had belonged to one of the physicians, or one of the priests. "Thank you," she said.

"Thank *you*."

And so November 2 found her aboard the *St. George* and headed up the freezing river. Along the banks she could see the ice extending further every hour. The breeze was icy as well, and low grey clouds scudded across the horizon. A few flakes of snow fell and she burrowed deeper into her cloak. Someone's cast-off, true. And yet the cloak was warm and whole and clean, the fabric wonderfully thick, the buttonholes frayed only slightly and the torn satin binding nicely mended. The boots she'd found were too big, but the newspaper she'd stuffed into their toes acted as insulation. Her feet were remarkably warm.

The sheer cliffs of Cape Diamond were a surprise; the bustling harbor, as busy as Liverpool, another. No one had told her the city was walled, or that the two addresses she'd asked Dr. Douglas to write out for her on a scrap of paper were not in the Lower Town, near the wharf where she disembarked, but high on the cliff and within the walls. Three times she asked strangers for directions to her first address; she got lost among the narrow cobbled streets and again emerging from the stairs at the top of the cliff. The strangers who looked at her scrap of paper and directed her on were distant but not rude. The dress, she thought, and blessed it. The cloak and the satchel and her boots. Later, when she would go in search of a boarding-house where she might spend a few nights, these clothes might keep her from unpleasant treatment.

Caleches passed her on the snow-covered streets, the horses pulling the runnered sleighs as cheerfully as if they pulled carriages. She had prepared herself for disappointment at the newspaper office, but still the clerk's flat words almost flattened her as well. No word of Ned and Denis, from either advertisement. In her mind's eye she saw the river, malignant and frozen, stretching for hundreds of miles through a country she could never penetrate, to cities that were only names. Kingston, Toronto—what were the chances of her finding her brothers in either place? What were the chances that Ned and Denis had not been pushed from those unreachable cities, looking for work as loggers or farmhands? What were the chances that they were still alive?

Two boys, out of the hundred thousand Irish emigrants who'd made the voyage to the Canadian provinces this season; two among all those who'd died on the passage over, or at Grosse Isle, or in Quebec and Montreal and further inland. But the numbers dead on the ships and the island meant nothing here in the city; the faces behind them could not be seen. As she walked toward her second address and came upon the market, she thought how the prosperous folk here forgot the numbers as soon as they sat down to breakfast or dinner, surrounded by this beautiful food—oh, the food in this market was astonishing!

She inched toward a tower of hot mutton pies, drawn by the smell and disguised by her blue dress. In her pocket was more money than she'd ever had before, and when the round-faced farmwoman told her the price of a pie she drew out a coin and ate her purchase right there. Flaky crust, hot spiced mutton, savory gravy that oozed with every bite; she closed her eyes as she chewed and thought how easy it would be to forget death in a place like this.

There was a cathedral just in front of her, where surely services had been held for the dead. But right here, within arm's reach, were muffins and large fried cakes and fresh butter and eggs. On the island food had been scarce and bad, cooked all at once in giant kitchens and distributed by the authorities: enough to keep them all alive, enough to make her give thanks every day, but by no means appetizing. Even back home, when there was still any food at all, a woman might have sat before a board on which were two or three eggs, a single ball of butter, perhaps a chicken or a goose. Here the eggs stretched like sand on a beach, the geese hung in rows by their beautiful feet, potatoes spilled from bags and oysters came not singly, nor even by the dozen, but by the barrel. As she watched, women with baskets over their arms made their purchases as if there were nothing unusual about the plenitude surrounding them. Haggling seemed like a sport for them; they bickered cheerfully. Some, having filled baskets with more food than Nora could comprehend, still had enough money left to buy odds and ends for sheer pleasure. Cedar boughs, balsam, candles.

She bought a heavy golden muffin and ate that too; her mouth watered and her head spun. She touched potatoes and onions and cabbages, apples and squashes and leeks, and then she pulled herself together and moved on, to the address on Palace Street.

The neat flagstone walk had been swept clear, and someone had knocked most of the snow from the shrubberies. For a minute she thought of going round to the servants' entrance, but this was no servant's errand she was on. She walked up to the handsome front door and knocked firmly on the center panel, below a carved decoration. Some kind of writing, she thought, staring at the intertwined shapes. Someone's name, perhaps? Annie Taggert opened the door.

The two women gazed at each other, each assessing the other's probable origins and position. Nora took note of Annie's worn shoes and reddened hands and coppery hair, but she also saw the care with which that hair was braided and pinned, the good-quality cloth of the simple dress, and the clean white apron, well-pressed and starched. Another Irishwoman, clearly, but one who had been here for some time and who was respected in this prosperous house. Annie, very busy this day, still registered the disparity between Nora's dress and boots, nicer than her own, and the worn, thin, absolutely Irish face. A new one, Annie thought. Another like Sissy. Who did this girl think she was, aping her betters in those clothes?

"There's no work here," Annie said frostily. "And you oughtn't be coming to this door—you go around back if you're looking for food, perhaps cook will have something for you."

Nora flushed. "It's not work I'm needing," she said, although soon enough she would. "Nor food."

Before she could finish speaking, Annie tried to slam the door on her. Nora wedged her satchel between the door and its frame and said, "I have a message for Mrs. Rowley. It's important. Would you fetch her for me, please?"

It was too much, Annie thought. Everything that had happened these past six months; it was simply too much. She owed this girl no explanations, but she did open the door a little wider. Perhaps she had not taken sufficient account of the quality of that blue dress. Perhaps this girl had important friends? "Mrs. Rowley is not available," she said. "You may leave the message with me."

"Is Mr. Rowley available, then?"

"He's busy," Annie said. "But you can be sure whatever you leave with me will reach him."

Nora shook her head and refused to move. "It's important. And I have a parcel as well. I will wait."

For a minute Annie considered making her wait downstairs, but Mr. Rowley was so changed these days, and so distraught, that she dared not risk offending him. Suppose the girl was a friend of someone he'd met on his travels? Grudgingly, she said, "You can wait here in the hall, I suppose. But it may be some time." She opened the door wider and led Nora in, pointing out a stiff brocaded chair. "Your name?"

"Nora Kynd. Please tell him I have a message from a friend." Just as Annie was about to say, "Don't you go touching anything here," Nora said, "From his friend Dr. Lauchlin Grant."

Annie drew back at the mention of Dr. Grant's name. "You haven't come from that island?"

"I have," Nora said proudly. "I worked there all summer. I was one of Dr. Grant's assistants."

"Are you . . . sick?" Annie whispered. "Have you brought the fever back to this house?"

"Of course not," Nora said. "I had the fever back in the spring, and recovered—you know you can't get it twice." She brushed her arm over her cloak and dress. "These are all newly boiled, completely cleaned. I touched nothing on the island after I changed."

"I'll tell Mr. Rowley you're here," Annie said. She opened another door, into a nearby room.

Nora could hear the sounds of men arguing in there, a constant rumble that broke only for a second when Annie interrupted them. Annie returned, said, "Mr. Rowley will be a while," and disappeared again. She forgot to close the door to the library behind her, and so left Nora inadvertently eavesdropping.

No faces, only voices; fragments of statements from which

she might try to deduce an attitude, a person. One of those voices, she supposed, belonged to Mr. Rowley. She waited on her stiff chair, wondering where Mrs. Rowley was. Wondering if Mr. Rowley had any idea of the relationship between his wife and Lauchlin; wondering what she would do with the things in her satchel if Mrs. Rowley did not appear and Mr. Rowley asked leave to pass them on to his wife. Was he the sort of man who'd consider his wife's belongings private? Or the sort who'd think his wife's possessions were his, as his wife was his possession?

As she studied the cut glass and the gleaming furniture, the knot of voices began to unravel and isolated phrases floated free. The men were forming some committee, or had already formed it and now were drawing up resolutions. Someone mentioned the *Lord Ashburton*; someone mentioned an article yet another someone had written about the terrible conditions aboard that ship. Someone reminded someone else of the recent deaths of both the mayor of Montreal and the Catholic bishop of Toronto. A man with a harsh, carrying voice said, "The stringent measures adopted by the Government of the United States have driven the poorer classes in Ireland to the more tedious but less expensive route up the St. Lawrence, with the result that a large mass of indolence, pauperism, destitution and disease has been thrown upon us."

"Fine," another man said. "That's fine, we'll end the summary with that. Now for the measures we recommend, to prevent a recurrence of the catastrophe next year—"

"Point number one," said a man with a fresh, light voice. "The emigration tax must be increased."

"No, no, no," said the harsh-voiced man. "We will list that second, even third. Most important is that we demand regulation of accommodations aboard the ships. No more than two tiers of berths six feet in length by eighteen inches in width, in the orlop deck no more than—"

Still other voices broke in. "A medical attendant must be present for every one hundred passengers—"

"Effective means for ventilation and cleanliness between decks must be assured—"

On and on the men went, throwing out numbers and rules and restrictions, suggestions, demands, and pleas. Nora balanced on her straight-backed chair, gazing at the blue-and-white glazed vases and the framed arrangements of flowers made from shells while the men began to argue about money. A great deal had been expended by the province in caring for the sick and destitute emigrants, she heard. A much smaller amount had been received in emigration tax receipts. Who had paid, was paying, would pay?

"Water, twenty-one quarts per week per passenger," someone said. "Specifications must be laid down for all provisions. Biscuits, two and a half pounds; oatmeal, five pounds; two pounds molasses . . ."

"Rice," someone added. "Don't forget an allotment of rice."

Would she have sickened, if she'd been given all that food on the bark? Would Ned and Denis have been stronger? She wished she had bought another muffin in the market and had the sense to stow it in her pocket. Had her father been here, she thought, he would have skipped the muffins and pocketed some of the expensive trinkets littering the tables. His right, he would have thought. They had it, he needed it. He would not have seen, as he had not back home, that the rich believed he had a right to nothing.

A voice she hadn't heard before, clear and yet somehow tired, said, "We have to keep in mind that the point isn't to discourage emigration of these poor people—what else are they supposed to do? Where else can they go, so long as this famine lasts? The point is to make their voyage more humane, and to make better arrangements for them once they're here."

The harsh-voiced man disagreed. "That you of all people should say that . . . no, we want to reduce the numbers as well as ameliorate the emigrants' passage."

"You'll excuse me for a minute. I have someone waiting to see me." And then Nora heard footsteps coming her way and a man wearing a beautiful fawn-colored coat suddenly stood before her.

"Miss Kynd?" he said. His features were youthful, but his face was pale and drawn. "I'm sorry to keep you waiting. I'm Arthur Adam Rowley. How may I help you?"

He was shockingly young, hardly older than herself although his poise and grace were those of an older generation. Perfectly groomed, and somehow very sad. She rose from her chair. "I'm sorry to interrupt you," she said. "I have a message for your wife."

His face, already pale, blanched further. But his voice continued courteous and controlled. "My wife is very ill," he said. "Of this fever that's come in the ships. Perhaps you could give the message to me."

Nora silently cursed both her clumsiness and Annie's secretive nature. "I'm sorry," she said. "Would you have known Dr. Lauchlin Grant?" Still, surprisingly, it gave her a horrible pain to speak his name.

"Of course. We were good friends. How did you know him?"

Briefly, Nora told him the story of how Lauchlin had found her and saved her, and how she'd gone to work for him on Grosse Isle and then cared for him during his illness. "Dr. Douglas has packed up his books and most of his belongings for his father," Nora said. "They'll be shipped to the house soon. But he had a few small personal things with him, and he told me he wanted Mrs. Rowley—and you, too, of course—to have them if he died."

She lied here: he had told her no such thing. She had made this up on her own when she cleaned his office the day after his death. During the worst of his fever he had several times called out Susannah's name, and she had linked this to the woman

Dr. Douglas had mentioned, and then to the "Mrs. Rowley" Lauchlin had spoken of when he returned from his one brief leave. Although she was unable to read Lauchlin's journal, she had seen him write in it so often that she believed it to be both important and personal. And surely the woman he thought of above all others during his last days deserved to have it.

But now this woman was too sick to read it, and there might be something in the closely written pages that would bring her husband sorrow. Quickly Nora made a decision; she reached into her satchel and took out the small parcel containing Lauchlin's good shirt and waistcoat, and his watchchain and his watch. She pushed the journal down deeper and then held out her gift.

"It's so little," she said. "But I know he would have wanted you to have it."

Arthur Adam unfolded the wrapping paper with his long white hands, pushed aside the folds of the shirt, and lifted a loop of the chain. "Thank you," he said. "You're very thoughtful, to bring these here. My wife would have—*will*—cherish them. I'll cherish them."

They were silent for a minute. Then Arthur Adam said, "They were very close, you know. Lauchlin and Susannah— they were childhood friends. It seems impossible that he's gone, and her so sick—over and over this month I've kept thinking that if he were here he could help her."

"He was a fine doctor," Nora said. "If you'd seen him with his patients. . . ." For a moment she almost thought of shouldering what she could of the burden Lauchlin had dropped, as she'd done on the island. She might say to Mr. Rowley, *Perhaps you need some help? I'm very good with fever patients.* She might walk up those wide and curving stairs, find her way down the hall to a room where a sick woman lay in a soft, clean bed, near a shining window. To that woman she might say, *Lauchlin called your name when he was dying. Over and over again. Let me bathe your face, let me smooth your hair, let me bring you a cool drink*. All those things she might do, in memory of Lauchlin. And then be caught here, in a web of obligation and sorrow. . . . She picked up her satchel.

"You look rather like my wife," said Mr. Rowley.

"Me?"

"In a certain way. Your hair, the shape of your mouth and forehead. Where will you go when you leave here? What will you do?"

"I'm not sure," she said, startled by his words. That she should look like Susannah, whom Lauchlin had cried out for—she knew then she was right in keeping the journal, and not just because she was protecting the Rowleys by doing so. That was her family tree in there, with its dead branches and withered fruit. She would find a teacher, a school, deciphering what Lauchlin had left behind and all he'd had access to: newspapers, books, the advertisements she'd place for her brothers and the ones that they, if they knew someone as kind as Lauchlin, might place looking for her.

Annie appeared in the hall just then, irritable and faintly ashamed. Downstairs, while Nora had been waiting, Annie had been cursing Sissy with more than her usual violence. It was Mrs. Rowley who had brought her to this; she had no love for her mistress, but she pitied her and also everyone in this house. No one deserved to suffer as Mrs. Rowley had. Six weeks she'd been wasting away, and Arthur Adam could not take much more strain. Nor could she herself: she was exhausted shuttling trays back and forth, running errands for the doctor, putting up with the whims of the high-handed nurse. And then the sight of Nora, and the recognition of where she'd been, had brought her own early years in this strange land back to her. That awful time, when so few people had been kind to her; at the thought of it she'd yelled at Sissy and then felt abashed and wondered what possessed her to be so mean. She had been mean to this stranger as well, or at least unwelcoming. She cleared her throat and said,

"Won't you come downstairs for a cup of tea before you go?" Nora, grateful to be released from Arthur Adam's gaze, followed Annie willingly.

In the kitchen, Nora sat in silence while Annie prepared the tea. "I'm sorry," she said finally. "I'm sorry about Mrs. Rowley. I didn't know. You should have said."

"I should have," Annie said. "I don't know what got into me." She thought about the vomiting and the delirium, the inability of the doctor to ease Mrs. Rowley's pain, her own fear and terror during the two weeks before Arthur Adam's arrival, when Mrs. Rowley had cried out in the night and there was no one to help but her. About Arthur Adam, who for all the good he might have done with his articles, had not arrived home in time. Now his wife didn't recognize him. "It's a hard sickness. You know. What was it like, on that island?"

Nora told Annie a little about Grosse Isle. "My brothers were taken from me," she said. "They were well, and I wasn't, and the doctors took them away and wouldn't let them join me on the island." She told Annie about her days in the church, what little she could remember; and about how Lauchlin Grant had saved her and become, almost, a friend. She spoke briefly about the work she'd done when she'd recovered, and about all she'd seen, but she didn't dwell on this; she could tell from Annie's face that the news was unwelcome. Finally she described Lauchlin's last days. "He was such a gentle man," she said. "He worked so hard, right up until the last. Even when he was dying, you could tell he tried not to be any trouble."

"I hardly knew him," Annie said. "But the Rowleys were very fond of him." Neither of them said anything about the attachment of Lauchlin and Susannah, but the fact hung in the air between them. And when Annie told Nora about Susannah's work among the emigrants at the hospital, and the way she'd fallen sick despite Annie's best efforts, Nora shook her head and said, "It's one thing I am thankful for, that Dr. Grant never knew she was sick."

The afternoon lengthened as they spoke. "What are your brothers' names?" Annie asked, and Nora found herself telling tales about Ned and his love for beetles, Denis snatching fish from the stream with his hands. Annie served tea and seed-cake. On the boat, Nora said, the boys had conspired to steal extra water for her. Her description of their passage over led Annie to talk about her own, which had been marked by the same crowding and insufficient supplies but was much easier to bear, as the weather had been fine and all her companions had been in good health. "But I've seen sickness," she said. "As bad as anything this time around. In '32, when the cholera came, I was in service down in Lower Town when I was taken with it. . . ."

She'd been a girl then, she told Nora; just turned twenty-one and only a few years off the boat from Leitrim. One day she'd felt hot and peculiar and then had fallen unconscious down the stairs she was scrubbing. She had only the haziest memory of being carried out of the city on a sick cart. When she'd woken she'd found herself in a tent on the Plains of Abraham, surrounded by the dying.

"It was a miracle I survived," she said, and she told Nora how the cholera burying-ground had swallowed her friend Mary MacLean, and with Mary their shared dream of making their way to the States together. Around them the shadows gathered in the kitchen. And in a corner, occupied with a bushel of beets, Sissy listened open-mouthed to their tales.

"Where will you go?" Annie said finally, echoing Arthur Adam. "What will you do?" She had changed her mind about Nora, and thought that after all there might be a way to find her a position in the Rowleys' house.

But somewhere in the course of this long day, Nora had reached a decision. "If I can't find my brothers," she said. She stopped and swallowed and started again. "If I can't find them, and I probably can't, I'm going to the United States. It's beautiful here. A beautiful city. But I could never live here after all that's happened."

"You could," Annie said. "You could stay. It gets better."

"There's a place called Detroit," Nora said. "I heard about it on the island; it's off one of the huge lakes that this river runs into."

Sissy, unnoticed until then by Nora, set down the beets and her knife and crept closer to the table. "I've heard about that place too," she said.

Because she had company, and because she was abashed by her earlier outburst, Annie restrained herself from snapping at the girl and only motioned her back to the corner with her chin. Nora, thinking of Denis and Ned, registered Sissy's shining, curious face before she turned. This one had lived, like her, somehow escaping the trail of bodies littered across the ocean. And like her was all alone. She said, now speaking to Sissy as well as to Annie, "A man who has some family there told me it's easy to sneak over the border, and that the city is lively, and there's lots of work. I'd like to be in a new place," she said. "Start fresh."

"Wouldn't we all," Annie said. "Didn't we all of us think that was what we were doing, leaving our homes for here?" She put down her saucer as Nora rose and grasped her satchel. "You're leaving already?"

"I am," Nora said.

Acknowledgments

I am indebted to Cecil Woodham-Smith's *The Great Hunger*, from which I first learned about the events on Grosse Isle. Robert Whyte's journal of his passage from Ireland to Quebec (published in 1848 as *The Ocean Plague*) provided key eyewitness descriptions of conditions on the ships and on the island.

The Grosse Isle Tragedy and the Monument to the Irish Fever Victims, 1847 (compiled by J.A. Jordan and first printed on the occasion of the dedication of a monument honoring the victims of ship fever as the *Quebec Daily Telegraph's* "Grosse Isle Monument Commemorative Souvenir"; later reprinted as a book by The Telegraph Printing Company, Quebec, 1909) is the definitive source for details of the typhus epidemic on Grosse Isle during 1847. The chapter "Medical History of the Famine" in *The Great Famine: Studies in Irish History* (edited by Dudley Edwards and Desmond Williams) provided much useful information about the diseases—particularly typhus—that follow in the wake of famine.

Drs. Douglas and Jaques are historical persons, as are Buchanan and the doctors and clergymen Lauchlin Grant records as having died on the island. The remaining characters, including Lauchlin Grant, are fictitious.

3